Scatterheart

LILI WILKINSON

Scatterheart

LILI WILKINSON

Catnip

CATNIP BOOKS
Published by Catnip Publishing Ltd
14 Greville Street
London EC1N 8SB

First published by black dog books, Australia, 2007

This edition first published 2009
1 3 5 7 9 10 8 6 4 2

A CIP catalogue record for this book is available from the British Library

ISBN   978-1-84647-077-6

Printed in Poland

www.catnippublishing.co.uk

For Agnes Nieuwenhuizen:
a terrific boss
an inspirational mentor
a feisty debating opponent
and a dear friend.

PART I:

London Town, 1814

one

Once upon a time, there was a poor man who had a daughter. She was very beautiful, but she was selfish and vain, and her heart was as fickle as the changing winds. For this reason, she was known as Scatterheart.

The turnkey pushed Hannah into the cell, and clanged the door shut behind her. Hannah's eyes stung and she felt a heavy churning in her belly. The smell of urine, vomit, sweat and rotting flesh was overpowering, and she broke out in a hot, prickly sweat, despite the icy night.

Her mouth filled with saliva, and she doubled over and threw up onto the grimy stone floor. Wiping her mouth, she drew a ragged breath, but the smell was so unbearable that her throat closed over and her stomach heaved again. She fell to her hands and knees, gasping and retching.

'Look here,' remarked a dry voice. 'This blowse must have a padlock on her arse, that she shites through her teeth.'

There was a ripple of coarse laughter.

Hannah closed her eyes, and breathed through her mouth. After a few moments, the nausea subsided, and she opened her eyes.

The cell was small; smaller than her bedroom at home. It was dark, with only a dim torch in the hallway outside to shine a weak light through the thick, black iron bars. The flickering torch seemed to create more shadows than light, but Hannah could make out the shapes of bodies: some moving about in the dark, others still. In sleep or death, Hannah couldn't tell.

There were more than fifty, to Hannah's count. Apart from the comment as she'd come in, no one paid any attention to her. They lay on the floor, some sprawled out with others in a dirty tangle of arms and legs.

Men and women.

She felt sick again.

There was a single window in the cell, high up and barred like the door, with iron rods thicker than Hannah's arm. Grey snowflakes were drifting down through the night sky, illuminated by the gas-lights in the street outside. There were no beds, and only one or two people had a blanket. At the back of the cell, there was a wooden bench that ran the length of the wall. A wooden plank was nailed to the side of the bench closest to the wall. People were curled up on the bench as if it were a mattress, and the plank were a pillow.

Hannah picked her way through the sleeping people, and crawled onto the bench, into a gap between two sleeping inmates. She curled up, her throat still stinging with bile. She would never be able to sleep in a place like this. Strange sounds came from corners of the cell: grunts and moans and snores. Even though it was freezing, the room felt stifling.

Hannah closed her eyes, and tried to pretend she was back in her own bed. She tried to think about Thomas's story, but all she could see was ice collapsing around her, and a white bear shaking his head and saying, over and over again, *What have you done? What have you done?*

⁂

There were only two men in Hannah Cheshire's life, and they could not be more different. Hannah's father, Arthur Cheshire, spent his evenings at respectable gentlemen's clubs, gambling and drinking porter with other men of Quality. Hannah was not exactly sure what her father *did*, but she knew that he was an important businessman.

Her father was always immaculately presented. His necktie was starched and extravagantly folded according to the latest mode. His hats and coats were crafted by the very best tailors. He wore knee-high black hessian boots with golden tassels. He spent a small fortune on a rainbow-coloured assortment of ointments and tinctures for his skin and hair, and he was always well-buffed and delicately perfumed with lavender.

Thomas Behr was Hannah's tutor. *His* coat was shabby and fraying about the cuffs. Holes had been clumsily mended, and his wrists stuck out from the too-short sleeves. The fabric was stretched and pulled across his broad shoulders, creaking when he bent down to pick something up.

Mr Behr was not fat, nor thin, nor did he seem particularly strong or solid. Hannah had the impression that he was ill-at-ease with his large frame. He hunched his shoulders to appear smaller, and seemed restless and awkward in his ill-fitting clothes. He had pale hair that had always slipped out of its neat style by the time he reached Hannah's front door. His silver-rimmed spectacles were slightly bent, and sat askew on his rather beaked nose. His pale skin was flushed and he was very quick to blush when embarrassed. Thomas Behr's modest necktie was carefully tied, but always sat a little crooked.

Arthur Cheshire had met Thomas's uncle at a gentlemen's club. On discovering that Thomas was an Oxford graduate (on scholarship), he immediately sent for him and employed him as Hannah's tutor.

The two men had vastly different opinions about her education. Arthur Cheshire had hired Mr Behr when Hannah was eleven years old, feeling that she had outgrown her nurse. He warned Thomas not to teach Hannah *too* much; he didn't want his daughter to turn into a blue-stocking.

'Just teach her enough to appear *accomplished* to her suitors,' he said.

Thomas Behr had ignored him. He taught Hannah about

history and poetry and mathematics and stars. He told her about the animals that lived in Africa, and about men who made houses from snow in the far north. He taught her French and German and Latin. He read to her from great works of fiction. He told her stories about glass slippers, poisoned apples and white bears.

Hannah didn't notice his worn cuffs. She loved the way he took off his glasses when he got excited – telling her about the Crusades, or about Copernicus's discovery that the earth revolved around the sun. He would pace around the room, talking, throwing his arms around. Hannah thought he looked like a wild animal, trapped in city-clothes. His grey eyes would shine, and Hannah thought that the ocean might be that colour – a sparkling, mottled grey.

Hannah started awake as someone grabbed her, and yanked her off the bench. She looked around, dazed. It was still dark, so she couldn't have been asleep for long. Her assailant grabbed the front of her dress and shoved a pock-marked, gap-toothed face before Hannah's.

'That's my bed,' it hissed through lips that were blotchy with red and white sores. The person – Hannah couldn't tell if it was man or woman – spat on Hannah, and its breath made her gag. 'Doxie slut. You have to pay to kip on the bed. So show us your blunt, else it's on the floor with the rest of the maggots.'

Hannah stared, uncomprehending. The person shoved her roughly, and she sprawled to the floor, colliding with several sleeping bodies, that grunted in protest. Hannah crawled to a small patch of floor beneath the window. A gust of wind blew a flurry of snow down on her, but at least it brought clean air in with it.

The stone floor was hard, and damp with urine and saliva. Hannah's hips and shoulders ached. She rested her head on her arm, and remembered the day when everything had changed. It had started well.

⚜

She and Mr Behr were in Hyde Park, their laughter billowing out before them in white clouds. Mr Behr was making snow animals. Hannah had to guess what they were. Sheep, elephants and tigers paraded across the white-blanketed gardens. Then he made something that Hannah had never seen before.

'Is it a rabbit?' she said.

'No,' said Mr Behr. 'Much bigger than a rabbit.'

'A hare?'

Mr Behr laughed, and Hannah felt his warm breath on her cheek. 'It's a kangaroo.'

'A what?'

'A kangaroo. From New South Wales.'

And he told her about the strange animals, as big as seven feet tall, who carried their young around in a pocket.

'What a funny creature,' said Hannah. 'I would like to see one.'

Mr Behr smiled. 'I can show you a picture of one when we go back to the house,' he said. 'I brought a book.'

Mr Behr always arrived with a parcel of books tucked under his arm. Her father didn't approve of books, and Hannah hid them in her bedroom, and read them by candlelight.

'I want to make an animal first,' said Hannah.

She pulled off the fur muff keeping her hands warm, and knelt in the snow. She frowned, concentrating. She was trying to make a giraffe, but she couldn't get the neck right. It kept breaking when she tried to add the head. Her fingers ached with cold, and icy water soaked through her dress.

'A chicken?' guessed Mr Behr.

'No,' said Hannah. 'I'm not finished yet.'

'A turkey? An otter?'

Hannah's creation crumbled again.

'Hmm,' said Mr Behr, looking at the shapeless mound of snow. 'A mole hiding under a molehill? An anteater disguised as an anthill?'

'It was *supposed* to be a giraffe,' said Hannah.

'Of course,' he said, the corner of his mouth twitching. 'I can see that now.'

Hannah heard the rattle of a carriage, and looked up to see a smart curricle, with lamps and silver moulding, go flying down Rotten Row. She wondered what people of Quality would think to see her playing children's games in the snow.

'We should go home, Mr Behr,' she said.

Mr Behr glanced at the curricle, and raised an eyebrow.

'You should call me Thomas,' he said. '*Mr Behr* makes me feel about a hundred.'

Hannah felt herself blushing, and looked away.

The twitch around Mr Behr's mouth curled into a real smile. 'How about one more,' he said.

He got down on his knees beside her, and scooped some more snow onto Hannah's failed giraffe. He smelled like cinnamon. He smoothed the snow, and shaped four short legs, a rounded body, and a long, angular head. Hannah watched him. His hat fell off as he bent his head, and landed upside down. The faded grey silk lining was so worn it was crumbling away. Mr Behr's hair was pale, almost as white as the snow. It was rumpled and stuck out at strange angles like ruffled goose-down. Hannah had a sudden desire to run her fingers through it.

Two little ears appeared on either side of the head of Mr Behr's creation. He felt in his pocket, and produced two currants, which became black, beady eyes.

'There.' He stood up, brushing snow from his knees.

It was a bear. A white ice-bear.

'Once upon a time,' he said. 'There was a girl called Scatterheart...'

two

One dark, wicked evening, Scatterheart and her father were sitting by the fire. The rain fell hard and the wind blew so fiercely that the walls of their little cottage shook. All at once, there were three taps on the window. The man looked out, and saw a great white bear.

When Hannah woke again, pale daylight was leaking in through the little barred window. She sat up, and the room spun a little. She was shivering.

Her gloves were gone. So were her bonnet and shoes. Even the lace from the hem of her dress had been torn off.

An old woman sat with her back against the wall. Her face was deeply lined, and Hannah thought she must be at least a hundred. She wore an old-fashioned pair of stays with no over-dress and a moth-eaten skirt of indeterminate colour. She looked at Hannah with glittering black eyes.

'Someone took my bonnet and my shoes,' said Hannah to the old woman. 'Did you see who it was?'

The woman spoke in a Scots accent so thick Hannah could barely understand her.

'Tis na more a pity to see a woman greit, than to see a goose go barefoot.'

Hannah watched a fat louse crawling up the woman's arm. All at once, the woman grabbed the tiny insect, and popped it into her toothless mouth.

She chuckled. 'There is none so crouse, as a new-washen louse,' she said, chewing.

The door to the cell banged open, and a turnkey tossed two buckets into the room, one sloshing with water, the other filled with scraps of bread. The other people quickly crowded around them, grasping and snarling at one another like dogs. Hannah's stomach rumbled, and she got up cautiously and went over to the bread bucket. It was empty.

'Is you hungry, little miss?' said a voice behind her.

Hannah turned around. It was the person who had evicted her from the wooden bench during the night. In the watery daylight, Hannah could now see that it was a young woman, not much older than twenty, but very tall, with broad shoulders and long legs. She was filthy, her face was scabbed and pock-marked. Several of her teeth were missing, and her hair was thin and wispy. She wore a dirty skirt and stays laced tight to push up her bosom. On her head sat Hannah's bonnet. She sat on the floor, skirt hitched up and bare legs spread out before her. She leaned against a dark, bearded man, who casually laid his hand on her leg. She stared insolently at Hannah, and held up a hunk of bread.

'You wants this?'

Hannah's mouth watered at the sight of the bread, but she tried to remain demure.

'I think you have my hat,' she said politely.

The woman laughed, and affected a posh-sounding accent. 'I'm sure madam must be mistook,' she said. 'This here is my bonney, bought for me by Black Jack, here. A bonney from my bonny love.' She patted the arm of the bearded man, who pushed her skirt back to move his hand further up her thigh. Hannah blushed.

The woman dropped the posh voice, and looked at the bread in her hand. 'I'll give you this here pannam. Does you want it?'

Hannah nodded.

The woman smiled, showing a few lonely grey teeth. 'I wants that coat you're wearin'.'

She put her hand up to the fur collar. The woman had already stolen her bonnet, and probably her shoes and gloves as well. She wasn't getting her pelisse!

'I'll give you my bonnet for the bread,' said Hannah.

'Sounds like a round deal,' agreed the woman. 'Let's see it, then.'

Hannah frowned. 'You're wearing it.'

The woman shook her head. 'You must think me a rum cull, tryin' to trade me me own hat! Give me that there coat, and the belly timber is yours.'

'No, thank you,' said Hannah. 'I think I'll just wait until nuncheon.'

The woman burst out laughing, a deep open laugh. 'Nuncheon!' She clutched the arm of the bearded man. 'Does you hear this moll, Black Jack? Nuncheon! She must've come from the royal palace I expect. Nuncheon, your ladyship!' She slapped her thigh. 'We don't gets nuncheon in Newgate, y'ladyship. Nor dinner, nor supper, nor high tea. This here,' she waved the bread around, 'is it. Until tomorrow.'

Hannah looked at the piece of bread, and her stomach ached. But she remembered the cold of the night before, and shook her head. 'I won't be staying long anyway,' she said. 'This is all a misunderstanding.'

This set the woman off into a fresh gale of laughter. 'Sure it is, y'ladyship. You ain't done nuffin.'

Hannah narrowed her eyes. 'You have no idea who I am,' she said. 'But sooner or later someone is going to come along who does, and then you will all be sorry.'

She went over to the water bucket, and dipped a cupped hand in. The water tasted like mud and metal, but her throat was parched and sore from being sick the previous night. She then picked her way over to the bars to wait for the turnkey to return.

Some of the inmates slept, others played at cards or dice, swigging great mouthfuls of gin from dark brown bottles. A heavily pregnant woman lay awkwardly on the ground, her hands resting on her swollen stomach. Another woman suckled an infant. Hannah watched for a moment, fascinated and faintly horrified, then blushed and looked away when the woman met her eyes. Did all babies feed like that? Hannah thought it quite strange. Had she drunk from her own mother's breast? Hannah couldn't remember anything about her mother, but she was sure she wouldn't have fed Hannah that way. Her father would have thought it vulgar.

Hannah and Mr Behr arrived home from Hyde Park just as Arthur Cheshire was coming down the stairs for breakfast. He wore a green brocade dressing gown embroidered with brightly coloured oriental birds and flowers. His eyes were ringed with dark circles, and his face seemed to be sagging with exhaustion.

He took one look at his bedraggled daughter, her hair slipping out from its pins, and pursed his lips. Thomas looked down at his feet.

'Go and change your dress,' Arthur Cheshire said to Hannah. 'I need to have a word with Mr Behr.'

They went into the dining room. Hannah crouched on the stairs, straining to hear what was going on. Her father's voice sounded low and angry.

'…anyone could have seen her…'

Mr Behr murmured a response. Arthur Cheshire's voice continued its lecture.

'…high expectations for my daughter… attract a man of great fortune…'

Hannah bit her lip and crept upstairs to her room to change.

After about an hour, her father called her down to the dining room. Hannah pinched her cheeks and smoothed her hair before she went in.

He was sitting, reading a newspaper. A large glass of brandy was on the table in front of him.

'Morning, my love,' he said absently.

'It's afternoon, Papa.'

'Is it?' He looked up. 'I'll be damned.' He reached for the brandy glass.

Her father's manservant, Adams, entered the room, followed by Lettie, the maid. They laid silver and porcelain dishes of soused herrings, buttered eggs, cold sirloin and wafer-thin slices of ham on the white linen tablecloth. Arthur Cheshire gestured for Adams to refill his glass.

'Did you have a late night, Papa?' asked Hannah, sitting down at the table.

'Devilish late,' he replied, loading his plate with food. He shovelled eggs into his mouth, and washed them down with brandy. Then he looked at her and narrowed his eyes.

'Angel, I want you to know I'm very disappointed.'

Hannah twisted the tablecloth between her hands, feeling that she might cry. 'Papa, please don't let Thomas go.'

Arthur Cheshire raised a well-plucked eyebrow. 'I have spoken at length to *Mr Behr* about his... methods of education. They are entirely inappropriate for a young lady of Quality.'

Hannah said nothing.

'When I hired him,' Arthur Cheshire continued, 'I expressly outlined the kind of education that I wished for you.'

'But Papa,' said Hannah. 'Thom– Mr Behr has been the very best of teachers. He has taught me all sorts of wonderful things.'

Arthur Cheshire frowned. 'That is precisely the problem,' he said. 'It is quite unnecessary for a young lady of Quality to know about the heathen gods of Egypt, or the voyages of Marco Polo. Unnecessary and undesirable.'

Hannah's lower lip trembled.

'Hannah, you need to understand that you must conduct yourself in a proper and dignified fashion if you want to find a good husband.'

Hannah looked at him. 'A husband?'

He smiled. 'Of course, my love. Isn't that what you want?'

She reached out and took a slice of ham.

'You're a beautiful young lady,' said Arthur Cheshire. 'You'll catch yourself a fine man.'

Hannah tore the ham into thin strips. *Was* she beautiful?

Her father leaned over and patted her on the knee. 'We shall find you a rich husband, and you shall have a grand house in Mayfair, and carriages, and fifty servants, and you will hold the finest parties London has ever seen.'

Hannah thought about that. It *did* sound wonderful.

'But what about Mr Behr?' she asked.

'I shall let Behr go at the end of the month.'

Hannah stopped, her hand half-raised to her mouth. She put the ham down again on a plate.

Her father sighed. 'You're nearly fifteen, Hannah. Much too old for a tutor.'

'Oh,' said Hannah. She wondered what she would do all day without Thomas Behr.

'You shall be far too busy going to parties and meeting rich men,' said Arthur Cheshire.

'Yes, Papa,' said Hannah.

'We'll get you tutors to teach you skills more appropriate for a young lady. Dancing. Pianoforte. Painting. Then, when you are fifteen, you shall be ready to enter Society.'

Hannah said nothing.

'That reminds me,' said Arthur Cheshire. 'Mr Harris is coming to dine with us tonight. Make sure you dress well.'

Hannah made a face. Mr Harris was a fat, asthmatic man who played cards with Arthur Cheshire. He was at least fifty years old, and was always pink and sweating.

'Now, Hannah,' said her father, downing the last of his brandy and standing up. 'Mr Harris is a very rich man. You'd do well to impress him. He has a house on Grosvenor Square, you know.'

He touched an elegant finger to her cheek, and then left the room, his dressing gown billowing behind him.

Hannah scowled at the thought of having to spend an entire evening in Mr Harris's company, listening to him wheeze and stammer, and watching the sweat stains under his arms grow as the evening wore on. Thomas Behr despised Mr Harris, calling him a toad-eater.

Hannah sighed, and poked half-heartedly at the buttered eggs with a fork. It didn't really matter what Thomas Behr thought, because Papa was letting him go.

When Hannah was younger, she and Thomas used to make up stories about the animals woven into the Turkish rug in the sitting room. Hannah would tell him about the outrageous adventures of the tiger and the elephant, and he would laugh and laugh, until his eyes filled with tears.

She put down the fork and stood up. She only had a few lessons left with Thomas. At the end of the month he would leave, and she would probably never see him again. She thought about Thomas, with his rumpled coat and snow animals. The way he looked at her sometimes. She thought about how she had wanted to touch his hair in the park. Then she imagined wearing jewels and beautiful dresses. She thought about riding through Hyde Park in her own carriage. Perhaps her father was right, it *was* time to grow up.

Most people in the cell just sat staring into space, waiting and wasting away. Hunger gnawed at Hannah. She could feel the water she had drunk sloshing around in her empty stomach. As the dim light in the cell started to fade, Hannah leaned her head against the cold iron bars of the cell. She felt weak and trembling.

'Oi! Y'ladyship!' she heard the woman with her bonnet call over to her. 'Stop polishin' the king's iron wiv your eyebrows and come over here.'

Hannah rose unsteadily to her feet and looked around. The woman was sprawled out on the wooden shelf with Black Jack, a brown glass bottle in one hand.

'Still hungered?' she asked.

Hannah nodded, and put her hands to the buttons of her pelisse. Her father had bought it for her birthday last year. It had been wrapped up in delicately scented tissue paper, in a white box with a green velvet ribbon. The woman looked at Hannah pointedly. Hannah sighed, and fumbled with the buttons.

The woman wedged her bottle between her knees, holding out both hands. Hannah held out the dark green garment. The woman stood up and put it on. It was tight around her shoulders and across the bosom, and only reached mid-calf, but she belted it up and paraded around the cell like a peacock.

'Ooh, I say,' she said in a posh voice. 'Aren't I devilish grand, old fellows? A diamond of the first water, ay?'

Black Jack chuckled. He was a tall man, bigger even than Thomas Behr.

'Wait!' said Hannah.

The woman stopped. 'I ain't goin' back on no bargain,' she said darkly.

'No,' said Hannah. 'I just–' she took a deep breath. 'There's something in the pocket of my – of your pelisse. It's … precious to me.'

The woman tilted her head on one side. 'Precious, eh? What is it then? Gold? Jewels? A note from your sweetheart? A pretty polly like you must have a handsome heart-splitter hangin' off your sleeves.' She dug her hand into the pocket of the pelisse and drew out a handkerchief. It was rumpled and a little dirty. She raised her eyebrows.

'This?' she said. 'This is precious?'

Hannah nodded. 'Please.'

The woman shrugged, and passed Hannah the handkerchief. Hannah wrapped it around her fingers.

⚜

At Hannah's next lesson, Thomas didn't talk about ancient Greek myths, or Columbus's travels, or tell stories about ice-castles and tricksy winds. He was formal, even awkward. Hannah yawned.

Thomas sighed. 'Shall we go for a walk? I'm sure your father would not disapprove of us visiting the British Museum–'

'Papa says it is too cold to go out. He says I have a weak chest.'

'Your Papa is full of concern,' said Thomas, stiffly.

Something was itching inside Hannah, making her restless.

'Was there something you wanted to say?' she asked. 'About my father?'

'Forget it,' said Thomas. He tugged his too-short shirtsleeve down where it had started creeping up his arm, revealing a thick tangle of pale hair on his wrist.

'No,' said Hannah. 'I want to hear your opinion of my father.'

Thomas hesitated.

'I'm waiting,' said Hannah.

He stood up and walked over to the fireplace. Then he turned and looked at her. 'Hannah, your father dresses you up like a china doll and then swans around town spending other people's money, leaving you in this big house on your own–'

'My papa is very important,' said Hannah. 'I don't mind at all that his affairs call him away from time to time.'

Thomas snorted. 'Affairs is right enough. Your father is known all over London for his *affairs*.'

Hannah stared at him, speechless. His eyes were sparkling again, and a part of Hannah was just happy to see his face lit up and excited, even if it was lit up with anger. But he shouldn't speak to her like that. Her father would be angry.

Thomas shook his head. 'Listen, Hannah–'

'Miss Cheshire,' said Hannah coldly.

Thomas looked away. The flush left his cheeks, and his eyes grew dull again. His shoulders hunched back over.

Hannah felt a tugging in her chest, and softened.

'I'm sorry,' she said, reaching over to touch his hand.

Thomas snatched his hand away.

'Your hands are *icy*,' said Hannah.

'It's cold outside,' he replied, not looking at her.

'Not as cold as the land where Scatterheart and the white bear come from,' she said with a smile.

Thomas looked surprised, but smiled back. 'No, not that cold.'

'Where is it, that land?' asked Hannah.

'The story comes from Norway.' He took off his glasses, which were fogging up in the warm room, and polished them with his handkerchief.

'How do you know it? Are *you* from Norway?' She wondered that she had never asked him that before, and realised that she knew very little about him. Where did he live? Did he have another job? Where was his family?

'My father is German, but his mother was from Norway. She liked to tell stories–' He broke off, as a door slammed somewhere in the house, and they heard the sound of glass breaking, and of sobbing.

'What on earth is that?' he asked, getting to his feet. The handkerchief slid onto the floor.

Hannah shrugged. 'It's probably Lettie. Papa let her go yesterday afternoon.'

'Let her go? Why?' Thomas turned his head upwards, as if he could see through the ceiling to where Arthur Cheshire was asleep in his bedroom.

Hannah waved a vague hand in the air. 'Papa wasn't happy with her. She always made the cup rattle in its saucer when she brought him tea.'

'She made the cup rattle?' asked Thomas. 'He's letting her because she made the cup rattle?'

Hannah rolled her eyes. 'He also thinks she stole his mother-of-pearl cufflinks. He can't find them anywhere. Shall we continue with my lesson?'

Thomas turned and frowned slightly. 'Of course,' he said, and came and sat down again. But he said nothing.

'Thomas?' said Hannah.

'That poor girl.'

This time it was Hannah's turn to frown. 'Poor girl? That poor girl stole from us,' she said. What was wrong with him? Who cared if the serving maid had been let go?

Thomas sighed. 'But what could have driven her to it? She seemed so happy here.'

'You never can tell with people like that.'

'People like what?' Thomas asked. 'Servants? Poor people? People like me?'

Hannah blushed. 'She was a thief. She deserved to be let go.'

Thomas stood up again, and paced over to the fireplace. 'Don't you pity her?' he asked. 'Your father turned her out onto the streets. She will steal, or starve, or worse. She could be sentenced to death, or transportation.'

Hannah felt a tug of guilt in her belly, but shook it away. 'You're being ridiculous. You didn't even know her.'

'Neither did you.' Thomas threw his hands up in the air. 'Last week a nine-year-old boy was transported for stealing three wrinkly old apples. The week before, a nineteen-year-old girl was hanged for taking a silver spoon from her mistress's cabinet. A single spoon!'

'Exactly,' said Hannah, relieved. 'Papa didn't turn her in. He just asked her to leave. She won't face any charges for her theft. Really, he is being very generous.'

'Why are you defending him?' asked Thomas, looking at her strangely.

'Things could be much worse for her,' said Hannah.

'I doubt that very much,' said Thomas. 'You have no idea what life is like outside this house. You've never been to Seven Dials and seen a woman feeding her baby gin because she can't afford to buy milk. Or a man so drunk that he beats his wife senseless and then drinks himself to death. Or a child, without family or shelter, frozen dead in an alleyway... You have all the silver spoons and apples you could ever want,' he said. 'You don't know what it's like.'

Hannah said nothing. Did *he* know what it was like? Had Thomas seen those things? Lived in those places? It was as if the ocean in his eyes had frozen solid. He looked disappointed in her. She felt a prickle of tears behind her eyes.

The frown-lines on Thomas's forehead faded, and the thin line of his lips softened.

'I'm sorry,' he said. 'I didn't mean to frighten you. Maybe I should talk to your father. Reason with him.'

'And what would you say?' said a smooth voice from behind them.

Hannah turned around to see her father standing in the doorway. He looked small and delicate compared to Mr Behr, like one of the china figurines on her mantelpiece next to a rough patchwork doll.

'Sir,' said Mr Behr. 'Please don't do this to Lettie.'

Arthur Cheshire wore an amused expression, but Hannah could tell that he was furious.

'I'm sorry, Thomas,' he said. 'But I'm afraid I don't take advice from servants.'

Hannah saw Thomas's shoulders straighten, and he stood up to his full height. Thomas's face was flushed with anger. 'You're a pathetic little man,' he said.

Arthur Cheshire didn't seem at all intimidated. He smiled blandly, and examined a perfectly shaped nail.

'Don't you think it's time you found a real job, Thomas?' he said. 'You've been here for nearly four years, dangling after my daughter. It's getting unseemly. You should go and find yourself some pretty serving-wench to marry. Someone who is closer to your own station in life.'

Thomas ignored Arthur Cheshire, and turned to Hannah.

'I'm sorry I said those things,' he said, his voice quiet and strangely gentle. 'I didn't mean to upset you.'

Hannah swallowed. She felt hot and angry and sick. She wanted Thomas to stay, but her father was right. She looked up at Thomas.

'Hannah?' he said.

Hannah looked away, saying nothing.

'You will address my daughter as *Miss Cheshire*,' said Hannah's father. 'If you address her at all, which I hardly think necessary any more.'

Thomas seemed to shrink. He reached down to put on his hat and gloves. He picked up the parcel of books. Then he sighed and looked at Hannah.

Hannah stared firmly at her hands, folded in her lap.

'Hannah,' said Thomas again.

She looked up. He was staring at her, a strange expression on his face that seemed urgent and sad and gentle all mixed up together. Hannah wanted to look away, but found she couldn't. She felt very aware of her father standing only a few feet away, watching.

She closed her eyes, and turned her head away, hot and trembling.

Thomas sighed, and walked into the hallway, closing the sitting room door behind him. It slammed loudly – Hannah wasn't sure if it had been Thomas's anger or just a gust of wind. The room trembled, and a blue-and-white porcelain vase toppled from the mantelpiece and shattered on the hearth.

Arthur Cheshire raised his eyebrows, and turned and left the room. Hannah heard the creak of stairs as he went up to his bedroom.

She went over to start picking up the pieces of broken vase, and saw Thomas's handkerchief lying on the floor where he had dropped it. She bent and picked it up, absently thinking she could give it to him at their lesson next week. Then she remembered he wasn't coming back. Her fingers curled around the handkerchief, and she dissolved into tears.

⁂

'What's your name, then, y'ladyship?' asked the woman.

Hannah swallowed. 'Hannah Cheshire.'

'Hannah Cheshire,' the woman mocked. 'Well, Hannah Cheshire, I is Long Meg.'

Hannah held out her hand. 'Very pleased to make your acquaintance, Miss Meg.'

Long Meg stared at the proffered hand, and burst out laughing. 'Ooh, ain't she posh, Black Jack! Did you hear that? *Very pleased to make your acquaintance, Miss Meg.* Did you ever hear such a thing?'

Black Jack shook his head. Hannah looked at Long Meg expectantly, who looked back.

'Is there sommit I can do for you, Hannah Cheshire?' she asked.

Hannah nodded. 'I– I gave you my pelisse. Do you think I might have some bread now?'

Long Meg slapped her forehead. 'Well ain't I just the most buffle-headed creature in all of the wit!' She reached under her skirt, and drew out the piece of bread. Hannah snatched it out of her hand.

'Careful now, else you'll be washing your shoes with it again like you did last night,' said Long Meg.

She watched Hannah devour the bread. 'So what you in for, eh?'

Hannah looked at her blankly, still chewing.

'What did you do? To get in here? Did you pilfer sommit? Those fancy threads, by the looks of it.'

Hannah looked indignant. 'Certainly not. I'm not supposed to be here. It's all a mistake. I haven't done anything wrong.'

Long Meg laughed her great roar of a laugh again. 'Sure you ain't. None of us have, have we lads?' She spread her arms wide. One or two people acknowledged her with a nod or a wink. She turned to Hannah. 'We's all innocent, pet. All of us.'

Hannah felt anger rise in her. She opened her mouth to issue a sharp retort, but said nothing. What was the point? She should be saving her energy to explain everything to the turnkey.

She swallowed the last crumb of bread. 'What did *you* do? To be in here?'

Long Meg stood up proudly, and linked her hands behind her back as if she were reciting poetry. 'One raven grey Coventry gown, one white ground cotton gown with red and laylock stripes, one Norwich crepe gown, one pink quilted petticoat, seven yards of black Calomanco, one pair of women's stays, one black satin cloak, one red duffin cloak, one fine white lawn apron, one chocolate ground silk handkerchief, one red and black silk handkerchief, one black silk handkerchief, one women's black silk hat, three white linen aprons, two checked linen aprons, one pair of leather shoes and one pair of plaited shoebuckles.' She sat down again.

'How did you steal it all?' Hannah was impressed, despite herself.

Long Meg just grinned, and reached for her brown glass bottle.

three

'Good evening to you,' said the bear through the window.
'Same to you,' replied the man.
'Will you give me your daughter to marry?' asked the bear.
'If you do, I shall make you as rich as you are now poor.'
'Well…' said the man.
'No,' said Scatterheart.

By the time Hannah woke the next morning, she found she had
almost grown used to the smell. But she had a new problem.
There was no water-closet in the cell, just an overflowing
bucket in a corner. Hannah's cheeks grew red at the thought
of using the bucket, with so many people watching, and yet
her bladder ached. She tried to put it out of her mind. She
wouldn't be there for long, after all.

When the turnkey came to deliver the meagre buckets of bread and water, Hannah was ready by the door.

'Excuse me, sir,' she said, whilst the other inmates scrabbled and fought for their scraps of bread.

The turnkey ignored her.

'I was apprehended mistakenly. I haven't stolen anything…'

The turnkey left the cell and slammed the door shut behind him.

'Wait!' called Hannah. 'I'm not supposed to be here! I demand to speak to someone in charge!'

The turnkey's footsteps echoed down the passageway, then died away. Hannah sank to the floor, trying not to cry. The toothless old woman touched her arm.

'Courtesy is cumbersome to them who kens it not,' she said, her words whistling through her empty gums. Hannah stared at her. Everyone here was mad. Tears began to spill over onto her cheeks.

'Don't you go listenin' to old Tabby,' said Long Meg, who had watched the exchange. 'She's as mad as a wet bullock.'

The old woman spat onto the stone floor, and sucked on a scrap of bread. Hannah looked at it longingly.

'Here,' said Long Meg, breaking her own bread in two and offering half to Hannah. 'Just this once.'

Hannah took the morsel, and found herself crying in earnest. She tried to remember the last time someone had done something nice for her.

'I'm sorry,' she said, hiccuping.

'Cry all you like,' said Long Meg. 'The more you cry, the less you'll piss.'

⁂

Thomas didn't come back. For the first three days Hannah cried bitter tears, but on the fourth day, her sorrow and shame turned into something else: a hard feeling like glass.

Why did she even care if he was gone? Thomas was just a servant, employed by her father to educate her. But she carefully washed Thomas's handkerchief, folded it neatly, and placed it in her dresser.

The other servants were colder towards her after the departure of Lettie and Thomas. Hannah's breakfast was plonked in front of her each morning, the toast often singed around the edges, the tea lukewarm. Hannah spent her mornings drifting around the house until her father rose, or one of her other teachers arrived for a music or dancing lesson.

Her father seemed in no hurry to find a new housemaid; he was distracted and vague – more so than usual, rising sometimes as late as three o'clock, and always out by six, returning home in the early hours of the morning, reeking of brandy and cigars.

One morning, nearly two weeks after Thomas's departure, Hannah was in the sitting room, embroidering a pair of slippers for her father. Snow fell heavily outside, making strange greyish swirls in the fog. A fire rumbled in the grate, but Hannah still shivered, and drew her shawl more tightly around her. She jumped as the front door banged open. There were footsteps in the hall. She frowned. No one had knocked, and surely her father was still asleep. She rose, and opened the door into the hall.

Her father stood there, brushing dirty grey snow from his hair and shoulders. His usually-gleaming hessians were scuffed and wet from the snow, and his hands shook in their yellow gloves.

'Papa!' said Hannah. 'What's wrong? Where's your hat and cloak! Didn't you come home last night?'

He turned to her, his eyes bloodshot and his face slack. He shook his head. 'Nothing to worry about, angel. Nothing at all.' He had an unfocussed look, and walked past her and began to climb the stairs, clutching the banister for support. Hannah followed him.

'Papa, are you sure you are all right? Have you been robbed? Where is your hat?'

He stopped, halfway up the stairs, and fumbled in his pocket, drawing out something wrapped in a stained handkerchief. He thrust it towards her. 'A gift, angel. Now be a good girl and let Papa go to his room. I have – business to attend to.'

Hannah took the handkerchief and watched her father stumble up the stairs. She unwrapped the bundle. It was a pair of silver earrings, glittering with tiny sapphires.

With a cry of delight, Hannah went to her room and clipped the earrings onto her ears, turning her head from side to side to admire them in the mirror. She must show her father.

She opened his bedroom door and stopped short. He was frantically throwing clothes into an open portmanteau on his bed.

'Papa?' said Hannah. 'What are you doing?'

Her father froze, and looked at her blankly. Then he shook his head. 'Business, angel,' he said. 'Going to Paris for a few days. On business. Nothing to worry about. You'll manage on your own.' He scrabbled about in his tallboy and drew out a handful of cravats.

'Why don't you get Adams to pack your case?'

He stuffed the cravats into the portmanteau. 'Adams ... I loaned Adams to a friend of mine. Nothing to worry about.'

'You *loaned* him?' said Hannah. 'You're going to Paris without a manservant?'

'No, angel. He will meet me at Newmarket. Nothing to worry about.'

'So you keep saying.' Hannah felt like she was about to cry.

Arthur Cheshire closed the portmanteau and jammed a hat on his head.

'Papa, you haven't even changed your clothes!'

'Can't you see I'm in a hurry?' he said. 'I have important business to attend to. I'll see you in a few days.' He dragged the case out of the room.

'Thank you for the earrings,' Hannah called out after him, her voice trembling. The portmanteau went thump, thump as Arthur Cheshire dragged it down the stairs.

⁕

The bread was hard and gritty, as if it had been mixed with ashes. Hannah started over to the water-bucket, but Long Meg reached out a hand.

'Shouldn't drink the water here if I was you,' she said. 'Got all sorts of wrigglies in it.'

She held out her brown bottle, and Hannah took a swig. The liquid tasted like fire, burning her throat and making her cough and splutter. Long Meg laughed her belly-laugh. 'You'll get used to it soon enough, y'ladyship,' she chuckled.

Hannah made a face. 'I think I'll take my chances with the water, if it's all the same to you.'

Long Meg shrugged. 'Suit yourself.'

Hannah learned from Long Meg that there were two sorts of prisoners in their cell: those awaiting trial, and those waiting for their sentence to be carried out. The next trial, or Session as it was called, was scheduled for the following Thursday. Hannah would have to stand before the judge and jury and plead her case, and hear her sentence. She spent her days practising the speech that she would deliver to the judge so there would be no doubt as to her situation.

The inmates who had already been to trial were different

from those who hadn't. They were quiet and subdued. Hannah thought they looked hollow, as if their bodies were just moving out of habit.

'What will happen to them?' she asked Long Meg.

'Transportation, mostly,' said Long Meg. 'And a few hangin's.'

Hannah swallowed. 'The people who get transported ... they all go to New South Wales?'

Long Meg shrugged. 'I 'spect so. They just calls it "Parts Beyond the Seas".'

Hannah thought that sounded rather romantic and said so to Long Meg, who laughed. 'Romantic? I hears it's hell. They say it takes nigh on two years to get there, on boats run by gangs with whips and chains.'

Hannah thought of Thomas Behr in an officer's uniform, brandishing a whip, and smiled.

⁂

Two days after Arthur Cheshire's departure, Thomas Behr came to see her.

Hannah had barely spoken since her father had gone. The servants muttered to each other in corners, stopping when she entered the room. Hannah rose at the usual time each morning, ate toast and tea for breakfast, worked on her embroidery, read and practised the pianoforte. Every afternoon, she would order a full dinner, in case her father came home, and every evening she would sit alone in the dining-room in her best dress, surrounded by cold buttered crab and haricot of mutton, congealing brown soup and sagging almond pudding. Asparagus and green beans grew limp in their dishes, as Hannah picked half-heartedly at the pheasant pie, and pushed beetroot around her white porcelain plate with a silver fork. Then, at ten o'clock, Jenny would come in and clear the dishes away, and Hannah would go up to her room and cry herself to sleep.

Thomas looked even more bedraggled than usual, standing at the door to the sitting room. The hem of his coat had fallen down, exposing the crooked stitching. He wore no gloves, and his fingers were white from the cold. Hannah wanted nothing more than to throw her arms around him and sob. But something stopped her.

'Mr Behr,' she said politely, inclining her head.

He took off his hat and bowed.

'Please,' said Hannah. 'Do sit down.'

He sat for a moment, saying nothing, then stood, and walked over to the fireplace.

'Is something wrong?' asked Hannah.

He looked at her, for the first time, a direct gaze that made Hannah turn away.

'Your father,' he said.

Hannah smiled. 'My father is in Paris on business. He will be back any day now, should you wish to speak to him about renewing your employment here.'

Thomas reached out and leaned on the mantelpiece.

'He isn't coming back.'

Hannah's jaw ached from smiling. 'I'm afraid you are mistaken.'

Thomas picked up a porcelain figurine and examined it carefully. Hannah heard the clock ticking in the hall. 'If he comes back, he will be killed.'

Hannah laughed nervously. 'Nonsense.'

'Hannah.' Thomas put down the figurine again. 'He's in a lot of trouble.'

Hannah began to tremble. She pushed herself deep into her chair and gripped the arm-rests so Thomas wouldn't notice.

'He's fled the country. He gambled away your mother's fortune. He's been living on credit for years.'

Hannah shook her head. 'My father is a good man, a man of business.'

'Last week...' Thomas pulled at his collar like it was choking him. 'Last week one of his creditors demanded his account be paid. Your father was drunk. He became violent ... He nearly killed the man, and took ... money and valuables from his person. The next day he disappeared. Now no one knows where he is.'

Hannah saw her father in the hallway, hatless and coatless, with vacant bloodshot eyes. She thought she might shatter into a thousand pieces.

'How do you know this?' she said, ashamed at the wobble in her voice.

'Everybody knows,' said Thomas uncomfortably. 'It's the talk of London.'

Hannah thought of the servants, whispering and muttering to each other.

'You're a liar,' she said.

A voice inside her protested. Thomas had never lied to her before. Hannah squashed the voice. He must be lying. Her father would never do something so … vulgar.

Thomas drew his chair closer to hers. 'Hannah. I can help you. You must know how…' he stuttered and looked away. 'You know how much I…'

He took a deep breath, and took her hand.

'Let me look after you,' he said. 'It won't be Mayfair and grand carriages, but I'm sure we can be happy … I have an uncle who is a naval Commander. He says he can get me a job in the marines.'

He stopped again, blushing furiously. Hannah stared at him.

'You want to *marry* me?' A hysterical giggle escaped her lips as she pulled her hand away. 'But you're so *old*!'

Thomas looked startled. 'I know you're a little young to be married, Hannah,' he said. 'But it's not unheard of. I'm only five years older than you.'

Hannah looked at him, as if for the first time. The pale hair, which she had always thought of as white, was really just the palest of pale yellows. He had been her tutor for nearly four years. Could he really be only nineteen?

She shook her head. This was ridiculous. Her father hadn't run away. Thomas Behr was lying. She had trusted him, looked up to him. And here he was, lying to her.

She stood up.

'Mr Behr,' she said. 'You came into my house, told me hateful and cruel lies about my father, all in some desperate and pathetic attempt to win my affections. I am not so easily bought. I will never marry you, or anyone like you. I am a gentleman's daughter, and I will marry a gentleman. Not some … some *commoner*.'

'Hannah, listen to me,' said Thomas, rising to his feet also, and reaching for her hand again. 'Let me explain.'

Hannah pulled away. 'Don't touch me.'

Thomas Behr shrank back from her expression, then lowered his head and left the room. This time he did not slam the door. He didn't even close it. He just left.

Hannah sank to the ground, her heart thumping. The front door closed. This time, Hannah didn't cry. She just sat there.

That evening, the servants packed up their bags and left, leaving Hannah alone in the house.

four

Scatterheart's father was a greedy man, so he told
Scatterheart to accept the bear's offer. She realised that
it might be quite nice to live in a castle and have beautiful
dresses. So she agreed, and climbed onto the bear's back.
As they travelled, the bear asked, 'Aren't you afraid?'
No, she wasn't.

'Well you might laugh, missy,' said Long Meg. 'But I hears
things. Storms that'll smash you into bits. Monsters as big as
mountains. Darkness when it should be blazin' noon. Islands
that can swim and has tusks like an elly-phant. And all of us,
chained up together in the belly of the boat, packed in as close
as God's curse to a whore's arse.'

Hannah raised her eyebrows. 'I think you've been listening

to too many fairy-stories.'

But Long Meg had an audience now. Several of the other inmates had turned their attention to her, and she continued in a deep, ominous voice.

'That's only the sea journey. They says when you gets to Parts Beyond the Seas, the worst of the monsters is yet to come. Men with dog-heads, dragons that'll turn us into stones, people with faces on their chests! The place is overrun with savages, skins as black as thunder, and they all wants to eat our flesh. It's a battle just to survive.' She looked around, her eyes wide.

Hannah snorted. 'Papa has read me a number of reports in the *Morning Post* about the colony in New South Wales, and none of them mentioned any dog-headed men or dragons.'

The old woman, Tabby, had obviously been listening. She clambered laboriously to her feet, and shuffled over to them, her back hunched.

'All things has an end,' she said. 'And a pudding has twa.'

There was a dead silence in the cell for a moment, broken only by the coughing of a man lying huddled in a corner, and then Long Meg laughed her belly-laugh.

'But we ain't got nothin' to worry about, do we friends? We's all innocent!'

A rumble of laughter went through the inmates, and they all returned to what they were doing. Tabby looked at Hannah then belched loudly, and shuffled off.

Hannah sat for a while, squirming uncomfortably at

the full, sloshing pain in her bladder. She crossed her legs
and balled her hands into fists. She bit her tongue. Finally,
she could stand it no more, and made her way over to the
bucket. She hoisted up her skirt and petticoat, and lowered
her pantaloons, burning red with shame. The noise of her
urine sounded so loud as it splashed into the bucket, she was
sure that half of London could hear it. But none of the other
inmates so much as looked in her direction, and the feeling of
release was so great that Hannah sighed with relief.

⁂

With the servants gone, the house felt empty and strange.

Hannah's bedroom was cold. Her fingers were stiff from
holding the handkerchief all night. The jug of water on her
nightstand had frozen. The fire had gone out. Her stomach
felt hollow and growly – she had not eaten anything since
early the day before.

She climbed out of bed, placing the handkerchief carefully
on her nightstand, and went over to the fireplace. It was cold
and dark. She paused. It couldn't be that hard. She looked
around and her eyes lit on the coalscuttle. She reached in
and pulled out a few hard black lumps. She tossed them into
the fireplace and wiped the black dust on her nightdress.
She looked at the fireplace, unsure about what to do next.
Lettie had done this in front of her a million times. Why had
Hannah never paid more attention? She picked up a poker
and jabbed the coal in the fireplace. A cloud of ash rose and

made her cough. She felt as if she might cry.

Hannah closed her eyes and counted to ten. 'Papa will come home today,' she said firmly to herself. 'He will make everything right.'

She stood up and went over to the window, drawing the drapes open. She could see nothing but a dark, yellowish void. Old, greying snow lay on her windowsill. Everything felt flat and suffocating.

Hannah closed the drapes again, and went to investigate her tallboy for warm clothes. The shelves were well-stocked with crisp white linen. Hannah opened drawer after drawer until she finally located some thick woollen socks. She pulled these on, and also found a knitted shawl, which she wrapped tightly around herself, rubbing her upper arms to warm them up.

She made her way out of her room and down the stairs. They creaked under her feet, the sound echoing in the empty house. Hannah had never been truly alone before. There had always been servants around. Hannah clutched the balustrade and breathed deeply. She would *not* be afraid.

In the sitting room fireplace, a single coal still glowed red. Hannah took fresh coal from the scuttle and piled the pieces in the grate. The cheery red coal went dull, and began to smoke alarmingly. Hannah looked around. She needed something that would *burn*.

She ran into the dining room. A pile of newspapers were folded neatly on a side-table, waiting for her father. Hannah glanced at the date on the top one. It was four days old. She grabbed the whole pile and hurried back to the sitting room.

The one hot coal was barely glowing. Hannah peeled a tiny strip of newspaper, and laid it gently over the coal. She didn't want to smother it any more than she already had. The edges of the paper glowed red, then suddenly a flame sparked into life, and, just as suddenly, was gone. Hannah tore off another strip, a longer one, and tried again.

'Catch,' she muttered. 'Catch.'

She wasn't sure if she were talking to herself or to the fire. She ripped off an entire page of newspaper, and scrunched it into a ball. She poked it into the fireplace, snuggled up against the hot coal. It smouldered, then went up in a sheet of yellow flame.

Nearly an hour later, Hannah had used up four editions of the *Morning Post*, and two of *The Times*. She sat back on her heels, exhausted but satisfied. It was not the cheery, lively fire that normally burned in the grate, but the lopsided arrangement of coal was definitely producing heat. Hannah brushed the coal dust and scraps of newspaper from her nightgown. Her stomach growled. It was time for breakfast.

She made her way down to the kitchen, feeling rather pleased with herself, and found a stale loaf of bread, a dish of butter and a knife.

Back upstairs, Hannah sat in one of the chintz armchairs, chewed on the hard bread and considered her predicament.

There were no servants. No food. The fire was burning

now, but for how much longer? There was only so much newspaper in the house.

She had no money of her own – her father bought her anything she wanted. He said it was vulgar for a woman to handle money. *Not ladylike*, he said. *Inappropriate*. But perhaps Papa would have some money in his room.

His tallboy contained yards and yards of unstarched white linen, ready to be pressed and folded into elaborate neckties. There were also some strange linen articles that Hannah could only assume were undergarments. Blushing, she replaced them hastily, and turned to her father's dressing-table.

It was covered in little pots and jars with the most enticing names. *Pomade de Neroles* was a dark, crumbly substance that smelled of violets. *Olympian Dew* was clear and sticky like honey. *Liquid Bloom of Roses* was red and waxy. *Pearl of India* was a fine white powder, delicately scented.

There were also nail-scissors, shaving equipment and other implements too strange to guess their uses. Hannah was astounded that such a handsome gentleman needed so many accessories.

There was no money.

⁂

The man who lay in the corner kept Hannah awake all night with a rasping, choking cough that made her throat hurt just hearing it. The next morning, he was sweating profusely, and shaking at the same time. Someone tried to give him a drink of water, but he wouldn't swallow. He took to sleeping in the darkest corner of the cell, shielding his eyes from the light, and moaning and muttering to himself as he shook and convulsed.

After two days, a red, angry rash appeared on his chest, and spread rapidly over the rest of his body. The other inmates kept as far away from him as they could, covering their mouths with scraps of fabric. A doctor came and forced a slippery silver liquid into the man's mouth, but he showed no sign of improvement.

On the fifth day, he was dead.

five

Scatterheart and the white bear travelled a long, long way, until they came to a castle, high up on a white mountain. In Scatterheart's chamber there was a bed as white as you can imagine, with silken pillows and gold fringe.

The bear told her she could go anywhere in the castle or its gardens. But there was one place she could not go. In the garden there was a great white wall of ice, with a little door set in it. Scatterheart was never to open that door.

Hannah stayed in the cell for twelve days. Each day when the turnkey came to dump the bucket of scraps on the floor, Hannah would plead with him to let her speak to someone in charge. The turnkey ignored her until the sixth day, when he saw the dead man in the cell. He immediately backed away, digging in his pocket to find a handkerchief, which he held over his mouth and nose. He barked a command, and two burly men appeared. They entered the cell, kicking aside sleeping prisoners. The women simpered.

'Fancy a tumble, mister?'

'I bet you dance the feather-bed jig very fine, sir.'

'Come on, love, let's blow the grounsils!'

The men ignored them, and bent over to pick up the dead man. His head lolled to one side, and a string of saliva dribbled from the corner of his mouth. As his head fell back, his eyes stared straight at Hannah. She let out a small scream. The dead man's head rolled back the other way as he was hoisted up between the two men. Hannah climbed over the sleeping bodies to the door of the cell.

'Please,' she said to the turnkey. 'I'm not supposed to be here.'

Hannah felt dizzy from hunger and fear and exhaustion. She touched the turnkey's arm.

'My name is Hannah Cheshire,' she said, her voice breaking. 'I'm a gentleman's daughter. I'm Quality. You know I don't belong here.'

❦

Hannah was in the sitting room, half-heartedly working on her embroidery, when she heard the knocker rap three times on her front door. Papa was home! She raced into the hallway and wrenched the front door open.

It was not Papa. It was Thomas. He loomed out of the sickly fog, his shoulders hunched against the cold.

He took his hat off when the door opened, then blushed madly and looked away when he saw Hannah still in her nightdress. Hannah wrapped her shawl around herself. He wore the red coat and brass buttons of a marine.

It made him look different. Younger, and at the same time more grown up. A part of her wanted to burst into tears and tell him about everything that had happened, but something stopped her. He had been so...forward last time. So inappropriate. Arthur Cheshire would have called it *vulgar*. Thomas Behr wasn't like her. He wasn't a person of Quality.

'What do you want?' she asked.

'I want to know if you've thought about my offer.'

Hannah sighed. 'Good day, Mr Behr.'

She moved to close the door, but he threw out an arm and stopped her.

'Hannah,' he said. 'Please. There is a bounty on your father's head. If he returns to London he will hang.'

The fog slithered about them.

'Listen,' said Thomas Behr. 'I don't have much time. I have a new job. As an officer in the New South Wales Corps. But our ship leaves the day after tomorrow. I've spoken with my commanding officer, and I've been granted leave to bring you with me, but we have to be married.'

'You can't seriously think I would consider this,' she said through clenched teeth. 'When I marry, it will be to a gentleman of Quality. My husband would never even dream of suggesting something as vulgar as taking me on a *boat*, to a prison on the other side of the world!'

'It's a ship, not a boat.' Thomas Behr grinned at her, and despite herself, Hannah smiled back.

'Come on, Hannah,' he said. 'It'll be an adventure! Like Robinson Crusoe!'

His eyes shone. She imagined them together on a ship, the wind rushing through their hair as they sailed over an ocean that sparkled grey like his eyes. For a moment, she believed him. It *would* be an adventure. Then she remembered who she was.

'Robinson Crusoe,' she said, 'was shipwrecked for twenty-eight years, and encountered savages, captives and mutineers. Hardly appropriate company for a young lady of Quality.'

'Who cares about *appropriate*?' said Thomas. 'Think of the adventure! Who cares about *Quality*?'

'I do,' replied Hannah. 'I care.'

'So you'd rather stay here and marry old Harris.'

Hannah thought about Mr Harris's sweat stains, and his moist fleshy lips. And she thought about his big house in Grosvenor Square, and his chaise-and-four.

'Yes,' she said. 'I would.'

Thomas took a step back, confusion and hurt on his face.

'Really?' he asked, his voice suddenly very quiet.

Hannah felt as if something were dying inside her, like a candle was being snuffed out.

'Really,' she said.

'Hannah,' said Thomas. 'He wouldn't have you, not anymore.'

For a moment, neither of them said anything. Hannah could barely stand to look at him. It was like he could see right through her, into her heart. The expression on his face frightened her. It was so raw, all hurt and angry and all sorts of other things that Hannah didn't understand. She wanted to reach out and touch his pink cheek, feel his ridiculous messy straw-hair under her fingers. She shivered.

'Let me help you,' said Thomas.

The fog rolled away in whirls and billows.

'I don't want you, Thomas.' She closed the door.

⁂

'Cheshire?' The turnkey looked at her. 'Not Arthur Cheshire's girl?'

Hannah found herself weeping with relief. Finally, someone knew who she was. He could explain the mistake to everyone, and she'd be free to go. *But where?* a niggling voice inside her wanted to know. She shook it away. She curled her fingers around the turnkey's sleeve.

'Yes,' she said. 'I'm Arthur Cheshire's daughter.'

The turnkey shook her hand from his arm. 'Then you belong in here as surely as night follows day,' he said. 'Criminality *descends*, you know. And your father was a criminal, all right.'

Hannah closed her eyes. Even the turnkey thought her father was a villain. It must be true.

The two men shuffled past, the corpse swaying between them. The turnkey slammed the door.

'Cheshire, eh?' said Long Meg's voice behind her.

Hannah turned around. There was a strange expression on Long Meg's face. It seemed almost … respectful. Hannah sniffed, and wiped the tears from her cheeks.

'My papa is a gentleman,' she said, her voice trembling. 'A good man.' She wasn't sure if she believed it anymore.

'Well,' said Meg. 'I don'ts know if he's a good *man*, but he sure is a good–' she paused and took in Hannah's tear-stained face, 'gambler.'

Hannah drew herself up. 'You don't know my father,' she said.

'Poppet, every girl in London Town knows your daddy,' chuckled Meg. 'Quality or no.'

⁂

'Everyone in London knows of Arthur Cheshire.'

Hannah froze. She was still in bed. There was someone downstairs. Unfamiliar voices in the hall.

Snatches of conversation drifted up to her.

'…Catch him, he'll have cotton in his ears.'

'…dine on a hearty-choke an' caper sauce…'

'…a right tangerine…'

The words meant nothing to Hannah. She listened to them

walk from one room of the house to another, the floorboards creaking under their feet. She wondered why she hadn't thought to lock the front door, then realised she didn't know where to find the key.

It was not until she heard their tread on the staircase that she looked around for a place to hide. Their voices grew louder and more intelligible.

'Well, if Newgate doesn't get 'im, it's only a matter o' time before one of 'is cent per centers does,' said one voice, harsh and common.

'They say he's been in dun territory for nigh on five years. Five years, and not so much as a monkey to his name.' The other voice sounded more educated, but didn't have the sophisticated air of a man of Quality.

The other man laughed. 'A monkey? Poor fellow doesn't even 'ave a pony. Pockets to let, 'e does.'

They reached the top of the stairs, and Hannah dropped to the floor and wriggled under her bed. The stench of her chamber pot, unemptied for many days, was almost unbearable. Her stomach heaved, but she bit down hard on her bottom lip. She thought about screaming for help, but who would hear her? All their neighbours had left town, and wouldn't return until the Spring.

'Terrible rake,' said the second voice, as they entered her room. 'Look here, this is a girl's room. They said he had a daughter, but I didn't believe it.'

Hannah's heart beat so loudly that she thought they must

be able to hear it. What would happen if they found her?

The first man swore. 'Keepin' a young lady in this kind of sit-choo-ashun? Where's 'er mama, then?'

'Died,' said the other man, shortly. 'Just as well, really. They says he only married her for the money. He was flashing his screens and chasing bits of muslin about town before she was cold in the grave. Now he's drowning in vowels. If he comes back…'

'A babe in the woods,' said the first man morosely.

'Pity about the girl, though.'

The other man spat. Hannah saw it land, not two feet away from her face. It glistened there, wet and shining.

'Well she ain't 'ere. Come on then, we've seen enough. Let's go tell Jones, before we both end up punting on the river Tick.'

The men left the room, and Hannah listened carefully as their footsteps grew fainter. It was only when she heard the front door bang that she allowed herself to breathe again. *He only married her for the money*, they'd said. Her father didn't mention her mother often. Hannah had always assumed that it was because his heart was still broken from her death. She remembered him describing how beautiful she was. Didn't that mean he had really loved her?

She lay on the dusty floorboards, waiting for her heart to calm down, and for the trembling in her hands to subside. He must have loved her. He loved Hannah, after all, didn't he?

Hannah crawled out from underneath the bed, and

brushed the dust off her nightgown. She caught her reflection in the mirror. A pale, frightened face looked back at her.

Food. She needed food. She combed her father's room again for money, but found nothing. So she selected her least favourite necklace from her dressing-table, and wrapped it in a linen handkerchief. She would have to sell it.

Hannah dressed herself with difficulty – she had never done it unassisted before. She found a clean linen corselet, lacing it clumsily behind her. Then she pulled on a pair of flesh-coloured pantaloons that reached to her ankles, warm woollen stockings and a flannel petticoat. Next, she selected her warmest dress – a pale pink gown made of fine wool and trimmed with lace. She struggled with the buttons, her fingers cold and stiff.

She pulled on a full-length, fur-trimmed pelisse in dark green, and a pair of kidskin ankle-boots.

She pulled a brush through her tangled hair, but it kept getting stuck. She tried to yank it through, but it pulled on her hair so hard that she yelped, and tears started to her eyes. She put down the brush and worked at the knot with her fingers. She remembered a story Mr Behr had told her about Alexander the Great cutting through an intricate knot with a sword. She thought about the little silver nail-scissors she had seen on her father's dressing-table, but decided against it. She didn't want to ruin her hair. Papa was so fond of it.

Once the knot was finally loosened, Hannah attempted to pin her hair into place. The pins slipped from her fingers, and more than once she stabbed herself in the head with their sharp ends. By the time she had finished, one of her fingers was bleeding, her head ached, and her jaw was clenched to keep her from crying. Hannah dabbed a little scent behind her ears, and pulled on warm gloves.

Finally, she clipped on the sapphire earrings her father had bought her, and admired her reflection in the mirror. Her hair was a little askew, and her pelisse did not sit *quite* right, but overall she looked like any young lady of Quality.

She dropped the necklace into a pink satin reticule, daintily embroidered and beaded in green. She lifted a velvet bonnet from its stand, and tied the strings under her chin. She tucked her reticule under her arm, and, almost as an afterthought, put Thomas Behr's handkerchief in her pocket. Then she swept from her room, down the stairs and out the front door.

She stood on the front step for a moment. It was the first time she had been outside – really outside, not just into the garden – for nearly two months. The fog hung thick and heavy over the deserted street, as cold and empty as the house she had left behind. Her cheeks and nose burned with cold. She pulled the door closed behind her and took a step forward. The hunger gnawing at her stomach pushed her on.

She thought about Scatterheart and the white bear. *Are you afraid?* he had asked her.

Hannah plunged into the fog.

six

Scatterheart was happy for a while, doing as she pleased, and dressing in fine silks and jewels, but soon she turned lonely, silent and sorrowful. She only saw the white bear at dinner-time, and all day she was alone. She began to wonder what lay behind the little door set in the wall of ice. So, one day, she ventured out into the garden.

On her twelfth day in the cell, Hannah woke covered in sweat. It was raining heavily outside, and the room was damp. Hannah's stockings were full of holes. Her hands shook. Today she would attend the Sessions.

'Gentlemen of the court,' she muttered to herself. 'A series of misfortunes and calamities…'

She ran her trembling fingers through her hair, splashed

some cold water on her face. Her dress was no longer a delicate pale pink, it was now an indiscriminate greyish-brown. But she smoothed it as best she could, and bit off the loose threads that hung where the lace had been ripped off. The other inmates watched her with some amusement, but made no effort to smarten themselves up. Long Meg was in a corner with Black Jack, giggling and whispering as if it were a day like any other.

Hannah scratched at her louse bites absently as she waited for the turnkey to arrive. The bites were red and angry-looking. Her heart pounded, and she felt a little light-headed from the lack of food and water. She drew Thomas's handkerchief out from inside her dress, where she kept it safe from thieving hands. It was now filthy, but she held it tightly.

Hannah followed the dim orange haloes of the gas lamps, which seemed to be suspended in mid-air, their lampposts obscured by the yellow murkiness. She turned right down Oxford Street.

The streets were dim and almost deserted. The occasional person would suddenly materialise out of the fog – tall, dark strangers in black cloaks. The fog muffled all sounds, so there was no warning of someone approaching. They would loom before her, and then pass silently by.

Where would she find a pawnbroker? Hannah had no idea where to look. She turned down a side street, and then another, trying to move quickly to stay warm. Down another narrow street, and Hannah found herself in a small square. Dirty children played at hussle-cap in the grey snow, shouting and squealing like skinny brown pigs. One of them looked up and saw her.

'Oi! Missus!' he called. 'Give us a shilling! Me little sister's catched the cold and me mam is laid up with the clap.'

Hannah hurried on, until their cries were swallowed up in the fog.

She was in a part of London where she had never been before. The elegant brick and stone houses had been replaced with wooden ones, which jostled against one another as if clamouring to reach the light. Few windows were paned with glass; instead they were stuffed with rags and brown paper. A rat scurried across the street and Hannah bit back a scream. A man staggered out of the fog and crashed into her. She clutched her reticule tight to her chest. The man had a red face, and wore a shabby brown coat and ancient breeches. His face was ruddy and his eyes unfocussed.

'Beggin' yer pardon, miss,' he said, belching, and reeled away into the shadows.

She turned another corner, and saw a man pressing a woman up against a wall. The man's breeches were unbuttoned, the woman's legs wrapped around his hips. Hannah felt cold and sick all of a sudden. The man's face was red. The woman saw Hannah watching, and met her gaze with a uninterested stare. Hannah blushed, confused, and hurried on.

A loose paving stone wobbled under her foot, shooting a jet of freezing, filthy water up her skirt. She broke into a run. A dog barked. She whirled around a corner, and found herself in a dead end. Tiny, rotting wooden houses leaned on each other for support.

A woman sat in the snow. She wore only a dirty petticoat and old-fashioned stays. A bottle lay on its side next to her, its contents spilled out into the snow. It smelled bitter and sweet at the same time. The woman stared fixedly at the ground in front of her.

'Excuse me,' said Hannah, her voice shaking. 'I appear to be lost.'

The woman didn't reply. She didn't even move. Hannah leaned forward to get the woman's attention. She brushed the woman's cheek. She was as cold as snow. Hannah turned and ran back down the street, down cluttered alleyways overflowing with rubbish and vermin, trying to make out a familiar landmark.

Hannah couldn't see the street signs for the fog. Her head was light from hunger and cold, and she was not sure how far she had walked.

What little light there was had faded, and the fog drew in, close and suffocating. Hannah peered to either side of her, but could discern no buildings at all. She felt the crunch of wild bracken and frozen earth under her feet, and panic rose in her throat. She couldn't even see her hand stretched out in front of her. Where was she?

A low cry sounded through the fog. Hannah ran again, blindly. Finally, her feet found solid earth once more – not a paved street, but some kind of dirt road. She reached out in front of her, and her hands met something hard and rough. Wood. Some kind of tree. She leaned against it and tried to catch her breath. The pounding of her heart seemed to beat in the air around her. Hannah dug her hand into her pocket and felt the comforting folds of Thomas's handkerchief. She heard the mournful cry again, but it was further away this time. She slumped in relief.

A breath of wind lifted the fog for a moment, and Hannah peered around her. She laughed nervously. She had become completely turned around. Behind her was the long stretch of Tyburn Road. Hyde Park lay to her left, and to her right, fields and farmland. That was the strange land she had wandered into, just the fields to the north of Tyburn Road. The strange cries she had heard had been nothing more than cows lowing. Hannah's heart calmed somewhat, and she felt rather embarrassed at having been so frightened.

She turned to examine the tree that had provided her with support. It was no ordinary tree. Its trunk was smooth and straight. It was a gallows.

She thought of Thomas, surrounded by swirls of fog. *There is a bounty on your father's head. If he returns to London he will hang.*

She began to shake uncontrollably. What if Papa never came back? Had he really abandoned her? Surely he would write, or send money, or something. What would she do? She had no aunts or uncles to go and live with. She was sure Mr Harris would have nothing to do with her now.

She leaned against the gallows, her breath coming in short, gulping sobs. She tried to be sensible, to think of a plan. But her mind was in a panicking whirl. She closed her eyes.

She thought of her bedroom, with the satin quilt and cheery fire. That was what she needed. Comfort. Normality. She ached to be in her bedroom, to climb into the four-poster bed and bury her head under the goose-down pillows.

The pawnbroker could wait until tomorrow. She took a faltering step away from the gallows, then another. She walked, still trembling, back down Tyburn Road, and turned right down New Bond Street, and Brook Street, until she finally found herself turning the familiar corner of her own street. A heavily-loaded wagon rumbled past, splashing freezing slush onto her dress, but Hannah didn't care. She was home. She ran to her house, and stopped short at the bottom of the steps.

The front door was open.

⚜

The turnkey rattled the cell door open. Hannah got quickly to her feet, and her head swam for a moment. She reached out to steady herself on the damp stone wall. The turnkey read out twelve names from a list, and Hannah and ten others stepped forward. The twelfth name belonged to the dead man.

In the corridor outside the cell, the turnkey fastened leg-irons to all the prisoners, and linked them together with a length of chain passed through the irons. Hannah tried to step forward, and nearly fell. The irons were heavy. With each step she felt like she was wading through thick sand. Her calves ached from the effort after only a few steps. She took small, clanking, shuffling steps down the corridor, past other cells full of wasted creatures with huge empty eyes. At the end of the corridor was a steep flight of stone stairs, leading downwards. The turnkey told them with satisfaction that this was Dead Man's Walk.

They stumbled down the stairs, into a dimly-lit underground passage. The rich smell of damp earth and stone seemed like the sweetest thing Hannah had ever experienced, after the fetid air of the cell. She breathed deeply, and the trembling in her hands lessened.

'Gentlemen of the court,' she whispered, rubbing Thomas's handkerchief with her thumb. '…at your mercy.'

When they came to the foot of the steps that led upwards into the Old Bailey, the turnkey stopped them, and unchained the first prisoner, leading him up the steps and out of sight.

The prisoners huddled together in the passageway. Hannah was third in line. A candlestick, a Bible and a prayer book were chained to the wall. Hannah kept her eyes firmly on the flight of stone steps, waiting for the turnkey to return, and rehearsing her speech over and over.

She would tell them about her father, and everything else

that had happened. They would nod understandingly, and take her to a hotel where she would be given hot soup and fresh bread, and a steaming mug of chocolate. And a four-poster bed with goose-down pillows... And then Papa would come back from France, and everything would be fine. She would see Thomas again and they would forget about the awkwardness and the arguments...

※

Had Hannah left the front door open? She didn't think so.

A flicker inside her hoped that it was her father, home at last, but it was only a weak spark, extinguished quickly in the cold evening air.

The grandfather clock was gone. The hats on the hatstand were gone. The umbrella stand was gone. The rug on the floor was gone. There were muddy footprints on the bare floorboards.

Hannah pushed open the door to the sitting room. It was empty. Even the Turkish rug that she and Thomas Behr had made stories about was gone. Hannah ran to the dining room. It too was empty. She ran up the stairs, only to be greeted by creaking floorboards, with clean squares where carpets had lain, and dusty ones where furniture had sat.

A great weariness came over her. She went into the room that had so recently been her bedroom. She felt like her heart was breaking. There was no four-poster bed. No satin quilt. No goose-down pillows. Her clothes were all gone. Her jewellery.

She felt dizzy from hunger and fear and cold. All she had were the clothes she had on, her sapphire earrings, the topaz necklace in her reticule, and Thomas Behr's handkerchief.

She lay down on the wooden boards where her bed had once been, resting her cheek against the dusty floor, and closed her eyes.

⁓

'We ain't got all day, missy.'

Hannah jumped. The turnkey was standing in front of her, staring down at her with a look of contempt on his face. He had unchained Hannah from the rest of the prisoners, and was waiting to escort her up to the courtroom. Hannah blinked. Could she have fallen asleep? She shook her head to clear it, but it only made her dizzy. Putting one hand out to steady herself on the damp earthy wall, she made her way slowly up the steps, the leg-irons tearing her stockings to shreds, and carving out red marks on her skin.

seven

Scatterheart lifted the latch of the little door.
On the other side was a garden made of ice.
White leaves tinkled overhead. In the centre of the garden,
an ancient ice-tree spread twisted branches towards the sky.
A single, blue fruit hung from one of its branches.
Scatterheart plucked it from its branch.
It was cold to touch.

The turnkey opened a door at the top of the steps, and pushed Hannah through. She was assaulted by a blast of icy air, followed by an overpowering smell of burning herbs and vinegar. The floor was wet, and the small cuts and grazes on her feet stang. The floor was red, like it had been washed with wine. Her eyes watered.

She was marched by two men in uniform to a barricaded wooden stand, where she would stand during the trial. The Old Bailey courtroom was packed with spectators, who covered their mouths with handkerchiefs as Hannah passed. She felt a hot mixture of shame and indignation. What were all these people doing here? It was vulgar.

The room was elegant, with a high ceiling and an elevated gallery where the public jostled for a view. The large windows and doors were all flung open to the raging gale outside, and the black velvet curtains were soaking wet from the freezing sleet which was driving diagonally in through the windows. Large, open braziers burned in every available space, pouring forth a noxious smoke which made Hannah's head swim.

She looked across the room to the jury and the judges. An enormous sword hung on the wall above the Lord Mayor's chair of office, larger than a man. Above it, a lion and a unicorn grasped a crown.

The Lord Mayor sat in his chair, wearing his black robe and golden chain of office. He looked stern. In front of him, the jury sat penned in a wooden enclosure, as did the witnesses and the defendant. The smoke made Hannah's eyes sting. She leaned heavily on the bench in front of her.

A clerk came up to Hannah, and held out a Bible. She put her hand out and touched the leather cover of the book. Her fingers were slippery with sweat.

'How will you be tried?' asked the clerk, chewing hard on a strange black and orange mass. His breath reeked of orange peel, caraway and garlic. Hannah felt sick, but she had already been told what to say.

'By God and my country,' she replied, in a quavering voice.

The clerk turned to the Lord Mayor and announced in a loud voice, 'Hannah Cheshire is accused with feloniously stealing a pair of sapphire earrings, value forty-one shillings.'

A murmur went around the assembled spectators when Hannah's name was announced. Hannah thought of the knowing smile on Long Meg's face when she had mentioned Arthur Cheshire, and the way the turnkey had shook her hand from his arm. She felt hot and prickly, despite the freezing room.

A man stood up and swore on the Bible. Hannah recognised him by his curly ginger whiskers.

'My name is Samuel Smith,' he said. 'I own a shop on Monmouth Street. The prisoner came into my shop some weeks ago and pawned a golden necklace. While she was there, she stole a pair of sapphire earrings that were on display.'

⁂

Hunger drove Hannah from the house the next morning.

It was difficult to tell what time of day it was, or even if it was daytime at all. Shops were dimly lit, their windows covered in frost. *John Wheeley, Scale-maker. Jack Picard's Paper Hanging Warehouse. Goodman & Flude, Purveyors of Tobacco & Snuffs.*

The smell of baking bread wafted from someone's kitchen and made Hannah's stomach growl. She licked her lips, and hurried on, until she found *Samuel Smith, Pawnbroker & Silversmith*. She peered in through the window, and saw jewellery, watches, fine china, silver cutlery and candlesticks, shoes, hats, coats and stays. A sign above the door read *Unredeemed goods fold Wholefale & Retail. Money lent.*

Hannah opened the door.

The man behind the counter looked up at her. He had ginger whiskers and close-cropped, curly hair. There were gravy spots on his shirt and something white and crumbly in the corners of his mouth.

'You lost?' His eyes were narrowed.

Hannah tried to look businesslike. 'I need some money. I have this necklace.' She opened her reticule, and deposited the necklace on the counter. It was gold, with topaz stones set along the front. The man – Hannah presumed he must be Mr Smith – reached out for an eyeglass and peered at the necklace. Hannah could hear him breathing, a wet, rasping sound.

'Where'd you get this?' he asked.

Hannah felt a hot burst of shame. She shook it away, angrily. She had nothing to be ashamed of. 'My father bought it for me,' she said.

Mr Smith licked his lips. 'Your father bought it for you, eh?'

Hannah gritted her teeth. 'His name is Arthur Cheshire.

He is currently away on business in Paris. He will be back any day now, but I need a little something for my expenses. He will redeem the necklace the moment he returns to London.'

At the mention of her father's name, Mr Smith looked up from the necklace and leaned over the counter towards her. Hannah took a step back. His breath stank.

Mr Smith's eyes roamed all over her body, and settled on her ears. Hannah put up a hand and felt the sapphire earrings.

'I'd rather take them pretty blue earrings,' he said.

Hannah swallowed. 'No,' she said, trying to keep her voice firm. 'Only the necklace.'

'Quite a famous design,' said Mr Smith, not taking his eyes from the earrings. 'They'd fetch a fine price.'

'Thank you, but no,' said Hannah. 'I think I'll keep them.'

'Are you sure they're yours to keep?' he said.

Hannah suddenly remembered Mr Behr standing on the front step. *He nearly killed the man, and took ... money and valuables from his person. The next day he fled the country.*

She thought about how her father had given her the earrings wrapped in a stained handkerchief. Why hadn't she wondered at the time why they hadn't come boxed, with a ribbon and tissue paper?

Hannah's clenched her fists to stop her hands shaking. Her fingernails bit into her palms. The pawnbroker grunted, and looked back down at the topaz necklace.

'Five shillings,' he said.

Hannah didn't know whether that was the right amount of money for her necklace, but she took the money and fled.

⁂

Hannah thought she saw the lion's tail twitch above the Lord Mayor's chair, but when she looked up, she saw only white plaster. Her eyes stung and she squeezed them shut.

'Hold up your head, young woman,' hissed the clerk. 'And look at his lordship.'

Hannah opened her eyes, and the room seemed to swim before her.

'My eyes–' she stammered.

The clerk ignored her. Another man stood up, and swore on the Bible. Hannah thought she had seen him before, but could not remember where. He wore a large ring on his finger, gleaming like new. She coughed again, her throat swollen and raw. The leg-irons seemed to burn into her skin.

'My name is John Huggins. Three weeks ago, I was selling tickets to an attraction at the Frost Fair, when the prisoner, along with other ruffians, pushed me down onto the ice, and scrambled into my theatre without paying.'

⁂

Hannah stepped out of the pawnbroker's, and felt like she was stepping into another world. The fog was lifting, and a faint glow of sunshine could be made out in an increasingly blue sky.

Where the streets had been empty yesterday, they were now occupied by a large group of young people. They were not people of Quality, but they spoke well enough. They all seemed to be dressed in their best clothes, and for a moment Hannah thought that she must have missed two whole days and it was now Sunday. They were heading east down Oxford Street towards the city, all laughing and talking.

One young man was waving a scrap of newspaper around.

'Hurry!' he said to his friends. 'Before the Frost Fair melts!' He tossed the paper into the air.

As the young man and his friends moved off, Hannah picked up the scrap of paper. It was a page torn from the *Public Advertiser*. The writing showed through from the other side, making it difficult to read, but Hannah could make out some of it.

This booth to let, the present possessor of the premises is Mr Frost. His affairs, however, not being on a permanent footing, a dissolution or bankruptcy may soon be expected and a final settlement of the whole entrusted to Mr Thaw.

Hannah had no idea what to make of this, but she found herself following their footprints in the snow.

They went down Oxford Street, past where it turned into High Holborn Road, and then turned right into Farringdon Street. Soon, the young people were joined by more people, commoners and cits and people of Quality, all flocking down towards Blackfriar's Bridge, laughing like it was a holiday.

When they came to the bridge, everybody stopped and gasped. Hannah couldn't see past the crowd, so she pushed her way through, until she stood at the place where the bridge met the riverbank. Then she caught her breath.

The river Thames was frozen solid. Instead of the usual rushing water, brown tipped with white, there was a strange, greyish-white strip that ran through the middle of London. But what was most peculiar were the traders selling their wares on this new, icy street. A sign had been crudely erected where steps led down to the River. *This way to Freezeland Street.*

There were booths and tents set up in the middle of the river, edging a thoroughfare that ran all the way from Blackfriar's Bridge to Three Crane Stairs. The makeshift street was thronged with people.

Frost glittered on everything, making the whole world sparkle and twinkle like some kind of fairyland. People on skates soared up and down the river like birds, swooping and spinning with easy grace. Others trod carefully on hessian sacking laid down to avoid slipping, buying souvenirs and drinking steaming hot chocolate and porter from pewter mugs outside makeshift taverns with names like *The City of Moscow* and *The Free and Easy on the Ice.*

Hannah made her way down the steps, and stepped carefully onto the ice.

The air was thick with the sound of traders calling out their wares.

'Baked ox cheek, fat and brown!'

'Your feet to mend, corns to cut!'

'Sheep hearts, livers or lights!'

'Newcastle salmon!'

'Gingerbread!'

The smell of baking hot pies reminded Hannah how hungry she was. She walked carefully over to the nearest stall.

'Afternoon, miss!' said the pieman, winking at her. Was it afternoon already? 'Toss you for a pie? Piping hot and mighty tasty, they are.'

Hannah smiled at him. 'I'm sorry? What do you mean by 'toss'?'

He chuckled. 'You give me a sixpence. I toss it. If it's heads, you get your pie, I get your coin. If it's tails, you keep your coin and get your pie as well!'

Hannah laughed, and handed over a coin, and the pieman tossed it high in the air, where it twinkled in the sunlight. It came down, and he caught it deftly and slapped it onto his wrist. He shook his head. 'Heads, miss. I keeps your coin.'

He whipped a pie out of his portable oven, and expertly cut a hole in the top. White steam rushed out of it. The pieman poured warm, thick gravy into the hole, and wrapped the whole thing in newspaper. He winked at Hannah again as he handed it over.

Hannah saw a familiar tuft of ginger whiskers in the crowd,

and felt the urge to spit out her mouthful of pie. It was Samuel
Smith, the pawnbroker.

'Are you all right, miss?' asked the pieman.

'Yes,' she said, touching her earrings. 'Thank you.'

She ducked into a crowd of people queuing up to try their
hand at the Wheel of Fortune. When she emerged out the
other side, she noticed a man with a black beard leading a
long-haired sheep across the ice. A one-eyed girl with a scarred
face scurried around among the crowd, collecting sixpences.
Hannah surrendered a coin to the girl, who bit it suspiciously,
to make sure it was real, then tucked it away in a pocket.

'Fanks, miss,' she said. Up close, it looked as if one side of
her face had melted, like candle wax. It was shiny and raw-
looking, standing out horribly against her otherwise filthy
person. There was a gaping black hole where her left eye
should have been. The girl wore a grubby red pinafore. Her
boots were so worn that Hannah could see a dirty toe peeking
through the tip of one. The girl wore no stockings. Hannah
turned away, feeling a mixture of disgust and pity.

The black-bearded man reached a metal spit on the
southern side of the river, and drew a long, sharp knife from
under his coat. The crowd watched with baited breath. The
man held the sheep between his knees, pulling its head back
with one hand. It bleated pathetically. The wax-faced girl
giggled. The black-bearded man moved with one swift, clean
stroke, and slit the creature's throat.

Blood cascaded onto the ice, the red standing out on the

white surface of the Thames. The sharp, metallic smell of blood filled Hannah's nostrils. Another stroke of the knife, and the sheep's entrails spilled out like coils of delicate pink rope.

Two other men moved forward and with sharp, deft movements, removed the dead animal's skin. The carcass steamed in the cold afternoon air. They skewered the animal onto the spit, and slipped a tray of roasting coals underneath it. The smell of roasting meat filled the air.

As the light grew dim, traders lit lamps and torches outside their stalls, casting a warm, flickering glow which glinted gold on the surface of the river. A man produced a fiddle, and another began to sing.

All you who are curious downright
And fond of seein' every sight
If to the Thames you 'ad repaired
You might get to see the famous fair.
Diversions of every kind you'll see
With folks all drinkin' coffee an' tea,
And dancin' too, I do declare.
Upon the Thames, the great Frost Fair!

Couples began to dance, but the ice was slippery, and the dancers more often than not ended up falling down.

The black-bearded man started to carve slices off the sheep.

'Lapland mutton!' he cried. 'Get your Lapland mutton! Shilling a slice!'

Hannah handed over a shilling, and was given a steaming slice of hot meat, wrapped in newspaper. She chewed it, even though it was tough and stringy.

The little one-eyed girl she had seen earlier was wandering through the crowd. She brushed past Hannah, nearly knocking her over, and then scampered away, calling out, 'Sorry, miss! King's pictures!'

Hannah noticed that the crowds of people, instead of milling around booths and chatting, were starting to drift to the East, where she could make out a hastily constructed wooden amphitheatre on the ice, surrounded by burning torches. Two men stood at the entrance, taking money from the crowd, which was now pushing forward, eager to get in.

'Half a crown!' shouted one man. 'Half a crown to see the most terrifying beast of the Arctic circle in fierce combat.'

Hannah opened her reticule, but it was empty. She looked around wildly, then remembered the little wax-faced girl bumping into her. She had picked Hannah's pocket.

She heard shouts coming from the entrance. A man had got into an altercation with one of the ticket-sellers. He tried to push past the ticket-sellers, who shoved him back. As they scuffled, the crowd surged forward, bursting into the amphitheatre, and sweeping Hannah along with them.

eight

As Scatterheart raised the blue ice-fruit to her lips, she felt
it soften and turn to liquid. Scatterheart looked up in alarm
and saw that the ice-plants were starting to melt. They
dripped and cracked, as the walls of the white garden began
to crumble.

The white bear suddenly appeared before Scatterheart.
'What have you done?' he cried.

John Huggins stepped down from the witness stand and left
the courtroom. Hannah stared at the white plaster lion above
the Lord Mayor's chair of office. It was definitely moving. It
wriggled and lashed its tail, growling at the unicorn, which
cowered behind the crown.

The clerk gave Hannah a shove. His touch was like a

thousand needles, and she cried out in pain. The light hurt her eyes.

The constable who had arrested her at the Frost Fair produced her earrings, which were examined by the Lord Mayor and the jury, then handed to Samuel Smith, who slipped them into his waistcoat pocket.

'Can you offer any reason that judgement should not be passed upon you?' asked the clerk.

⁂

The amphitheatre was little more than a central ring, open to the star-studded sky. The ring was surrounded by a wall of wood, seven feet tall. Wooden benches were perched above the wall, so the spectators could look down into the ring. A small door was set into the side.

Hannah squashed herself onto a bench, beside two young men who stank of ale and a woman wearing too much rouge. The torchlight flickered and cast strange shadows on the wood and inside the ring.

One of the ticket-sellers appeared in front of them.

'Ladies and gentlemen,' he called out, his voice echoing strangely between the ice and the wooden benches. 'Tonight we have a wonder such as never before been seen in London. An enormous creature, a terrible monster, vicious and cruel and murderous. It is a white bear from the North Pole, the cruellest and most dangerous of all bears. And tonight you will see it do battle with some of the very best and most destructive dogs that London has to offer.'

The crowd cheered and stamped their feet. Hannah didn't move. She felt cold all over.

The man climbed out of the ring, and rang a brass bell that hung near the wooden benches. The door opened.

'You may go anywhere, do anything you like,' said the bear. 'But never *open that little door.'*

There was a pause. The crowd was silent, waiting. A woman laughed hysterically, and was hushed. The wooden amphitheatre creaked.

Then there was a noise which shattered the night and made the women scream. A hoarse cry, like no sound Hannah had heard before. It was a strong cry, powerful and huge, but full of pain and anger.

Then the creature came out through the door and into the amphitheatre.

It came slowly, putting one paw in front of the other hesitantly. It sniffed the air, and a growl rumbled in the back of its throat.

It was not as big as Hannah had expected. It was larger than a sheep, but smaller than a cow, a scrawny creature with fur that hung in great folds off its emaciated shoulders and long, sloping neck. It was nothing like the white bear that Hannah had imagined in the story. Its fur was matted and filthy, more of a dirty yellow colour than the pure, snow-white she had pictured. It tossed its head, agitated and frightened.

Hannah felt sick. Where its eyes had once been, were

messy, weeping open sores. Its eyes had been burnt out, and it now groped blindly around the ring.

The creature pressed itself against the wall of the amphitheatre. People jeered and threw bottles and food scraps at it. The creature cried out again, a deep, crazed roar.

A shrill whistle sounded, and two dogs were let in. They were large – almost as large as the bear. One was a mottled grey, with a pointed snout. The other was black, with a tan-coloured muzzle. Frothing at the mouth, they made straight for the bear, slashing at its side with their teeth. The crowd cried out with joy as blood was splashed onto the ice. The bear whipped around, quicker than Hannah would have believed possible, swatting at the dogs with a great clawed paw. The black one was tossed across the ring, yelping, but it sprang back to its feet again. Fur was torn from flesh. Hannah sat very still, fearing that if she moved she would vomit. The bear continued to cry out as it groped for its attackers.

The mottled grey dog darted up and ripped into the bear's flank. The bear spun around with a great roar, snarling. It caught the grey dog in its mouth and crushed it, bones crunching and splintering. The limp body of the dog fell to the ground. The bear looked up and roared again, the yellowish fur around its mouth stained red.

The bear shook its head, spraying blood and slaver into the air, spattering the excited onlookers. Hannah felt the warm wetness splash on her cheek, and felt bile rise in her throat.

While the bear's head was raised, the black dog leapt at

its throat. The bear let out a cry so loud and terrible that the wooden amphitheatre shook.

Hannah couldn't watch any more. She turned her eyes to the stars, but they were gone. Instead, there was blackness, boiling and churning in the sky, seeping in over the frozen river and into the amphitheatre, blocking out the carnage in the ring, blocking out the other spectators. There was panic and confusion as people struggled to their feet and fled the amphitheatre.

The fog rolled in fast, thicker and darker than Hannah had ever seen before. It was not the usual London particular, the sickly greenish-yellow pall that normally hung over the city; this fog was pitch black and suffocating.

The bear ceased its howling, and was silent. Hannah pushed with everyone else, desperate to escape the choking blackness and the thick, sweet smell of blood. She felt the solid slipperiness of ice under her feet, and realised she must have escaped the amphitheatre, but she couldn't see a thing. She tried to run, but she slipped on the ice and fell down.

There was a loud, booming noise, and the ice under her shuddered. Then there was an ear-splitting *crack!* and people began to scream.

The burning torches of the frost fair were tiny, weak spots, as if they were very far away.

Hannah felt the ice shift and move below her, quaking and buckling. One of the distant lights was moving, coming closer to her, getting larger and brighter. She reached out to it, and a large, strong arm clamped down on her wrist. The lamp came even closer, until it hurt her eyes, and she could feel its warmth on her cheek. She saw two faces peering down at her.

One was wearing a constable's cap. The other had ginger whiskers.

'Them's mighty pretty earrings,' said the constable. 'This is the end of your career, little miss.'

Hannah stared up at him, her eyes wide and terrified. She was hauled her to her feet and dragged away, as the frozen river broke into pieces behind them.

⁂

Hannah opened her mouth to deliver her speech. 'Gentlemen of the court,' she said in a hoarse voice, and then broke off in a fit of coughing.

Her eyes were streaming, and sweat poured from her forehead. Her hands felt clammy and slippery, and Thomas's handkerchief was soaked through.

The white plaster lion lashed out with a paw, and slit the unicorn's throat. Blood poured down the wall, over the enormous sword, and dripped onto the Lord Mayor.

Hannah was shaking uncontrollably.

The lion turned to look at her and snarled, revealing rows of white pointed teeth. It climbed down the wall and began to make its way over to her, stepping daintily between the desks and chairs of the assembled jury and other officials.

'Hannah Cheshire, can you offer any reason that judgement should not be passed upon you?' repeated the clerk.

The lion drew closer. Its eyes burned. The spectators in the upstairs gallery whispered and giggled amongst themselves. The lion crouched down on its haunches, preparing to pounce.

'No,' she whispered, and threw up her hands to protect herself, dropping the handkerchief.

Everything tilted, and she slid to the floor, shivering and burning at the same time. The wine on the floor soaked into her skirt. The jury rose to its feet and spoke a single word aloud, but it was mixed up in the roar of the lion, and she couldn't make it out.

Dimly, she heard the Lord Mayor's voice, booming. 'It is therefore ordered and adjudged by this Court, that you be transported upon the seas, beyond the seas, to such place as His Majesty, by the advice of His Privy Council, shall think fit to direct and appoint, for the duration of seven years.'

She wondered vaguely who they were talking about, and then the lion sprang at her. She had just enough time to reach out and rescue Thomas's handkerchief before the world went dark.

nine

'What have you done?' cried the bear. 'Now you have
brought a curse down on both of us. If you had just waited
a year, I would have been set free! But now all ties between
us are broken. I must leave you and go to a castle that lies
east o' the sun and west o' the moon.'
The white bear vanished.

Someone was standing over Hannah, talking to her, asking
her something, but it sounded like they were miles away, and
all she could hear was a vague, fuzzy echo. She blinked, trying
to clear her vision.

The person put out a hand and felt her forehead. The hand
burned like hot coals. Hannah trembled. The person leaned
down and spoke again.

'Mr Behr?' she said. Her voice also sounded far-off.

The person spoke again. It *was* Thomas. Tears of relief welled in Hannah's eyes.

He was trying to tell her something. His voice was urgent.

She shivered, wondering why it was so cold in her bedroom. She tried to tell Thomas to put more coal on the fire, but the words came out all mixed up, and he clearly didn't understand, because then it started to snow.

A sharp pain stabbed at her forehead. The snow was the whitest snow she'd ever seen. It settled on Thomas's head and shoulders like a blanket, or a coat of white fur.

Hannah reached out to touch it, but her sense of direction was all confused, and she ended up reaching out in the opposite direction. Her hand brushed something hard and cold. A tree made of ice.

She was in the ice-garden!

Mr Behr had told her not to go into the ice-garden. Why had he said that? Something about her father spending all her mother's money and getting arrested. He had been terribly angry, and yelled at her, and asked her not to go into the ice-garden. She wished the snow would stop.

Thomas pressed something hard into her hand, and she curled her fingers around his wrist. It was covered in lots of wiry pale hairs. She ran her fingers through the hairs, and was startled to realise that it was actually fur. The white snow that had fallen had turned into a thick coat of white fur.

'So you *are* the white bear,' she said. 'I thought so.'

She examined the object that he had given her. It was a blue fruit, the same size and shape as a pear.

Hannah opened her mouth, and raised the blue fruit to it. But it didn't feel right. Her lips and teeth closed on something much smaller, and hard and cold like metal. A tasteless, thick liquid filled her mouth, and she swallowed automatically.

'Good girl,' said an unfamiliar voice. For a moment, everything came sharply into focus. She was back in the cell again, and a man wearing a black coat and hat stood over her, holding a silver spoon. Then she was back in the ice-garden. Thomas stood over her, his fur standing on end.

'What have you done?' he cried.

Hannah reached out a hand to grasp his paw. It was as cold as ice.

Thomas roared in pain.

His paw was melting in her hand, growing smaller by the minute. Cold water dripped from her fingers. Water poured off his fur, and he shrank visibly before her.

'What have you done?' he cried again.

His voice, which had become just a whisper, faded out altogether. Hannah's hand closed in on itself as the last piece of him melted, leaving her with just a puddle.

ten

**When Scatterheart awoke the next morning, the castle
had gone, and she was lying on a little green patch, in the
midst of a dark, gloomy forest. By her side was the same
bundle of rags she had brought with her from home.
Scatterheart sighed, and began the long journey back to
her father's house.**

Hannah drifted in and out of consciousness. The doctor came
from time to time, putting the silver spoon in her mouth and
making her swallow the tasteless, slippery liquid. After his
visits, Hannah was often violently ill, then slept for many
hours.

When she awoke, her limbs were sluggish and heavy, her
vision was blurry, and her hearing weak. She was visited by

many people: Long Meg, her father, and once, a petite, frail woman who Hannah thought must be her mother.

But Thomas didn't come again, no matter how many times Hannah called out for him. She longed to see him. But he didn't come. He had gone away to exile. Where had he gone? Somewhere. East of the sun, west of the moon. Hannah wondered how to get there, and if she could follow him.

Hannah scratched feverishly at her arms and legs, which were covered in a hot red rash. Someone grasped her fingers.

'Enough,' said Long Meg. 'You'll rip your skin clean off.'

Hannah held her hand out in front of her. Her fingers were bloody.

'Why am I here, Meg?' she asked. 'Didn't I already have my trial?'

Long Meg lifted a brown bottle to Hannah's lips. 'We is waitin' for a ship,' she said. 'Now drink.'

Hannah drank, and the gin burned. Everything went blurry again for a time. Then, Tabby was standing over her.

'Bourd not with Bawty, fear lest he bite ye,' she said, and cackled to herself. She looked at Hannah with her glittering dark eyes. Hannah stared back. They were like a bird's eyes. As she watched, Tabby hunched over further, and her nose grew long and pointed. She sprouted black, glossy feathers and hopped up and down. She cackled again, and spread her wings, launching herself into the air and hovering above Hannah, before beating her wings, once, twice, and soaring out of the tiny cell window.

Hannah felt for a moment as if she were flying too, grasped in Tabby's yellow claws, soaring and wheeling above the streets of London. Then, without warning, Tabby let go, and Hannah was falling, plummeting, spinning down into darkness.

She woke to pain. A jolting pain, as if she were being tossed about like a cork in the ocean. Hannah opened her eyes, and the pain doubled. White, searing light cut into her head. She cried out and closed her eyes. Was she blind? She struggled to sit up, feeling dizzy and sick. She fell back down again.

'Easy, y'ladyship,' said Long Meg's voice.

Cold air was rushing by, and Hannah could smell smoke, and cooking food. They were outside. She opened her eyes a crack, and saw wooden slats in front of her. Between them, she could make out buildings moving past at a steady pace. The regular clopping of horse hooves drummed in her ears. She was in a wagon. But going where?

The wagon jolted sharply, and Hannah screwed her eyes shut in pain. The horses snorted and, in the distance, she thought she could hear something roar. She opened her eyes again with a snap. Was it a bear?

Through the gap in the wooden slats, Hannah could see a wide brown stretch of river. The ice had all melted, and the Thames was rushing past with its usual brown fury.

Great ships lay anchored in lines on the water, bow to stern. They seemed to crumble before Hannah's eyes, their swollen wood bulging and warping, covered all over in patches and strange platforms and lean-to's. Rows of dirty grey linen were strung out between the broken-off stumps of the masts, and empty eyes peered out through tiny gaps in the rotting wood. A corroded figurehead clung to the front of one of the hulks, a giant woman whose once proud and beautiful face had all but been eaten away by mould and decay.

The wagon rumbled on. For a moment, Hannah saw a blur of white struggling in the rushing brown water of the river. It was the white bear, fighting with the plaster lion that had attacked her in the courtroom. They were swept downstream, clawing and biting one another. Hannah struggled, trying to raise herself onto her elbows.

The next thing she knew, the wagon was stopping.

'We're here,' said Long Meg.

Hannah clutched at the rail of the cart, hauling herself into a sitting position. 'What happened? Did the bear escape?'

'Shh,' said Meg, sharply. 'The surgeon's coming.'

Hannah began to tremble. Everything went dark around the edges, and there was a furious ringing in her ears. She sank down onto her back again. Her breathing was shallow and her chest ached.

'What about this one?' said a man's voice, cold and silky. An icy hand felt her forehead. Hannah could feel the prick of long fingernails. 'She isn't fit for a sea voyage. She has gaol fever. I doubt she will live out the week.'

Hannah opened her eyes and saw the face of Death. The face was long and pale and elegant, but seemed to be crumbling away at the edges. The nose was sunken and grey.

White pustules sprouted from the corners of the eyes, and along the cheekbones. Death opened his mouth, and Hannah saw glistening black saliva.

'Send her back to the gaol,' he said.

Hannah groped for Long Meg's hand. 'Please,' she whispered. 'Don't let me die.'

Long Meg squeezed her fingers. 'It ain't gaol fever, mister,' she said loudly. 'She's just got her monthly visitor, if you catch my meanin', sir. It always takes her this bad, but you know they says as that's a good sign. She's like to bear many children, sir. She'll be right as rain in a day or two.'

There was a pause. Hannah gasped for air.

'Fine,' said Death. 'Lieutenant Belforte! Kindly escort this lady to her cabin.'

A blanket was thrown over Hannah, and she was lifted in strong arms. She breathed in the smell of lavender.

'Mr Behr,' she murmured. 'You're alive. You came to rescue me.'

She leaned her head against his firm chest. The arms tightened around her. 'Hush now,' said a man's voice. 'I'll look after you.'

Hannah stirred. It wasn't Mr Behr. But she felt so safe in his arms that it didn't matter. The man carried her for some distance. The sweet scent of lavender was overcome by the smell of rotting fish. Hannah heard the crying of gulls, and a low, gentle roar that rocked her to sleep.

PART II:
The White Bear

eleven

Scatterheart walked day after day, until she came to a high cliff. An old woman made of sawdust sat nearby, playing with a copper acorn. Scatterheart asked her how to find her father's house.

Hannah sat bolt upright, banging her head, and looked around wildly.

'Calm down,' said Long Meg, yawning. 'It's sparrow's fart early.'

It was dim and dingy. Weak light trickled in through a sort of hatch in the ceiling. It took Hannah a moment to realise that they were in a long, wooden room with low ceilings and exposed beams. She was surrounded by women sleeping in bunks that ran along both sides of the long room, leaving a narrow passageway between. At the other end of the room a pool of brighter light illuminated a steep flight of stairs with a rope rail. The women were sleeping on straw mattresses, with rough hemp blankets and no pillows. They were all wearing identical dresses of grey serge. Hannah looked down to find that she was wearing the shapeless grey dress as well. She realised that she had on no stockings or underclothes and blushed. Long Meg also wore the grey dress, but she still had on Hannah's pelisse, buttoned over the top of it. It looked faded and dirty, and the fur trimming was matted and worn.

'Am I in hell?' Hannah asked. She had to raise her voice to be heard over a dull, constant roaring noise that seemed to be coming from all around them.

Long Meg laughed. Like the gaol, the room smelled of urine and vomit. But there were other smells. Damp wood, fish and salt. Hannah wrinkled her nose, then the whole world tilted on its side, and she fell over back onto the bed. The ground below her pitched and rolled. Hannah's stomach lurched, and she was filled with a terrible dread.

'I need to go home,' she said, clambering to her feet.

'Bit late for that,' said Long Meg.

Hannah cracked her head on the low beams above. Crouched over, with one hand on the ceiling to steady herself, She crawled over the sleeping women, towards the white light at the bottom of the stairs.

At the top of the stairs were long rows of hammocks, swinging from side to side. Some were occupied by sleeping bodies, but most were vacant, tied up neatly into a bundle. To her left, Hannah could see six closed doors. A thick, round post rose from below, where she had come from, and pushed through the wooden ceiling out of sight, like the tall trunk of a tree. Another flight of stairs led upwards after it. Hannah gripped the rail again and climbed.

It was much brighter on this level. To her left were the same six doors, and to her right was … a blinding whiteness. She walked into the brightness and looked up, her mouth falling open.

She was on a ship.

She was standing on a wooden deck that was open to the air, yet with other open levels above it.

The ship was huge. Men ran back and forth, swarming up the masts and securing ropes. Incomprehensible commands were shouted by men in uniform, standing above her on a higher deck, and a shrill whistle cried out orders.

Hannah squinted. Ropes hung everywhere, over everything, stretching up to the top of the tallest mast and crossing and winding like the most tangled and complicated of spider webs. Hannah's hair rose up around her in the wind, and with the wind the damp fishy smell became fresher. It was strong, but not unpleasant.

'No,' whispered Hannah. 'This is a mistake.'

'Hey!' cried one of the sailors. 'You're not supposed to be up here yet. Bracegirdle hasn't rung the bell for breakfast.'

He grabbed Hannah around the waist with thick, burly

arms, but she wriggled free and ran across the timber deck to the side, where round holes studded the ship's hull. The ship rolled on the swell, and Hannah fell down onto her hands and knees, tasting salty spray on her lips.

She clutched the railing and hauled herself up. Her despair had vanished, to be replaced by a strange kind of wonder, mingled with fear. She looked out at the ocean, open-mouthed.

'You're awake, then,' said a voice.

A man in an officer's uniform and straw hat stood beside her. Hannah thought he must be older than Thomas, but younger than her father. He had dark brown hair that curled around his ears and was tied in a neat ponytail at the nape of his neck, secured with a black velvet ribbon. His eyes were a startling blue, fringed with long dark lashes. His skin was pale, his lips full and red.

He smiled at Hannah, and she blushed and looked back out at the ocean. Hannah felt a flutter inside her stomach. Then she remembered that she was a convict, and felt rather sick. Why was he even talking to her?

'Not what you were expecting?' he said.

'It's *blue.*'

The young man laughed. 'What did you expect? Red? Purple?'

Hannah shook her head. 'I didn't expect it to be so…' she trailed off. She had always imagined it would be grey, like Thomas Behr's eyes.

'So blue? Haven't you ever seen the sea before?' The sea was actually the colour of the young officer's eyes. She blinked. They were *very* blue.

'No,' said Hannah. 'Never.'

'But surely you've seen pictures.'

'Of course,' said Hannah. 'But I thought – I thought that it was just artists … In some paintings the Thames is blue.'

The officer chuckled. 'So what do you think?'

Hannah stared out at the vast expanse of water. 'It's terrifying,' she said at last. 'And beautiful. And the sky is so…'

'Blue?' suggested the man.

Hannah nodded. 'Very blue,' she agreed.

'I'm James,' he said. 'James Belforte, lieutenant.'

'Hannah,' said Hannah. 'Hannah Cheshire, convict-by-mistake.'

He tipped his hat politely, his eyes warm. 'Pleased to make your acquaintance, Miss Cheshire.' He leaned in towards her. 'Now tell me Hannah Cheshire, what on earth is a young lady of Quality like you doing in such terrible company?'

Hannah sighed with relief. 'My father…' she said, then shook her head. 'It all went wrong.'

Hannah felt tears prick her eyes.

The lieutenant smiled. 'Don't worry,' he said. 'I'll make sure you stay safe.'

Hannah blushed again and turned her face upwards, letting the sun's warmth soak into her skin. The breeze was crisp and clean, and smelt fresh and salty. Hannah breathed deeply, her earlier panic forgotten. She felt more alive than she had done in many weeks. She turned to the lieutenant.

'I'm *hungry*,' she said, with some surprise.

He grinned. 'Breakfast is in half an hour. Welcome aboard the *Derby Ram*.'

'Well if it ain't her ladyship, come to eat her vittles with us mongrels,' said Long Meg, grinning at Hannah as she made her way into the crowded mess on the upper deck.

The women pushed and shoved to get to the front of the line, where a burly man stood sweating over a black iron hearth containing an enormous copper kettle. Two younger men were dishing out lumps of stewed meat in broth. Hannah lingered at the back of the crowd, but Long Meg grabbed her elbow and dragged her into the fray.

'Comin' through then, shift yer bob,' she shouted, pushing the other women, who bristled and hissed back at her.

'So many people,' murmured Hannah.

Long Meg looked at her over her shoulder. 'This is only half,' she said, shoving viciously at another woman. 'There be two hunnerd an' four of us girls in here, with only a handful of sailors to keep us warm at night. And we's all as hungry as dogs.'

At the front one of the men handed her a square wooden pannikin and slopped a ladleful of indescribable liquid into it. She looked at him, wide-eyed.

'And don' forget, sir, one for me poor friend Hannah, who is confined to her bed with a dreadful malady.'

The man eyed Meg suspiciously, and his eyes flicked to Hannah. Meg shook her head. 'Oh, no, sir. I sees what you is thinkin'. But this here is–' she barely paused. 'Mary. Me new friend Mary.' She winked at Hannah.

'Mary,' said the man, looking Hannah up and down. She felt uncomfortably hot. 'Ain't you a pretty one, then.'

The man filled another square pannikin and handed it to Long Meg. Another was pushed into Hannah's hands with a suggestive look. 'Feel free to come back for seconds,' he said.

'Well, Mary,' said Long Meg, grinning. 'Let's bugger off, then, so we can eat our breakfast in peace.'

Long Meg led her across the upper deck to the stairs. She balanced the two pannikins, one on top of the other, and scampered down the steps like a monkey.

'How long was I asleep?' asked Hannah, looking around the lower deck before following Meg down the next flight of stairs.

'Four days, more or less,' said Meg.

Hannah blinked as her eyes adjusted to the dim light of the women's quarters.

'Are there no windows?' asked Hannah

Meg didn't look back as she made her way down the aisle to their beds. 'This is the orlop deck. We is below the ocean, down here.'

Hannah imagined the water pressing in on them on all sides, and shivered. They sat down. Meg carefully set down one of her wooden pannikins, and placed the other on her lap. She felt about on the shelf above their heads, and fished out two spoons. Hannah saw four straight lines scratched into the wood above Long Meg's bed.

'Thank you, Meg,' said Hannah.

Meg raised her eyebrows. 'For what?' She handed Hannah a spoon.

'For getting my food for me. When I was sick.'

Long Meg looked away. 'Don't mention it.'

Hannah frowned. 'You *did* get me my food, didn't you? That's what you said to the man with the ladle. That you'd been getting my food.'

Long Meg looked down at her pannikin. 'More or less,' she said, and started eating. Then she put down her spoon and dug in her mattress. 'Here,' she said shortly, holding out a ragged grey square.

It was Thomas Behr's handkerchief. Hannah's fingers closed around it.

'Thought you might want it,' said Meg, picking up her spoon again.

Hannah thought for a moment that she might cry. 'Thank you,' she said, tucking the handkerchief away.

'What happened to Black Jack?' Hannah asked.

Meg shrugged. 'Hanged, I spect,' she said, her mouth full.

'Aren't you upset?'

'Upset, no. *Hungry*, yes. Shut your bone-box.'

Hannah examined the contents of her pannikin. The liquid was thin and watery, and she couldn't tell what sort of meat was floating in it. She looked at Long Meg.

'Is– is there anything else?' she asked timidly.

Long Meg rolled her eyes, but said nothing, slurping busily.

Hannah sniffed the meat, then dipped her spoon into the broth and raised it to her lips, taking a cautious sip. She spat it out immediately.

'I can't eat this!' she said. 'It's disgusting!'

Meg finished the first pannikin, and started on the second.

Hannah watched her. Her stomach growled. She sighed, pinched her nose with one hand, and held the spoon up to her mouth again with the other.

The ship lurched to one side, and the hot liquid splashed out of the pannikin and down Hannah's front. The lump of meat went tumbling onto the floor. She heard a high-pitched giggle and turned around. A single brown eye peered at her from a nearby bunk.

'You!' said Hannah.

The crippled girl with the melted face clambered down from her bunk. 'Any more king's pictures, miss?'

Hannah scowled at her. 'You robbed me! It's your fault I'm here!'

The little girl grinned and Hannah clenched her fists.

'Stay them fightin' claws,' said Long Meg, looking amused. 'Ain't no use brawlin' over spilt broth.' She chuckled at her joke, then looked at the girl and made a face. 'What happened to you, then? You're as ugly as a pig's arse.'

The girl shrugged. 'Polly put the kettle on,' she said softly. 'Molly took it off again.'

Long Meg nodded. 'Scalded,' she said. 'Poor thing. Your name's Molly?'

The little girl shrugged again. Then she giggled and scampered down the passageway out of sight.

Hannah got down on all fours to pick up the lump of meat. It had gone.

'Little monster! She stole my breakfast!'

Long Meg roared with laughter.

Molly was not the only familiar face on board the *Derby Ram*. Hannah recognised a number of women from her cell in Newgate, including Tabby, the crazy old Scots woman, and the pregnant woman Sally, who suffered terrible seasickness and rarely left her bed.

After the morning meal, Hannah made her way onto the upper deck, to stare again at the vast expanse of ocean. One of the sailors whistled at her as she walked past, and she looked around to find a less-crowded area.

There were two higher decks towards the back of the ship, but they were swarming with important-looking officers in blue coats, so she headed towards the front, where a smaller deck rose above her. She climbed up the steps, passing the bell that rang at meal-times.

One of the ship's three masts sprouted from the decking, rising above her so high it seemed to touch the sky.

There were two cannons on either side of the deck. Hannah stood between them, looking at the wide open ocean. The front of the ship cut smoothly through the water. The wind was strong and fresh. It was exhilarating.

She turned her back to the ocean and watched the men working on the ship. There were women on the upper deck too, bent over piles of what looked like rope-ends. Lieutenant James Belforte was standing on the highest deck at the back of the ship, talking to a tall man wearing black. The man had his back to Hannah, so she could not see his face. James tipped his straw hat again when he saw Hannah.

She sat down, leaning against the sun-warmed timbers of the ship, and watched him. A chimney in the middle of the deck was emitting some very appealing smells. Hannah realised that she was sitting above the Mess, and that she could smell food cooking. Thinking of the gristly lump of meat they'd had for breakfast, she wondered if the officers ate different food to the convicts.

After some time had passed, a man in an officer's uniform standing near James raised a silver whistle to his lips and blew a series of high pitched notes. The sailors all abandoned what they were doing, and scattered about the ship, some going down into the ship, others spreading out in the sunshine, playing cards and dice. A new wave of men emerged from various parts of the ship to take their places. A man wearing the black knee-breeches and crisp white shirt of an officer, but with no jacket or hat, emerged from the rooms at the back of the second-highest deck. He had grey hair that was neatly pulled back into a ponytail.

James climbed down the stairs to the next deck, where he paused to speak to the man with the grey ponytail. Hannah watched them, curious. Even though the man was not dressed like an officer of high rank, James seemed to be deferring to him, and saluted him as he turned to leave.

Hannah looked up again at the man in black. He turned. His face was grey and spotted with pustules. It was Death. Hannah remembered his icy hands on her forehead on the quay before boarding the *Derby Ram*. She felt cold, despite the sunshine. He was walking towards her. To Hannah it was as if he wasn't walking at all, but gliding. Slithering. She squinted, trying to make out his face. It wasn't Death. It couldn't be.

'Hello, there.'

Hannah looked up. James was smiling at her. She looked back, but the man in black was gone.

'Are you all right?' asked James.

'You startled me, is all.' She returned his smile when she could no longer hear her heartbeat. 'Who is that man?'

'The ship's doctor,' he said. 'His name is Ullathorne.'

He sat down beside her. He smelled like cedarwood and

violets. It reminded Hannah of her father. 'Making yourself at home?' asked James.

Hannah nodded. 'It's lovely up here. So bright and fresh.'

'It's all right,' said James, stretching in the sunlight and yawning. 'But I'd rather be at White's playing hazard.'

White's had been Arthur Cheshire's favourite club, too. Hannah felt a surge of fondness towards James Belforte. He was like a little part of home.

He took off his straw hat and rubbed the top of his head with the palm of his hand. Hannah chanced a sideways look at him. His skin was alabaster-pale, his cheeks so perfectly blushed that Hannah couldn't believe he wasn't wearing rouge. He caught her glance, and she looked away.

'Who were you talking to, before, on the officer's deck?' she asked.

James glanced over to the other side of the ship, where the man with the grey ponytail was now talking to another officer.

'That's Captain Gartside,' he said.

'He's the Captain?' she asked. 'He doesn't look very Captain-ish.'

'He says he finds the full uniform too constrictive.' James leaned forward and lowered his voice. 'He's a commoner. Distinguished himself in the war, and was promoted to Captain. But he isn't a gentleman. Still thinks he's just one of the sailors. He even sleeps in a hammock.'

'Oh,' said Hannah.

'Only the sailors sleep in hammocks,' explained James. 'They say it helps with seasickness.'

'But you don't sleep in one?' asked Hannah, then caught herself – she couldn't believe she'd just asked about a gentleman's sleeping arrangements.

James shook his head. 'Officers have proper beds. It's more civilised.'

There was a pause, where Hannah tried to think of something else to say.

'Why aren't you still on the officer's deck?' she asked.

James smiled. 'Just checking up on the welfare of our cargo. And it isn't called the officer's deck. It's the quarterdeck. The one above it is the poop deck. This one we're sitting on is the fo'c'stle, or forecastle.'

'Oh,' said Hannah again, trying to sound like she understood.

James chuckled. The whistle blew again, and he sighed. 'Back to work.'

Hannah watched him leave. He moved gracefully with the rhythm of the ship.

'Far fowls have fair feathers,' said a voice. Hannah jumped to her feet and looked around.

It was Tabby. She had been hiding behind the mast, but came over to Hannah and stood hunched over to nearly half Hannah's height. Hannah remembered the dream where Tabby had turned into a crow and she had plummeted out of the sky.

'You frightened me,' said Hannah.

Tabby licked her bare gums. 'Soon ripe, soon rotten.'

'You're mad,' said Hannah, all of a sudden feeling defensive and angry. 'Everyone on this ship is mad.'

Tabby blinked. 'Mad? Mad as Tom o' Bedlam? Or shamming Abram? No. Not mad. But a fool may give a wise man counsel.'

Hannah put her hands on her hips. 'Really?' she said. 'What counsel do you give me, then?'

'Not counsel. A warning.' She was staring at a fly that had alighted on the ship's rail.

'Well?' said Hannah impatiently. 'What is your warning?'

Tabby turned back to look at her, her black eyes glittering. 'Blaw the wind nere so saft, it will lowen at the last.'

Hannah stared at her. 'I don't understand a word you say.'

Tabby's hand flew out so fast that Hannah barely saw it move. But she did see the wizened and gnarled old fingers grasping the struggling fly, and she heard the smacking of the old woman's lips. She turned away in disgust.

'Be ye so eager to flee the past?' asked Tabby. 'Bears have the longest memories, ye ken. Longer than elephants.'

Tabby sauntered off, leaving Hannah thinking of the white bear.

She heard a step behind her, and turned to watch a boy no more than twelve years old climb the stairs to the forecastle and walk past, ignoring her completely. He went to the very front of the ship and raised a spyglass to his eye. He was dressed in an officer's uniform that seemed too large. His head was almost swallowed up by his bicorn hat.

'Hello there,' Hannah said, smiling. 'Are you here with your father? Do you want to be a sailor when you grow up?'

The boy lowered the spyglass and turned to face Hannah, his expression cold.

'I am Second Lieutenant Robert Bracegirdle,' he said in a high, reedy voice. 'Please return yourself to the prisoners' quarters.'

Hannah swallowed, staring at the boy.

'Now, woman!' he yelled, his voice cracking. 'Or you will face discipline!'

twelve

'Your father's house?' asked the old woman, and shrugged. 'All I know,' she said, 'is that you'll get there too late or never. But maybe my neighbour can help you. And you're welcome to this copper acorn.'

It didn't take long for the ship to settle into a routine.

Once the surgeon's mate had declared that Hannah was recovered from her illness, she was put to work. The convict women sewed, cooked, cleaned and scrubbed. Hannah's delicate pale fingers soon became red and calloused from hot water and rough linen.

Every day, the women were woken by the young Lieutenant Bracegirdle, who rang a bell four times to call them to breakfast.

After eating, they would get to work. The women who were skilled at needlework were set to mending and sewing shirts and trousers for the sailors and officers. They did not assist with mending the sails – that work was the sole domain of the sailors.

The rest of the women were divided into work teams. At first, Hannah was horrified to find out that she was expected to scrub the ship's decks with grey lumps of holystone, or polish the brass fittings. She protested to one of the supervisors, and was threatened with a beating.

'Keep yer trap shut, yer ladyship,' said Long Meg, who saw what had happened. 'Else we'll all feel the bite of the pussycat's tail.'

Every three days, the women dragged their straw mattresses and blankets up on deck for airing. There wasn't enough fresh water to wash the bedding, but the airing helped.

Hannah soon came to appreciate the work that kept her on deck in the sunshine, although she still felt uncomfortable under the appreciative gazes of the sailors. Other jobs were more unpleasant. Helping the cook prepare the lumps of salted meat and thin, watery stews that were the daily fare on the ship filled Hannah with nausea. The galley was stuffy and smelly, and often as not the barrels of supplies contained more rats and weevils than actual food. To make things worse, the cook would often find excuses to squeeze past her in the cramped galley, pressing himself up against her.

The worst job was picking oakum. Fragments of old

rigging were supplied to the convict women, who had to untwist the hemp rope to form individual fibres. The resulting fluffy pile was then mixed with tar and packed between the ship's timbers to keep her watertight. The oakum was very rough on Hannah's hands – already sore from the hot water in the laundry – and the wiry fibres got stuck between her fingernails, causing them to swell and become infected.

As the notches above Long Meg's bed increased to seven, then ten, then fifteen, Hannah began to understand the language of the ship. She stopped thinking of the forecastle as being at the front of the ship, and started thinking of it as fore. The quarterdeck was aft. Their sleeping quarters were on the starboard side of the ship, not the right-hand side. She learned the difference between the main mast and the mizzen.

At night, the women sat on their bunks and played cards. They drank their daily allowance of rum, and giggled as they ran up the stairs to the sailors' hammocks. Hannah was usually so exhausted by the end of the day that she fell into her bed and was asleep almost immediately, despite the scratchy straw and rough blanket, and the muffled bangs and moans from the sailors' quarters.

Hannah and Long Meg were sitting on the forecastle deck with some other women. They were sewing linen shirts which Captain Gartside intended to sell when they reached New South Wales. Hannah was amazed at how fast the other women could sew – she had only ever picked up a needle for her own entertainment, and had never had to repair anything or make clothes.

As the whistle blew to indicate the sailors' shift change, Hannah looked up, searching for James. Instead she saw the doctor on the upper deck. Long Meg followed her gaze and made a disgusted sound.

'Do you know him?' asked Hannah. 'The ship's doctor? I thought he was Death.'

Long Meg barked out a laugh. 'He is,' she said, and raised her voice. 'Oi! Dr Death!'

Dr Ullathorne turned, and glided up the stairs to the forecastle, where he stood over them. Hannah caught her breath.

The ship's surgeon was very tall, and his face had certainly once been handsome, but was now ravaged with white, fleshy pustules. There was an open sore on his upper lip which oozed constantly, and the grey flesh around his nose looked as if it were rotting away. One of his front teeth was missing, and his saliva was as black as pitch.

'You filthy animal,' he said to Long Meg. 'How dare you?' His voice was smooth and educated. He was clearly a man of Quality – or at least, had once been.

Long Meg stared insolently up at him. 'Filthy, is I?' she said. 'I is no filthier than Lizzy, or Pam, or Katie. But you didn't mind dallyin' with them, did you, Dr Death?'

Dr Ullathorne snarled at Meg, who put down her sewing

and stood up. She was tall, but he towered over her. His black saliva glistened.

'We all knows about you,' said Long Meg. 'You is the doctor who hands out coffins instead of cures.'

She moved closer to him, pressing herself up against his body. Hannah felt frozen, just as revolted by Long Meg's vulgar movements as she was of the doctor's hideous face and contemptuous expression.

'Don't touch me,' he said, shoving Long Meg, who fell onto the deck. She looked up at him and grinned without humour.

'Whyever not, doctor?' she said. 'Fraid you might catch something?'

He spat on her, his dark saliva sliding from her cheek like a fat slug, then made a curt gesture to a sailor called Jemmy Griffin who had been watching the exchange.

'Put her in the brig,' he said as he walked away.

'Aye, Dr Ullathorne,' said Jemmy, grinning at Meg and grabbing her by the waist. Tattoos of snakes twisted around Jemmy's wrists, and letters spread all over his back. Cathy, a scraggly blonde convict woman with a hooked nose, had told Hannah that the letters were the initials of every woman Jemmy had ever loved.

'Ahoy there,' said Meg, leaning against him. 'Fancy a bit of split mutton?'

Jemmy winked at Hannah, and hoisted Meg over his shoulder. Hannah felt herself blushing.

Long Meg laughed. 'I sees,' she said to Jemmy. 'You likes it rough. Happy to oblige.'

It was not Long Meg's only trip to the brig, a tiny, box-like cage on the orlop deck in amongst the cattle and pigs and chickens. Something about the doctor enraged her, and she never passed up an opportunity to taunt or insult him.

'Why do you hate him so?' Hannah asked Meg.

Long Meg wrinkled her nose. 'He's a bad man.'

'Why?'

'He's a whore-monger. *Infected*. Goes around to all the flash pannery houses tipping girls the token.'

Hannah frowned. 'The token?'

'The French disease,' said Meg. 'The pox. That's why he's such a looker. He is dyin', and he's going to take as many whores as he can with him to keep him company in hell.'

'No,' said Hannah, shocked. 'I can't believe that.'

'It ain't just ladies, either,' said Meg. 'There's many a stripling lad who's felt the bite of the wasp's sting. He is like a public ledger – open to all parties.'

Hannah said nothing, but wondered if it could be true.

The brig became a second home to Meg. She slipped into the forbidden parts of the ship, the offices on the quarterdeck, and the storage compartments deep in the hold. She stole tobacco and wine, trading it with the other convicts and sailors for favours. She was often out of her bed at night – Hannah would press her hands against her ears as she fell asleep, trying not to hear the strange noises from above, trying not to think of the man and woman she had seen pressed up against the wall back in London.

Long Meg would always get caught, and end up back in the brig. It reeked of bilge and animals, and had no windows, not even the dim light that came from the overhead grating in the women's sleeping quarters. The combination of the foul air, the constant irregular movement of the ship, and the suffocating closeness of the room would have made the most hardy sailor ill, and after a few hours, Meg was let back on deck again, with a pale face, an empty stomach, and a temporarily subdued demeanour.

By the end of the third week the blue skies had gone, replaced by dark clouds that hung low in the sky. A strong wind picked up, making the ropes swing and crack against the canvas sails. It made everyone on board jumpy as they waited for the storm. Sailors hurried about the ship, securing rigging and stowing away any loose objects. The women were told to stay on the orlop deck, out of harm's way.

Hannah stretched out on her bed. Long Meg sat cross-legged, tearing strips of paper from a Bible to use for curling her hair. Molly sat next to her, shredding a page from the Bible into tiny pieces.

'What I wouldn't give for a drink,' Long Meg muttered. 'Cooped up in here like chickens. We'll all be in Davy Jones's locker before suppertime. Ragin' storms. There'll be sea monsters before long, as sure as God made little apples.'

'Who's Davy Jones?' asked Molly.

Long Meg made a scary face. 'He is the devil of the sea,' she said ominously. 'He has red burnin' eyes like saucers, horns, a pointy tail, hunnerds o' sharp teeth, an' blue smoke comin' out o' his nose.'

Molly shivered with delight. Hannah rolled her eyes.

'You've been spending too much time with the sailors,' she said. 'What nonsense.'

Long Meg winked at Molly. 'I likes the sailors.'

Molly gathered all the tiny white specks of paper in her palm, and blew them towards Hannah. They drifted down and settled on Hannah's lap.

'It's snowing!' said Molly.

'Get out of here, you monster,' said Hannah, brushing off the paper. Molly squealed, and scampered away to the other end of the room.

Meg made a rude noise. 'Ooh-er, look what's got up her ladyship's nose.'

'I don't know why you let her hang around you.'

Long Meg raised an eyebrow. 'What made you cross as two sticks? It must be hard on 'er, so young an' all. No mama or papa. Funny little thing.'

'She didn't seem so young or so funny when she stole my money back in London.'

'Have some pity,' said Long Meg. 'Not all of us had the luxuries that you had, growin' up.' She nodded towards Molly. 'And with a mug like that, she'd have had no choice but to steal. Ain't no gentleman that's going to pay to spend a night with that face.'

Hannah said nothing, rolling over onto her stomach. Meg put down the Bible for a moment, got out her spoon and, with the flat end, started to scratch the twenty-first notch in the wood above her bed.

'How long will it take, Meg?' Hannah asked, looking at the notches.

Long Meg shrugged. 'The winds ain't good,' she said. 'One of the boys tells me it's been slow goin'. We is barely past Spain.'

Hannah tried to remember the jigsaw map of the world that she and Thomas Behr had played with. Then she thought about the question that had been sitting at the back of her mind. She'd tried to ignore it, but it wouldn't go away.

'What happens when we get there?'

'*If* we gets there,' said Long Meg.

Meg picked up the Bible again.

'I dunno,' she said. 'We'll prolly be made servants to rich folk. Or sold as slaves to the natives.' She shuddered.

Hannah tried to imagine what it would be like. She thought about the strange animal that Thomas Behr had made in the snow. A *kangaroo*. Would there be buildings? Or would everyone be living in tents? The colony in New South Wales had been around all her life, but how civilised was it?

'I also heard about a place called the factory,' said Long Meg.

'The factory?' said Hannah. 'What sort of factory?'

Long Meg shrugged. 'Dunno,' she said again. 'But it's where the bad women go.'

Hannah had read about factories in her father's newspaper. It was where you made a lot of things all at once. She wondered what they made in the factory in New South Wales, and what the women did.

There was a groan from one of the other beds. Sally was sick again, covered in a film of sweat.

'Should someone fetch Dr Ullathorne?' asked Hannah.

'He'd slit her throat soon as look at her,' Meg said. 'Probably eat her unborn child as well.'

Meg raised her eyebrows at the expression of disgust on Hannah's face.

'He's a snake,' she said. 'Deserves to have his slithery black tongue cut out.'

'You shouldn't make him so angry,' said Hannah. 'He's an officer. You're a prisoner. You know you can't win.'

Long Meg rolled her eyes. '*He's an officer!*' she mimicked. 'You got stars in yer eyes, missy. Officer ain't some ticket to bein' a gentleman. They is all the same. Snakes and animals, the lot of them. Yes, even your precious James Belforte,' she said, catching the look on Hannah's face. 'Animals. They'll strum you until your strings break, grind you down to nothing. That's all your lieutenant is after. Something to tickle his tail.'

'I don't believe you,' said Hannah, feeling sick. Long Meg

was clearly a liar. She had probably made up the story about the doctor, too.

'Don't, then,' said Long Meg. 'Why don't you come up and see for yourself one night?'

Hannah shivered. 'Why do you do it then?' she asked. 'If you hate them so much, why do you go up there?'

'It's a negotiation,' said Meg. 'I gives them what they wants, they gives me what I wants.'

Hannah said nothing.

'Shocked, yer ladyship?' Meg chuckled, wrapping her hair around a paper strip and pinning it into place.

'Do you really think you should be doing that?' asked Hannah, looking at the emaciated Bible.

'Doing what?' asked Meg. 'Churning butter with Jemmy Griffin upstairs? Or curling my hair?'

Hannah scowled at her. 'You know what I meant.'

Long Meg shrugged. 'I likes it curly.'

'But with a Bible?'

'Why not? I don't got no other paper, and I don't know me letters. Bible ain't much use to me, exceptin' as curlin' papers.' She paused, and looked thoughtfully at the Bible. 'I s'pose I could fashion a deck of cards…'

Hannah rolled over, turning her back to Long Meg.

There was a sudden explosion of noise from the women, whistles and cat-calls. Hannah propped herself up on her elbows and peered down the aisle. James was making his way towards her. He smiled at the women who were offering him their services, and stopped in front of her bunk.

Hannah stared at him, not quite sure what to say.

'Would you like to come up on deck with me?' he asked. 'It hasn't begun raining yet.'

'Of course,' replied Hannah.

'*Of course*,' mocked Long Meg, as she turned to James. 'Hallo, sir. Come to board our ladyship, have you?'

Hannah scowled at her. James helped her down from her bunk, and they made their way back up the aisle.

'You looks like you could use another dance with a short-heeled wench, mister,' called Long Meg.

Hannah turned red, but James grinned over his shoulder at Meg.

'Many thanks, Meg, but I'm not really in the mood for dancing today,' he said, and touched his knuckle to his forehead in a mocking salute.

The forecastle was eerily quiet. The sailors had done all the preparation they could do, and now had nothing to do but wait for the storm. Most of them were on the lower deck, getting a few precious moments sleep, or steeling themselves for the long night ahead with a stiff drink. One or two stayed on the upper deck, coiling ropes, and a handful of officers stood on the quarterdeck. Dr Ullathorne was there, talking to Captain Gartside.

The sky was hung low with suffocating clouds. The wind whipped Hannah's hair around her face. James sat down on the deck, and Hannah settled herself beside him.

In the half-light of the evening, James's pale skin seemed almost blue, his red lips nearly black. A lock of dark hair had escaped its ponytail, and hung over his eyes. He looked delicate and beautiful, like a prince from one of the fairy stories Thomas told her when she was younger.

'I thought you might have had enough of the other women,' he said.

'It smells down there.'

James nodded. 'That's the ballast you can smell.'

'That's in the bottom of the ship, right?' she asked.

James nodded. 'It weighs the ship down and makes it more stable.'

'Why does it smell so bad?'

'It's a mix of sand and gravel. It sloshes around in the bilge-water for years. You can't clean it, and it collects compost and dead rats and all sorts of other filth.'

Hannah made a face.

'You should count yourself lucky,' said James. 'I've been on ships that smelled much worse. On one, the air coming off the bilge was so foul that it turned our buttons black.'

Hannah turned her head as the wind lifted her hair from her shoulders. James sighed.

'That's what I miss the most,' he said. 'Sweet-smelling air. Clean linen. A freshly starched necktie.'

'Toast,' said Hannah. 'I miss toast. In a silver toast rack. Butter in a white china dish.'

'A decent tailor. Kidskin gloves.'

'My Abigail to do my hair each morning.'

'A glass of port, a fine cigar and a few rounds of piquet at White's.'

A whistle sounded, and sailors came streaming out of nowhere, shimmying up the ship's masts and out onto her beams like monkeys. Ropes were slackened, and the air was filled with the booming and flapping of sails and shouted commands.

Hannah watched them. 'How do they know where we're going?' she asked. 'There's no land in sight.'

James smiled. 'There will be barely any land in sight,' he said. 'Not until we put in at Cape Town to take on supplies, and after that not until New South Wales.'

'How long will it take?'

'Hard to say,' said James. 'The voyage can take anything from two to seven months. It's not the best time of year for it, so I'd say it'll be six weeks to the Equator, another couple of weeks to get to Cape Town, and then maybe another two months to New South Wales. I don't see us getting there before September.'

'September?' said Hannah. 'But it's only April.'

'New South Wales is far away. I don't know if you can get any further.'

Hannah shivered. 'Do you think we'll get lost?'

'No,' chuckled James. 'Mr Dollard, the navigator, is one of the best. He may well look like a drunkard, but he's following a track that none of us can see, all the way from Portsmouth to the other side of the world. Thirteen thousand miles that just look like salt water to us, but he can see the road beneath us as clear as I can see you.'

'Parts Beyond the Seas,' said Hannah. 'How does he do it?'

James smiled. 'Calculations, charts, compass,' he said. 'And there's always the stars.'

'The stars?'

'You can navigate by the stars. If you were to come up here one night, I could show you.' He glanced at Hannah, and she looked away, blushing.

'So...' she said hastily, 'if it's the wind that makes the ship move, doesn't that mean that when the wind changes direction, we're sailing the wrong way?'

James laughed. 'It doesn't matter which way the wind is blowing,' he explained. 'We can harness it to take us wherever we choose.'

'But how do you know when it changes?'

'See that man up there?' James pointed to the quarterdeck, where an officer was looking up at the sails. 'He's watching the wind.'

'Watching the wind?'

He nodded. 'At every hour of every day and night, an officer watches the wind. If there is any change, he tells the mate. The mate tells a midshipman, who in turn tells the bosun. The bosun blows out the code on his pipe, and the seamen trim the sails.'

Hannah looked up again at the men, who had spread out all over the ship, to the top of the tallest mast. They looked like the acrobats she had seen at Vauxhall Gardens with her father.

'And what about you?' she asked. 'What exactly is your job on this ship?'

'I'm a lieutenant,' he said. '*The* lieutenant, actually.'

'What does that mean?' asked Hannah.

'I make sure that Captain Gartside's commands are carried out. He tells me what needs to happen, and I make it happen.'

Hannah was impressed. 'So, you're the second in charge?'

James nodded.

'Will you be a captain, one day? Like Captain Gartside?'

'I will never be like Captain Gartside.' James adjusted his cuffs. 'He may be a captain, but I'm a gentleman. I'm only here because my fool of a father wrote in his will that I had to serve for three years before I could inherit. My time will be up in a year, and then I'm off this rust-bucket and back to civilisation.'

'Your father is dead?' said Hannah. 'I'm very sorry.'

'Don't be,' said James, his eyes growing hard and cold. 'He was a fool. Had all sorts of ridiculous notions about *work* and *earning a living*. He was always uncomfortable with his money.'

'You remind me of my father,' she said, but the memory

was shadowed by the last meeting her father had had with Thomas.

'Something wrong?' asked James.

'I was just thinking of my tutor. He didn't understand either. What it means.'

'What it means to be a person of Quality,' said James.

Hannah nodded.

'You don't belong here, do you, Hannah Cheshire?' James said softly.

'Toad goes a-courting!' said a crackled voice. Hannah looked up to see Tabby emerging once more from behind the foremast.

'Fickle Toad. Mucky Toad.' Tabby scowled at James, and levelled a piecing gaze at Hannah. 'There is many a fair thing full false,' she said.

The ship lurched suddenly, and Tabby went sprawling on the deck. She grunted as she tried to get up, but her old body was too brittle and frail. Her fall caught the eye of Dr Ullathorne.

James reached out a hand, but Tabby shrank from him.

'Take him up there with his five eggs, and four of 'em rotten,' she muttered.

James shook his head. 'Let me help you up, grandmother.'

Tabby spat onto his hand.

'Fickle. False. Grey and clammy is the Toad in a mucky pond.'

James went pale. 'You will show me proper respect.'

Dr Ullathorne climbed the steps to the foredeck and made his way over to them. James met him a few paces away. Hannah couldn't hear their conversation as she helped Tabby to her feet. 'What's the matter with you?' she asked.

''Tis dear bought honey that is lick'd from a thorn,' Tabby said.

The doctor came over to them and grabbed Tabby by the arm. She swore at him.

'Disgusting vermin,' he said. 'You'll have your rations suspended for the rest of the week.'

'You can't do that,' said Hannah. 'She's old – she'll starve. We barely get enough as it is.'

Dr Ullathorne turned his cold gaze on Hannah. 'That is the punishment for insulting an officer.'

'But she didn't mean it. She's just a bit mad.'

His eyes narrowed. 'Rules are rules,' he said, and dragged Tabby off by the arm.

Hannah looked up and saw James watching her. He nodded curtly, and then left for the quarterdeck where she could not follow.

thirteen

Scatterheart took the copper acorn and walked on, not bothering to thank the sawdust-woman. After a long, long time, she reached another cliff, where a woman of middling age sat. She was made of glass, and held a silver acorn. Scatterheart asked her if she knew the way to her father's house.

Long Meg was drunk. Not happy-drunk, or muddled-drunk, or sleepy-drunk. She was roaring drunk. It had been raining for three days and the women were going stir-crazy. Fights broke out over the smallest slight, and the hold stank of sweat and stale vomit. The ship was being buffeted by rain above and savage ocean below, and the stuffy air did nothing to relieve the seasickness that nearly everyone was experiencing.

Long Meg lay sprawled on her bed, telling bawdy jokes, and laughing raucously. A dangerously empty glass bottle was clutched in one hand. It was after lights-out, and the women's sleeping quarters were lit only by the odd stuttering candle. Hannah was terrified someone would hear Meg, and come down to investigate.

'A party! A party of one,' Long Meg squealed, waving her bottle around.

'Shush!' hissed Hannah. 'Where did you get that from, anyway?'

'Get what?' asked Meg, pulling an innocent face, then snorting with laughter. 'I don' knows of which you speak.'

Hannah shook her head. 'I don't know how you managed to get so drunk in such a small amount of time.'

'Drunk?' slurred Long Meg. 'I is not a bit drunk.' She giggled. 'I is a *lot* drunk. I is as drunk as a lord. No, as a emperor. Drunk as a wheelbarrow.'

She grabbed Hannah by the front of her dress and breathed boozy breath onto her.

'Don't do that face at me, y'ladyship.' She belched. 'I is as drunk as Davy's sow.'

'Enough,' said Hannah. 'You need to go to sleep.'

Long Meg shook her head. 'No. No. I needs to tell you about Davy's sow. You are–' she waved a hand around, searching for the right word. 'You are…somefing. Bonnets an' ribbons an' invitations. You know what I mean. High tea an' little cakes with icing flowers. You don' know about

Davy's sow, and I needs to tell you.'

Hannah laid a hand on Meg's arm. 'Maybe you could tell me in the morning.'

Long Meg shook off Hannah's hand. 'Now. You needs to hear it now.' She closed her eyes for a moment, concentrating. 'Davy was a Welshman. An' he had a piggy. An' a wifey. An' the piggy, she had six piggy legs.' Meg paused, and gave Hannah a meaningful look. 'Six, and not a leggy less. An' his wifey, she had two legs. An' she was a nazy mort, much addicted to drunkenness.' Meg giggled. 'Like me. Excepting as she was ashamed. And I is not.'

Hannah heard the tread of officers' shoes above their heads. 'That's a lovely story,' she said hurriedly. 'But I think that's enough, don't you?'

'One day,' continued Meg, as if Hannah had not spoken. 'One day, the wifey got herself as drunk as day, an' was much afeared of what her man would say. So she turned out the piggy, an' laid herself down in the sty to sleep herself into...' Meg had lost another word. 'Into being not-drunk-anymore. But Davy came home, and he had a friend with him who wanted to see the piggy with all the piggy legs. 'Look you!' said Davy, full o' pride an' love for his six-legged piggy. 'Did you ever see such another sow?' And here, you must know that Davy was not a very clever cove, not knowin' the difference between his wife and a piggy. So Davy's friend, who was really quite clever, said that it was the drunkenest piggy he had ever beheld. And whence the woman was ever after called Davy's sow.'

Long Meg wagged a finger at Hannah. 'So now you knows, that you should never, never–' she looked confused. 'Never pretend to be a piggy. Unless you is drunk.' She nodded firmly, and then her eyes rolled up in her head, and she passed out on her bed.

Hannah breathed a great sigh of relief, and lay down on her own bed. But she had barely closed her eyes, when someone tapped her on the shoulder. It was James.

'What are–'

'Shh,' he said. 'You'll wake the other women. It's stopped raining. Come upstairs.'

Hannah climbed out of bed, grateful for the first time that the convict women had to sleep in their day-clothes.

'Wait.' It was Long Meg, still half-asleep, and still very drunk. She reached out and grabbed Hannah's arm.

'You should be careful,' she said, slurring. 'You is only small, and very, very stupid. The lieutenant is used to getting his way. You don' want to make him angry. Trust me.'

She let go of Hannah, and began to snore. Hannah glanced at James, but he was already halfway down the corridor. She hurried after him.

On deck, stars glittered overhead in the night sky. It was the first time Hannah had seen the stars in months. They were so rarely visible through the London fog, and the convicts were normally not allowed on deck after sunset. Hannah wondered if she would get in trouble, but remembered she was with the ship's second-in-command.

They made their way up to the forecastle. The wood was still wet and slippery. James shrugged off his jacket, and laid it down on the wet boards. Hannah stepped forward, assuming it was for her to sit on, but James sat down on it himself. He reached into a pocket and drew out a hip flask. He unscrewed the lid, offering it to Hannah. She shook her head, and sat down next to him.

James chuckled and took a swig. 'You didn't join in on your friend's party tonight, then?'

Hannah looked at him. 'How do you know about that?'

'She broke into the officers' wine supply,' said James. 'Ullathorne found an entire hogshead of empty bottles in the hold. He's calling for her to be flogged.'

'Will she?'

James grinned. 'No, but we've got a bit of a surprise for her tomorrow.'

'What are you going to do?'

James said nothing, but his eyes stayed bright. He looked up at the stars, and pointed.

'See Orion?'

Hannah followed his gaze, and tried to make out the shape of the hunter.

James moved his gaze down near the horizon. 'And that's the Great Bear, do you see?'

Hannah squinted. 'I can't see it.'

'Look,' said James, moving closer to her. He bent his head close to hers so he could follow Hannah's eyeline with his pointing finger. He smelled of whisky, a smell that reminded Hannah of her father. 'He's walking over there, and his head is turned towards us. Those three stars there are his tail.'

'Her tail,' said Hannah, remembering something Thomas had once told her. 'It's a she-bear. It's Callisto.'

'Who?'

'Callisto. She was a nymph. Zeus fell in love with her, and seduced her. They had a son called Arcas. Zeus's wife was so angry she turned Callisto into a bear. Arcas nearly killed her in a hunt, but Zeus put them both into the sky as the Great Bear and the Little Bear.'

James raised an eyebrow. 'How do you know so much about the stars?'

Hannah smiled. 'Thomas taught me. He liked the stories.'

'Who's Thomas?' he asked quickly.

'My tutor.'

'A tutor taught you astrology? I'm surprised your father permitted it.'

'He didn't,' said Hannah. 'Thomas was … he was let go.'

'Quite right,' said James. 'No man wants his daughter to become a blue-stocking.'

'Knowing stories about bears hardly makes me a blue-stocking,' said Hannah.

James shrugged. 'That's the Little Bear over there,' he pointed. 'But I don't think it looks much like a bear. The tail is too long.'

Hannah smiled. 'Thomas always used to say he had a long

tail because he had been spinning around the North Pole, by his tail, for thousands of years.'

'Your Thomas has all the answers, doesn't he?' said James.

Hannah's smile faded, and she watched the stars spinning slowly above them.

'No,' she said, after a moment. 'He didn't have all the answers. He thought he did, but he didn't.'

Hannah thought of Thomas's white bear. She sighed.

'What is it?' asked James.

'Nothing,' said Hannah. 'Just remembering another story.'

James took another swig from the hip-flask. 'I've had enough stories for one night.' He looked at her, his head on one side. 'I'd like to see you in some proper clothes,' he said. 'Muslin. Pale pink. Perhaps some lace.'

'My favourite dress was pink muslin,' said Hannah.

'And I'm sure you looked beautiful in it.'

'You always look beautiful,' said Hannah without thinking. Her cheeks burned. 'I...I should go,' she said, climbing to her feet. 'It's late.'

She hurried over to the stairs.

'Hannah,' called James.

Hannah turned, very aware of the wet patch on the back of her dress where she had been sitting on the damp wood.

James was smiling. His teeth seemed so white in the darkness. 'Sweet dreams.'

The next day it was cloudy, but it stayed dry. The convict women poured onto the upper deck, desperate to breathe fresh air.

Leaning against the railing, Hannah told Meg about her evening with James and what a gentleman he had been. Molly loitered a few steps away – she had taken to following Meg around like a puppy.

Long Meg snorted. 'If he was a gentleman he would of given you his coat to sit on,' she said. 'You isn't doing yourself no favours, flirtin' with the pretty-boy lieutenant. They is all the same. We women should stick together.'

'That's rich, coming from you,' said Hannah. 'You spend every night in a different sailor's hammock.'

Molly giggled, and Hannah glared at her.

'That's different,' said Meg. 'That's for money, and grog, and protection.'

Hannah shrugged. 'Well maybe that's what I'm doing too, but just in a more ladylike manner.'

'Ladylike? Now who's callin' the kettle black-arse? There ain't nothin' ladylike about what you're doin'. You is like a bitch on heat makin' doe eyes at him. You is fallin' in love with the pretty-boy, and no good will come of it.'

'What if I am?' asked Hannah angrily, then turned away, surprised at herself. Was she falling in love with James?

Long Meg spun Hannah around to face her. 'Be careful, missy. Be very careful. He's dangerous.'

Hannah brushed Long Meg away.

'He is a gentleman. We are both people of Quality. What's wrong with that?'

'If there's one thing I can say for sure,' said Long Meg, 'it's that Lieutenant James Belforte is no gentleman.'

'How would you know?' said Hannah.

'Well, for starters, his name ain't really 'Belforte'. It's 'Buffet'. And his daddy ain't no gentleman. He's as common as I is. Made his fortune in buttons.'

Hannah blinked. James wasn't Quality? He seemed such a gentleman.

'But that ain't got nothin' to do with why he ain't a gentleman,' Long Meg said, turning and walking away. Molly trotted after her, casting a superior look back at Hannah as she linked her arm through Long Meg's.

Hannah sat fuming. Meg was talking to Jemmy Griffin. The cheeky look on her face, and the shrill giggles of Molly, left Hannah in no doubt as to what their subject of conversation was. Love? Long Meg knew nothing of love. She only knew about self-interest. She looked up at the quarterdeck, where Dr Ullathorne was watching Meg like a hawk. It looked like she would be sent down to the brig again. Hannah sighed and looked back at the heaving, rolling ocean.

A raucous squawk made her turn around again. Long Meg had abandoned her sailor for a midshipman. She was hurling forth a blazing string of insults about his appearance, his mother, and his sexual activities. Hannah glanced up to the doctor, waiting for Long Meg to be dragged away. But

Dr Ullathorne stood unmoving, watching Meg with a slight smirk on his face. The midshipman was ignoring her. Hannah remembered that James had mentioned a surprise, and looked around for him. He was nowhere to be seen.

Frustrated that her invective wasn't having any effect, Long Meg moved on to another officer. The same thing happened. Finally, she marched over to the ladder to the quarterdeck. Molly shoved a fist in her mouth and hovered at the bottom of the ladder. Hannah held her breath. She had seen sailors flogged for being on the quarterdeck without permission. Meg climbed the ladder, and found herself face-to-face with Captain Gartside.

Hannah couldn't hear what she was saying, but the occasional word drifted over the ship to her. *Common as muck ... mother had the clap.* By now, the convict women, sailors and officers were all watching the show. Molly was jumping up and down with excitement.

Captain Gartside nodded absently to Long Meg, and wandered off to talk to the bosun. Meg stood, shocked at his bland indifference. Hannah saw Dr Ullathorne nod to someone and then James and another officer appeared from behind the ship's wheel. Between them they carried a wooden barrel, with holes cut in the top and sides. They sprang forward, and forced the barrel over Long Meg's head. Her head came out of the top hole, and her arms poked out the side holes, like she was wearing a great round wooden tunic.

The sailors all laughed. Meg turned to them, as awkward

as a turtle on land. They laughed again. Hannah saw Captain Gartside frown. Meg grinned at the sailors, and did a little dance. The convict women cheered. Molly squealed with delight. Hannah looked at James, who was grinning.

'Do you like me new frock?' said Long Meg. 'I think it most elegant.'

'Elegant indeed,' said James. 'For a tortoise!'

'A tortoise?' said Long Meg. 'Then you'd better listen carefully, because we all knows what we learns from a tortoise.'

'What?' asked James.

'At school,' said Meg. 'A tortoise taught-us!'

Everyone laughed. 'Tell us another joke!'

'A joke?' said Long Meg. 'Well then. How about this one?'

She cocked her head on one side, thinking. 'There was a fellow walkin' through a forest, and he was mightily famished. He comes to an Inn, called "George and the Dragon". He knocks on the door,' – here Meg rapped her knuckles on the barrel – 'and the innkeeper's wifey sticks her head out the window. The fellow asks for some vittles, and wifey shouts "No!". The fellow asks for a pint of ale, and wifey shouts "No!". Then the fellow asks to use the privy, and wifey shouts "No!" again. "Well," says the fellow, "do you think I might–" but wifey screeches "What now?" before he can finish. "Do you suppose," says the fellow, "that I might now have a word with George?"'

The sailors and the convict women laughed uproariously
and applauded. Dr Ullathorne moved back into the crowd
– he was standing a few paces forward of Hannah, and to
her left. She could not see his face. Hannah looked over at
Captain Gartside again, who was watching Long Meg with a
strange expression on his face. Was it pity?

'What next, old tortoise?' asked Hopping Giles, a sailor
with a thick black beard and a limp.

'A distinguished old tortoise like meself needs a hat!' cried
Meg.

A battered old top hat was found, and placed on Long
Meg's head. Meg winked at Molly.

'Me pipe!' she cried. 'Where is me pipe?'

Molly went scurrying off, giggling, and returned presently
with a clay pipe. Long Meg gestured to her, and Molly, glancing
nervously at the officers, climbed the steps to the quarterdeck
and put the pipe in Meg's mouth. The doctor had turned and
Hannah saw his face, half-averted. But he wasn't watching
Meg, he was looking at Molly. It was as if he was seeing her for
the first time. Molly scurried back down the ladder, her good
eye wide with excitement, and one fist stuffed in her mouth.
One of the officers had produced a light, and Meg strutted up
and down on the deck, puffing out great clouds of smoke.

'Oh, I say,' she said. 'This is an absolutely corking boat,
you know. A real ripper! A fine and distinguished tortoise like
myself could really make himself at home here.'

'Dance, tortoise!' said Jemmy Griffin. 'Dance for us!'

The tortoise shook its head. 'Oh, I really don't know, old fellow. It doesn't seem very dignified thing for a distinguished gentleman tortoise to do.'

'Dance!' roared Hopping Giles. 'Or we'll put you in a pot and have tortoise soup for dinner.'

The tortoise let out a frightened whoop, and made a little jump into the air. The crowd laughed. The tortoise began to dance slowly and ponderously.

A sailor in a top hat who Hannah learned was called Tam Chaunter produced a fiddle, and began to play a lively jig. The tortoise began to dance more frantically, bobbing up and down and moving its little legs back and forth. The assembled crew and convicts cheered and clapped, and Long Meg grinned. But Hannah noticed sweat on Meg's brow.

Tam Chaunter finished his song, and started another. The sailors and women stamped their feet in time to the music, and the tortoise spun and cavorted before them.

When the second song had finished, one of the officers said something to the bosun, who blew his whistle shrilly. The sailors groaned, but returned to their work. Captain Gartside turned and made his way back into his office.

Sailors came out and distributed holystones to the convict women, and set them to clean the decks. Hannah took hers, and got down on her hands and knees. She looked up at Long Meg, who was making her way down the quarterdeck ladder with some difficulty. When she reached the bottom, Long Meg was panting and sweating. She tried to sit down to catch her breath, but the barrel was too awkward.

She crouched sullenly by the main capstan, until one particularly strong roll of ocean sent the ship leaning to one side, and she lost her balance. She fell heavily onto the wooden deck with a grunt. The barrel caught the movement of the ship, and rolled over to the other side of the deck, taking Long Meg with it. The sailors all laughed again, but there were tears in Long Meg's eyes.

The ship heaved again, and Meg rolled back the other way, only narrowly avoiding tumbling down the steps to the lower deck. She tried to scramble to her feet, but the barrel was too large and heavy. She waved her arms and legs about pitifully.

'Help me, you nazy morts!' she hissed to the other convict women. 'Help me or I swear I'll stick a darnin' needle in your eye while you sleep!'

James was watching them from the quarterdeck.

'You trumpery, wrinkle-bellied pack of hedge-whores!' said Meg, her voice choking with tears.

The other women looked at their feet and pretended not to notice that Long Meg was crying.

'Come on, lasses,' said Cathy.

The women slunk away, avoiding Long Meg's angry gaze.

Hannah bit her lip, and then stepped forward. Out of the corner of her eye, she saw James shake his head.

Hannah bent down and grabbed Long Meg's arm. Meg stumbled to her feet and grabbed the edge of a gunport to stop from falling over.

'Get out of here,' she said to Hannah through clenched teeth.

'What?' said Hannah, surprised. She had thought she was helping Meg.

'You'll just get into more strife,' said Meg. 'Go.'

By nightfall, Meg was begging to be released, and promised sobriety and good behaviour for the rest of the voyage. The barrel was removed.

When she came down to their sleeping quarters, Hannah was shocked. Long Meg was covered in enormous purple welts and bruises from the hard wooden barrel.

As she walked past Cathy's bunk, Meg spat onto the ground. 'Tratler,' she said, under her breath.

'See?' she told Hannah, wincing as she lay wearily down on her bed. 'The officers is the enemy. They hates us just as much as we hates them. Even your pretty-boy lieutenant.'

Hannah remembered James's expression as he forced the barrel over Long Meg's head.

fourteen

'I know nothing about your father or his house,' said the glass-woman, 'except that you'll get there too late or never. But take this silver acorn, and ask my neighbour on the next cliff.'

Hannah dreamed she was back at home. She and Thomas were putting together a jigsaw map of the world. They were in a silly mood, telling jokes and laughing.

'This piece looks a bit like a cow,' said Thomas, holding up Poland.

'Or Mr Burchill, with his long whiskers,' said Hannah.

She found Africa, and snapped it into place underneath Europe. North and South America came next, then China and Russia. Hannah frowned. There were no pieces left.

'There's some missing,' she said. 'There's a great big hole in the bottom right-hand corner, under Asia.'

Thomas shrugged. 'There aren't any pieces for that.'

'Why not?'

'We don't know what it looks like.'

'Nonsense,' said Hannah. 'There's a colony there. I've read articles.'

Thomas shook his head. 'Just fairy tales. Nobody knows what's there.'

Hannah looked at the ragged gap in the puzzle. She was sure she knew what was meant to go there.

'What's it called?' she asked. 'That bit.'

'Parts Beyond the Seas,' said Thomas.

Hannah closed her eyes, trying to remember. That was wrong, that wasn't what it was called.

'I thought it was called something else,' she said.

'Oh it is,' said Thomas. 'Some people call it east o' the sun, west o' the moon. It's the same thing.'

Hannah yawned. 'Perhaps that was it…'

Thomas smiled at her. 'You look tired,' he said. 'Why don't I read to you for a bit?'

Hannah climbed up into an armchair – it seemed bigger than she remembered – and listened. Thomas sat by the fire, with a book in his lap. He told her the story of Scatterheart and the white bear, and the land that lay east o' the sun and west o' the moon. Hannah dozed in her chair, and Thomas kept scolding her.

'If you don't listen,' he said, 'you won't know what to do next. You won't be able to finish the jigsaw.'

But try as she might, Hannah could not keep her eyes open.

Hannah woke the next morning covered in sweat.

She felt sick and dizzy and sore. She lay still for a moment, but her body was abruptly racked with a spasm, like someone was twisting her abdomen. When the spasm subsided, Hannah was left with a dull, nagging pain. It was as if someone had attached a weight to the flesh inside her belly, and that the weight was dragging her flesh downwards, slowly tearing it from her body. She felt a strange, trickling sensation between her legs, and sat up. She pulled back her blanket and looked down. Spreading from between her legs was a reddish-brown stain. Blood.

A terrible fear took hold of her. What was happening? Was she dying? Had the gaol-fever come back?

'Meg.' Hannah leaned over and shook Long Meg, who rolled over and grumbled. Her cheeks wet with tears, Hannah shook Meg again.

Long Meg opened her eyes.

'You had better be dyin', to wake me up,' she said.

Hannah bit her lip, trying to hold back the tears. 'I don't know, Meg. Something terrible's happened.'

Long Meg sat up. 'Well, then?'

Hannah swallowed. 'Everything h–hurts, and I'm bleeding.' She blushed, and pointed. *'Down there.'*

Long Meg looked at her seriously.

'How old is you?' asked Long Meg.

'Fourteen,' said Hannah. 'Why? What does it mean? What's happening?'

Long Meg looked at her pale face and wide eyes, and laughed. Hannah began to panic. Here she was, perhaps *dying*, and all Meg could do was laugh? Was she mad?

'Am I dying?' asked Hannah.

Long Meg nodded, still laughing. 'Oh yes, dearie. You is definitely dyin'. You will be dead within about a minute. Dead as mutton.'

'Don't play games, Meg,' said Hannah.

Long Meg grinned. 'You got your visit from Aunty Rose,' she said. 'You're a mite young, but they says it comes earlier to those with money.'

Hannah stared at her. 'What?'

Long Meg was still laughing, but it was a gentle laugh. 'You is a woman, now,' she said. 'It happens every month. It means you can bear a child.'

Hannah looked horrified. 'You mean this is *normal*?'

Long Meg nodded.

'But it *hurts*!'

Hannah was dumbfounded. This happened to everyone? Why had no one ever told her before? Did it happen to the women with parasols who walked through Hyde Park? Did they feel like this?

'And it happens every *month*?' she asked.

Long Meg nodded again.

'Here,' she said, getting up. 'I'll show you what to do.'

There was a trunk at the far end of the orlop deck that was filled with scraps of cotton. Meg showed Hannah how to tie the cotton between her legs to stop the blood from leaking onto her skirt.

'Change it every day,' said Meg.

Hannah nodded. 'What do I do with the old ones?' she asked. 'Do they get washed?'

'Don't wash 'em in sea-water,' said Long Meg.

'Why not?'

Long Meg winced. 'The salt chafes,' she said. 'There ain't enough fresh water to wash 'em, so we just keeps them until we get a new supply of water.'

'Keep them where?' said Hannah, suspecting that she wouldn't like the answer.

Long Meg went back over to her bed and lifted up the corner of her mattress. A sharp, heavy smell like rotting meat wafted out. Nausea rose in Hannah's throat.

Long Meg shrugged. 'Welcome to the club.'

Long Meg kept her promise of good behaviour for three days. She refused to see Dr Ullathorne to get a poultice or cream to put on her bruises and welts.

'Bastard,' she said. She examined the wounds left by the barrel, groaning as the bruises met her mattress. 'I'll get him. Him and your pansy loverboy.'

'James was only doing his job,' said Hannah, who was curled up on her bed. She sighed. She'd been avoiding James. The wad of cotton tied between her legs felt as thick and bulky as an entire bolt of cloth, and she was sure that he'd notice it. The very thought was mortifying.

Meg snorted. 'His job, is it? Is it his job to torment and torture innocent women?'

Hannah raised her eyebrows. 'I'd hardly call you innocent, Meg.'

'I may be as common as the barber's chair where the whole parish sits to have their beards trimmed,' said Meg. 'But no one should treat other folks like that. Be they convict or captain.'

Hannah thought about the pity on Captain Gartside's face when he had seen Long Meg in the barrel. She sighed, and reached under her mattress for Thomas's handkerchief. It was the only reminder she had left of her home.

'I wonder how your sweetheart back home'd feel, seein' you go all calf-eyed over your lieutenant.'

Hannah put the handkerchief down. 'It's not like that,' she said. 'Thomas was just a friend.'

Long Meg raised her eyebrows.

'I mean it,' said Hannah. 'He was my tutor. He wanted to marry me after my father left. But there was never any chance of anything else happening between us. He wasn't a gentleman.'

She remembered the expression on Thomas's face when

she had refused his offer of marriage, and something inside her ached.

'You really was rocked in a stone kitchen, wasn't you?' said Meg, shaking her head.

'Pardon?'

'You is paper-skulled. You is a ninny.'

Hannah frowned. 'I don't really want to talk about it.'

Long Meg ignored her. 'You should see your face,' she said. 'When you holds that hanky. A fellow offered to save you from all this,' she waved a hand around, 'and you refused, because he don't powder his nose or get his coats tailored for him?'

'We were just too different. I'm a gentleman's daughter.'

Meg groaned. 'Don't I know it,' she said. 'But what you ain't seein', is that you can't pick a gentleman by who his daddy was or how much blunt he carries. Gentleman is as gentleman does, and it sounds as if Mr Hanky was twice the gentleman that old Arthur Cheshire ever was.'

'I don't expect you to understand,' said Hannah.

'You noddy fool,' said Long Meg. 'Does you think that buttons the lieutenant is a gentleman? His blood ain't no more blue than mine.'

Hannah frowned. 'James may not come from Quality,' she said. 'But that doesn't mean he can't be a gentleman.'

She folded the handkerchief, and tucked it under her bed.

A whistle sounded, and they made their way up on deck

for breakfast. As they climbed the stairs, Dr Ullathorne came down, going to the orlop deck.

He put out a hand and stopped Hannah. She looked up into his face, and bit her lip in fear. The greyish flesh that surrounded his nose was spreading to his cheeks, which seemed puckered and sunken.

'Where is the child?' he asked. 'The crippled one. With the hideous face.'

Long Meg made a rude noise. 'That's rich, coming from such a prime article.'

The doctor ignored her. 'Well?' he said to Hannah.

'I haven't seen her,' said Hannah.

He made an exasperated noise and pushed past them. Meg stuck out her foot, and the doctor tripped over her ankle. He stumbled down several steps, and grabbed the hand rail, pulling himself upright again.

'Oops, sir,' said Long Meg. 'It can get awful slippery down here.'

Dr Ullathorne turned to face her. Hannah winced as she saw his crumbling face twist into an expression of pure hatred.

'You are nothing but a filthy whore,' he said.

Long Meg shrugged amiably. 'You is the expert in whores, sir,' she said. 'Filthy or otherwise.'

Dr Ullathorne climbed the few stairs between them.

'You will hold your tongue,' he said, quiet and dangerous.

'Course,' said Meg, ignoring him, 'if they ain't filthy before they meets you, they sure are once you've finished with 'em. You knows what they says,' she said with a wink. 'One night in the arms of Venus, a lifetime on mercury.'

Dr Ullathorne grabbed Long Meg by the arm and pushed his rotting face in hers.

'Say that again, and I will open your carcass and put your liver in a jar.' Flecks of his black saliva spattered Long Meg's face, but she just chuckled.

'You don' fritten me,' she said. '*Sir.*'

The doctor gave Meg a shove, and she went sprawling backwards up the staircase.

'A spell in the rigging should sort you out,' said Dr Ullathorne, hauling Meg to her feet and up the remaining stairs to the upper deck.

Hannah followed them. He gestured to two midshipmen standing by the midmast, who came and lifted Long Meg up under the armpits. She was hoisted up onto the latticework of ropes that hung on one side of the ship, and her arms and legs were tied in place.

'You will stay there until you apologise,' said Dr Ullathorne, and marched off.

Meg began to sing lustily.

'Ye good folks of the "Ram" attend to my ditty,
It is of a bold doctor that dwells in this city
Though poxy and grey yet still it appear
He is a famous old doctor for pleasing the fair.'

She stayed up there throughout the day, as the other women sewed and scrubbed and picked oakum. She stopped singing after an hour, and started calling out insults to the sailors and officers. But she would not apologise.

Dinner came and went, and James came down to the orlop deck to find Hannah.

'It's starting to rain,' he said. 'Perhaps we could go into my cabin.'

James saw her doubtful look and smiled. 'I promise you will be safe with me,' he said. 'My cabin is dry, warm and private.'

One of the convict women whistled at James, and Hannah nodded hastily. It didn't matter where his money came from. After all, her own father had hardly been a model for gentlemanly behaviour.

James led Hannah up the stairs, and past the sailors' hammocks and the cable tiers to the fore of the ship. Hannah listened carefully to see if she could hear Long Meg up on the rigging above her, but she could hear nothing.

'Are they just going to leave her out there?' she asked James. They went down a narrow wooden corridor, past a number of closed wooden doors. One was open, and Hannah saw three men bent over great white sheets of canvas, patching a sail.

'She needs to be taught a lesson,' said James. 'Otherwise she'll never settle down and behave.'

'But she'll catch her death out there!'

'Nonsense. People like her – they're like animals. Like

insects. They could survive anything.' James unlocked a door with a small brass key, and ushered Hannah inside.

The room was cosy, with a cheery lamp swinging from the ceiling. A neatly made bed took up most of the space, along with a wooden nightstand with a porcelain basin and mirror. There was a chest of drawers on which was placed a hairbrush and comb, and an assortment of little glass pots and bottles that reminded Hannah of her father's dresser back in London.

Opposite the chest of drawers was a little desk and chair. The desk contained an assortment of papers, inks and a quill. Above it was a shelf containing a single leatherbound book. Hannah gave a soft squeak and went over to run her fingers along the spine.

'Don't,' said James. 'It wouldn't interest you.'

Hannah peered at the title, embossed in gold on the spine. 'I haven't read a book for so long.'

James took her gently by the shoulders and pressed her into the chair.

'It's not a novel. It's the officers training manual, not appropriate for young female eyes.'

Hannah nodded. Her father didn't like it when she read either. She looked around again. There was a little round window above the bed, framed with a red curtain.

'It must be hard,' she said, 'not having a manservant.'

'It certainly is,' he said with a smile. 'Dressing, eating, remembering to get someone to press my shirts – everything is harder. There's no butler to introduce my visitors. No maid to turn down my sheets. I can't wait to get out of here and back to London.'

There was an uncomfortable pause. Hannah suddenly very aware that she was alone with a man. In his *bedroom*. She had never really been alone with a man before, except for Thomas Behr. And he didn't count. Hannah swallowed nervously. James just looked at her. Hannah looked down at her hands folded in her lap.

'What did you mean, "people like her"?' she said suddenly.

James looked blank.

'When you were talking about Long Meg. You said "people like her".'

James shrugged. 'They're animals. Criminals. They'll do anything for the glint of a coin. They don't care about anyone but themselves. People like her would sell their own child for a bottle of gin.'

Hannah felt very cold. 'Is that what you think of me? Do you think I would sell my family for a bottle of gin? Am I an animal too?'

James looked slightly irritated. 'Of course not. You're not like them and you know it.' He took her hand and smiled. His hands were soft and strong. 'You are beautiful and accomplished and well-born. You are a gentleman's daughter. You're nothing like them.'

Hannah was silent for a long while. She thought of what

Meg had said about James's father making his fortune by selling buttons.

'Hannah,' said James quietly. 'I'm sorry if I offended you. You know you're nothing like them.'

Hannah nodded slowly. 'I do. All this–' she looked around. 'All this is just … temporary.'

He was still holding her hand. Hannah could feel how calloused and rough her hands were against his. His fingernails were curved, white crescent moons. Hers were brown and ragged.

'Hannah?' James was still staring at her.

She stood up, dropping James's hand. 'I'm sorry,' she said. 'It's late. I should go.'

Meg's bed lay empty. Molly watched silently as Hannah crawled into her own bed. Hannah closed her eyes, but was too unsettled to sleep. She heard the shuffling of feet, and opened her eyes. Tabby stood at the foot of her bunk, her black eyes glittering.

'A fair bride is soon buskt,' she said. 'And a short horse is soon wispt.'

Scatterheart didn't thank the glass-woman, but took the silver acorn and travelled on, until she reached another cliff. A child made of wax sat on a patch of grass, tossing a golden acorn into the air and catching it. Scatterheart asked her if she knew how to find her father's house.

Hannah woke to the sound of groaning. At first, she thought that it was Long Meg, relieved from her spell in the rigging. But Meg's bed was empty.

Hannah sat up, looking around. The groaning was low and monotonous. It was Sally, the pregnant woman from Newgate. She had been confined to her bed with seasickness since their departure, and had been sick and quiet and sallow. But now her belly was swollen so large it seemed she might burst, and she groaned and whimpered. Clear liquid soaked into her bedding.

'What's wrong with her?' asked Hannah.

Cathy looked at her. 'Her time is come.'

'She's having her baby? Now?'

Cathy nodded. Hannah climbed out of her bunk.

'I'll go and get Dr Ullathorne,' she said.

One of the other convict women hissed at her. 'Nay,' she said. 'This is women's business. Just leave her be.'

Sally cried out in pain, and Hannah bit her lip, and climbed to the upper deck to check on Long Meg.

Hopping Giles, supervised by the doctor was cutting her down as Hannah arrived. The black-bearded sailor worked slowly, being careful not to cut Meg with his knife. But one of the ropes snapped, and Meg fell down onto the deck with a heavy thump, and lay there, unmoving. Her wrists and ankles were bruised and swollen where the ropes had cut into them.

'Is she all right?' Hannah asked Hopping Giles.

'Take her to the brig,' said Dr Ullathorne, ignoring Hannah.

Giles glanced at Hannah, and she saw sadness in his eyes. He lifted Meg gently, and limped away with her.

'Is there something I can do for you?' asked Dr Ullathorne.

'Meg…' stammered Hannah. 'Don't you think she might need some help? You– you are the ship's surgeon…'

Dr Ullathorne smiled coldly. 'I am here to look after the welfare of the crew and passengers. Your friend is not sick.'

'But she fainted … and her wrists…'

'If I were you, I should go down below before you share her fate.'

'One of the women … she … she's having her baby. She needs help.'

Dr Ullathorne spat. 'Do you think I care if some convict brat lives or dies?'

Hannah backed away, and went downstairs.

She felt jittery and nervous, listening to Sally's cries. She reached under her mattress and felt for Thomas's handkerchief. It would bring her comfort.

It wasn't there.

Hannah climbed off her bed and lifted up the whole straw mattress. It was nowhere to be seen.

Sally screamed, and the other women crowded around her.

Hannah heard a high, reedy voice singing softly.

'Little Bo Peep has lost some sheep, and cannot do aught to find 'em.'

Hannah was quickly filled with a white-hot anger. She sprang forward and pounced on Molly, who was crouching underneath a bunk. They both went sprawling to the floor, Molly squealing.

'Give it back,' hissed Hannah.

'Give it back? What back?' said Molly, struggling

underneath Hannah's weight.

'Don't play the simpleton with me, monster. Where is it?'

Molly giggled. 'Have you cracked your pitcher?'

Hannah pulled her hair. Molly squealed again and reached out and scratched Hannah's face. Hannah tightened her grip on Molly.

'Where is my handkerchief?'

Molly struggled. 'A hanky? Or blanky? Hanky the horse was whipped to death, and Blanky the badger killed him.'

Hannah shook Molly violently. 'Tell me where it is!'

Molly blew a loud raspberry into Hannah's face.

'I'll kill you!' said Hannah. 'I know you're not mad. Give it back before I shake you to death!'

Molly scrambled away from her, tears in her eye. She ran to the stairs and vanished.

Hannah got to her feet and pulled back the blanket from Molly's bed.

Lying on the bed was a little doll made from twisted bits of straw and rope. Thomas's handkerchief was pulled up around the doll's ears like a blanket, all tucked in neat and tidy. For a moment, Hannah felt a swelling of pity. Molly was just a little girl, playing with dolls. But she swallowed the feeling, yanking the handkerchief off the doll.

Sally's cries were becoming more frequent. She was panting, taking long, ragged breaths. Hannah smelled a sweet, sharp smell that was entirely foreign to her. It made her feel ill. She felt very trapped, in the small, low-ceilinged room. Sally's cries were almost constant now. The ship pitched and rolled violently. Hannah fled the sleeping quarters, and climbed up to the forecastle.

Outside, everything was a clear, deep blue. White clouds danced across the sky. The wind was crisp. The ship's sails were stretched taut, propelling the ship forward at a great speed. Hannah made her way over to the side of the ship. Her hands were shaking, and she couldn't stop thinking about Molly's little doll bed. But James was coming over to her. She took deep breaths and smoothed her hair. James leaned against the ship's rail.

Good morning,' he said. 'Look.' He was pointing at the sea below them.

Smooth, grey shapes were sliding alongside the ship, under the water. One of the shapes broke the surface, and a shining grey fin appeared.

'Porpoises,' said James. 'They're good luck.'

Hannah watched the creatures as they leapt and dove, matching the ship's pace.

'They're beautiful,' she said.

James smiled at her. The tip of his little finger brushed against Hannah's, and she felt a slight shock, and a strange warmth.

When Hannah finally made her way back down to her sleeping quarters at dusk, everything was silent. Hannah screwed up her nose at the sweet smell of blood, and another smell, sour and strange.

Sally lay on her bed, her blanket and mattress soaked through with blood. She looked pale, but she was alive. A strange, wrinkled, purple thing lay beside her, squirming weakly. Hannah made a face. It was the ugliest thing she had ever seen. Sally looked over at it, and smiled. Then she closed her eyes, exhausted.

Hannah flopped down on her bunk and stretched, yawning. A small, huddled shape nearby indicated that Molly had returned. Hannah ignored her.

She was just drifting off to sleep, when the bunk next to her creaked. It was Long Meg.

Her head had been shaved. Two great red welts streaked diagonally across each of her cheeks, oozing blood. One of Meg's eyes was blackened and swollen shut, and her lip was split.

'Meg!' said Hannah. 'What did he do to you?'

Long Meg said nothing, just lay down on her bed and turned away from Hannah.

sixteen

'I don't know your daddy,' giggled the wax-child. 'Nor do I care. But mark my words, you'll get there too late or never. Take this golden acorn.'

Long Meg wasn't speaking to her, or to anyone it seemed. She stayed in her bed for most of the day, picking absently at her straw mattress and staring into space. She only left the orlop deck to eat. The ugly gashes on her cheeks became swollen and infected, but she would not ask Dr Ullathorne for help.

She still scratched each day into the wood above her bed though, and the little notches grew crowded, until one morning Hannah realised they had been at sea for two months. James told her that they were sailing south past Cape Verde, the westernmost part of Africa.

Hannah didn't see much of Molly, but she didn't care. The girl was off somewhere during the day, and only crept down to the orlop deck after lights out.

As they travelled south, the weather grew warmer. Sally was slowly regaining her strength, and the infant seemed to spend most of its time either suckling at her breast, or emitting great, lusty howls that Hannah couldn't quite believe came from a creature so small.

There were chores to do – scrubbing the decks clean, sewing and mending, and helping in the mess – but Hannah had the best part of each day to do as she pleased.

She and James spent many hours sitting together in the sun, talking and reminiscing about their lives in London. Hannah enjoyed these conversations, but occasionally wondered if there was anything else they could talk about. The few times she had brought up books, or art, or history, James would look disapproving. 'That tutor,' he would say. 'Filled your head with all sorts of inappropriate things.'

One morning, James sought out Hannah as she was polishing the brass rails that ran between the upper deck and the quarterdeck.

'Come to my cabin,' he said. 'I have a surprise for you.'

Hannah put down her rag and wiped the polish from her hands. 'What sort of surprise?'

He didn't answer, just grinned and took her hand.

When he opened the door of his cabin, Hannah froze. The writing implements on his desk had been cleared away, and the desk had a piece of white fabric draped over it, like a tablecloth. Sitting on the tablecloth was a silver toast-rack containing three slices of toast.

'You made me toast?' she asked, her eyes filling with grateful tears.

James led her to the chair and sat her down. 'Not exactly,' he said. 'It's leftovers from the officers' breakfast. There's no butter or jam, I'm afraid, we finished it all.'

Hannah hesitated.

'Go ahead,' said James.

'Do you want some?' said Hannah.

He shook his head. 'I had plenty this morning.'

Hannah reached out and took a slice. It was cold, and very dry, and after the first few mouthfuls, the crumbs began to stick in her throat. She wished she had a cup of tea to help it go down, but didn't say anything.

He watched her as she finished the first slice, and started on the second. She wondered if she'd be able to get through all three without choking. She cleared her throat.

'Everything all right?' asked James, smiling.

He looked so proud of himself. She had wanted toast, and he had found it for her.

'Everything's perfect,' said Hannah, trying not to cough.

James nodded, pleased. Hannah swallowed hard, trying to dislodge the dry mass stuck in her throat. She took another bite, and her eyes started to stream.

James continued to talk, but Hannah wasn't listening.

She wondered how soon she could escape and get a drink of water.

'...my inheritance...' said James, and then looked at Hannah. 'Are you sure you're all right?'

Hannah stood up, knocking the chair over. 'I'm sorry,' she gasped. 'I have to go.'

She caught a glimpse of her own reflection in the mirror over the washstand. Her face was red, both from holding in her coughing and from sunburn. Skin peeled on her nose. Her cheeks were covered in ugly brown freckles, and her lips were cracked and peeling. Her hair was greasy and unbrushed, hanging in an ugly horse-tail from the nape of her neck. Her shapeless dress was dirty and smudged with polish and stained where she had spilled food on it.

'But you haven't finished your toast,' said James. 'It wasn't easy to get it for you, you know.'

'I'm sorry,' said Hannah again. She needed to get out of there.

James looked away and shrugged. 'Suit yourself,' he said. 'I'll see you at the festival tomorrow.'

When Hannah returned to the orlop deck, she found Long Meg shivering and sweating in her bed. The infected weals on her cheeks were more swollen than ever, and were oozing.

Hannah felt Meg's forehead. She was burning with fever. Hannah pulled her own blanket from her bed, and placed it over Long Meg. Then she fished out Thomas's handkerchief, dipped it in the bucket of water that sat by her bed, and placed it on Long Meg's brow.

Satisfied that she had done all she could, she left the women's quarters in search of Dr Ullathorne.

His rooms were also on the orlop deck, but at the fore end of the ship, so Hannah had to climb up to the lower deck, and then back down by a different flight of steps.

Apart from the surgery, there were only storerooms in this part of the ship, and it was strangely quiet. The whistling of the wind in the sails, and the creaking and sloshing of the ship were muffled, and the sound of Hannah's bare feet padding across the floor seemed unusually loud.

She knocked hesitantly on the door, and started when a voice inside barked, 'Enter!'

Hannah pushed the door open, and entered.

The surgery was cluttered with little bottles and jars with labels like *Pulvis Humani Cranium* and *Volatile Salt of Millipedes.* A set of knives and other instruments lay carefully organised on a table against the wall, and there was a bucket of water, a bed, and some linen in the corner. A steel operating table stood at the back of the room, bare and shining.

To Hannah's surprise, Dr Ullathorne was not alone in the surgery. Molly was there too, clutching a brown glass jar with a label on it reading *Amalgam of Mercury.* She held a spoon in her other hand, and looked a little frightened to see Hannah at the door.

Dr Ullathorne looked at her expectantly.

Hannah swallowed. 'It's Long Meg, sir. She has a fever – I think the cuts on her face are infected.'

He raised an eyebrow, and for a moment, Hannah saw again how he must have once been a very handsome man.

'And what do you expect me to do?' he asked.

'Come and look at her,' said Hannah.

She glanced uncomfortably at Molly, who stood, stock-still, her eye wide. Dr Ullathorne's eyes flickered to Molly, and then back to Hannah.

'I'm busy at present,' he said, smiling and revealing his missing tooth, and black-tipped tongue. 'Preparing for the festival.'

Hannah frowned. 'Then perhaps you could give me something – a poultice or some medicine I can take her.'

Dr Ullathorne looked around. 'I'm afraid that there is no cure for wickedness.' he said.

'But there must be something for her fever–' said Hannah.

'I don't believe I have anything,' said Dr Ullathorne coldly.

Hannah turned to leave, but Molly crept forward, holding out the brown jar to Hannah silently. Dr Ullathorne saw her, and snatched the jar from Molly's grasp with one hand, and struck her across the face with the other.

'Insolence!' he roared. 'You want a physick for your friend? Take her this!' He hurled the glass jar at Hannah's head. Hannah ducked, and the jar shattered on the doorframe, dripping silvery liquid onto the floor.

Hannah fled his rooms and went up onto the deck, leaning against the ship's railing and breathing deeply, trying to stop her hands from trembling.

Hannah awoke that night to feel cold, small fingers grasping at her. She sat bolt upright and banged her head on the wooden ceiling.

It was Molly. Her melting face seemed whiter than usual in the half-light. Hannah glanced across to Long Meg, who was sleeping. Her wounds looked a little better, and her breathing was steady.

'What do you want?' said Hannah, glaring at Molly.

Molly said nothing, only took shallow, gasping little breaths as if she had been running.

Hannah shoved her hands away and lay back down again. Her head smarted where she had hit it.

Molly's fingers brushed Hannah's face again.

'What?' asked Hannah.

'I do not like thee, Dr Fell,' she whispered.

Hannah rolled her eyes. 'Go away and let me sleep.'

seventeen

Scatterheart scowled at the wax-girl, and took the golden acorn. Then she walked on for many a long day, until she reached a grand house where the east wind lived. She asked him if he could help her find her father's house.

'Of course I can,' said the east wind. 'If you climb on my back, I'll take you there.'

But the east wind was a tricksy wind, and blew Scatterheart far, far away, to the land of the west wind.

Hannah was shaken awake in the middle of the night.

'Go away, Molly,' she muttered. 'I'm not interested.'

'Wake up,' said Long Meg's voice.

Hannah opened her eyes with a start. Long Meg was leaning over her. Her head was covered in soft bristles. The wounds on her face were an angry red, but were no longer weeping pus. Long Meg swayed a little, and put up a hand to steady herself on the timber beams overhead.

'Meg,' whispered Hannah. 'Are you all right?'

'I need your help,' said Long Meg shortly, turning and walking up the corridor.

Hannah watched her for a moment, still trying to shake off the heaviness of sleep. But it had been so long since Meg had spoken to her that Hannah was eager to humour her, no matter what she was up to.

They crept up the stairs, tiptoeing past the six cabins on the lower deck and rows of sleeping sailors in hammocks. They passed the trunk of the mainmast which pierced the ship like a needle, and Hannah glanced down the corridor which led to the officers' cabins. She wondered if James was asleep yet. They reached the stairs that led back down to the orlop deck on the other side of the ship.

'Where are we going?' whispered Hannah.

'He's taken Molly,' said Meg, starting down the stairs.

'Dr Ullathorne? I saw her there today,' Hannah said.

Meg stopped, and looked back at Hannah. 'He's hurting her.'

Hannah followed Meg down the stairs, and they turned down the corridor that led to Dr Ullathorne's rooms. She laid a finger to her lips and pointed.

There was light shining under the door of the surgery, and through the cracks in the wooden panelling. Hannah threw

Meg a sharp glance but Meg just shook her head and pointed again. Hannah crept towards the door. A board creaked under her foot, and she froze for a moment. Long Meg gestured frantically. Hannah peered through the crack between the door and the doorframe.

At first, all she could see was Dr Ullathorne, his back to her. A small knife glinted in his hand. He leaned forward, and fiddled with something Hannah couldn't see. Then he stood back.

Molly was in there, sitting stiffly on a wooden chair. Her arms were tied to the chair's arms, wrists facing upwards. There were a number of cuts on her arms, in various stages of healing. Some looked infected. A fresh gash on her right arm was dripping blood into a metal dish. Molly's face was deathly pale.

Dr Ullathorne scooped some of the blood into a small glass bottle, and held it up to the light. He made a note on a piece of paper, and then walked out of sight. Hannah heard the clinking of jars and bottles.

'What shall we try this time?' asked Dr Ullathorne. 'Ammonia? Sulphur? I read a paper once about curing disease with the water of the victim ... Ah.'

He appeared again, holding a green glass jar filled with some kind of powder. He opened the jar, took out a pinch of powder then rubbed the powder into Molly's wound. Molly screamed.

'Interesting.' Dr Ullathorne made another note.

Long Meg had crept up next to Hannah.

'What's he doing?' whispered Hannah.

'The devil's work,' muttered Meg.

Molly was whimpering and trembling. Dr Ullathorne took out another jar.

'Hush now, my dear,' he said to her absently. 'Don't want to wake anyone, we'll never find the cure then. You don't want me to die, do you?'

Molly bit her lip and shook her head.

Dr Ullathorne reached into a chest, and took out a wooden box. He picked up a pair of tweezers and reached into the box, drawing out a white, wriggling maggot. Molly whimpered.

'He looks a hungry fellow, doesn't he, my dear?' said the doctor.

Long Meg turned to Hannah. 'This has to stop,' she said in a low voice. Hannah nodded.

Dr Ullathorne poked the maggot deep into Molly's wound. Molly bit her lip so hard that blood appeared. He reached for a long silver needle and a spool of thread.

'Better make sure he can't escape, eh?'

'I'll distract him,' said Meg. 'You get the child away from here.'

Before Hannah had a chance to answer, Meg burst through the door. 'Oh doctor!' she cried. 'You must help me, or else I may die!'

Dr Ullathorne looked up from threading the needle. 'You,' he said quietly.

Meg threw herself at him, clutching his collar. 'Doctor, I am suffering of a broke heart!'

She threw a glance back towards the door. Hannah started, and then ducked in. She fumbled with the knots tying Molly's wrists to the chair.

'Get off me!' said Dr Ullathorne, struggling with Long Meg.

'Yes!' cried Meg. 'A broke heart! You see, doctor, I had falled quite in love with you, with your bonny eyes and your sweet voice and your gentle, caressing fingers.'

Hannah undid the first knot and started on the second.

'But you have broked my heart, Oh doctor,' said Long Meg, weeping hysterically. 'Because I 'ave realised that you are not the kind, gentle, loving doctor I thought you to be.'

Meg reached out with one hand and snatched up Dr Ullathorne's knife.

'No,' she said, her tone suddenly quiet and dangerous. 'You are nothin' but a vile, disgustin' maggot. And I hopes you suffer for every single second of sufferin' you have brought to others.'

She lashed out with the knife, striking the doctor across the face, in a mirror of the gashes that Meg wore on her own cheeks. He grabbed her wrist before she could strike again, and tried to force the knife to her throat. She bit him and he yelled out in pain. Hannah finally loosed the second knot.

'Meg!' she said.

'Go,' said Long Meg. 'Take Molly back to bed.'

Hannah hesitated for a moment, then hauled Molly to her feet, and half-dragged, half-carried her from the room, and up the stairs to the lower deck.

She turned to make her way aft to the stairs that would take them back to their side of the orlop deck, but paused. Something made her turn around and head up another flight of stairs and down a corridor to the officers' quarters.

She tapped on James's door. Nothing. She banged louder. Molly was trembling with fear. The door was pulled open.

James's eyes were rimmed with sleep, but he was fully clothed. His hair was rumpled and Hannah caught a faint whiff of brandy about him.

'Hannah,' said James, surprised. 'What–'

'Dr Ullathorne,' said Hannah breathlessly. 'And Long Meg. She needs help.'

James frowned. 'What do you mean? What happened?'

'He– he was hurting Molly,' she indicated the wounds on Molly's arm. 'Meg tried to stop him. She's still there.'

'Are you sure Ullathorne was hurting her?' asked James. 'You're sure he wasn't helping her? And this was all one of Meg's pranks?'

Hannah shook her head. 'Of course I'm sure,' she said, beginning to cry. 'I was there. He was cutting her…'

She choked up, and James nodded.

'Stay here,' he said. 'Don't wake anyone else. I'll take care of it.'

He left quickly and quietly. Hannah dragged Molly into

the room, and lifted her up onto James's bed. She yanked open the dresser and pulled out a linen shirt, tearing a strip from it and binding it around Molly's arm. Molly was still shaking uncontrollably.

'I do not like thee, Dr Fell,' she whispered.

'I know,' said Hannah. 'I'm sorry. Lie down now, James will fix everything.'

Molly closed her eye. After a few minutes, she stopped shaking.

Hannah waited for what seemed like hours. She couldn't sit still, and kept standing up and fidgeting. She went to the gunhole and peered out, her breath fogging up the thick glass. Stars smouldered in the sky. She looked for the Great Bear, but clouds scudded over the night sky and swallowed the stars.

Finally, she heard footsteps outside, and the door swung open. James paused on the threshold, looking at Hannah.

'What happened?' she asked.

He came inside, picking up the torn linen shirt.

'Everything's taken care of,' said James. 'You should get the child back to the orlop deck before anyone notices. Is this my shirt?'

'Long Meg–'

'She's fine,' said James. 'She … hurt her arm. You'll see her again tomorrow.'

He held up the shirt and frowned at the missing strip, then sighed and wiped his hands on the white linen. Hannah saw smears of red. He took her by the shoulders and looked into her eyes. All rumpled from sleep, he looked more beautiful than ever. 'I'd never lie to you.'

She looked back into his blue eyes, and for a moment all she wanted to do was curl up inside them and forget about Molly and Long Meg and Dr Ullathorne and the *Derby Ram*. But Molly was still lying on the bed. James squeezed her shoulders and smiled gently at her. He was telling the truth. He'd never lie to her. Hannah nodded, and stood up.

She bent over the hammock and picked up the sleeping Molly. Molly muttered something, and reached her skinny arms around Hannah's neck, resting her melted face on Hannah's shoulder. Hannah turned to look at James.

'Thanks for helping us tonight,' she said.

She left the cabin and made her way silently back down the wooden corridors and down the steps to the women's quarters. None of the sleeping sailors in the hammocks stirred.

She laid Molly on Long Meg's bed, and lay down on her own. She felt so full of nerves and fear that she was sure she'd never sleep. But before she knew it, a thin trickle of morning light was coming in through the grate.

Hannah sat up, glancing over to Long Meg's bed. Molly was there, blinking sleepily. Long Meg was nowhere to be seen. When Molly saw Hannah looking at her, she climbed out of her own bed and crawled into Hannah's.

'It's okay,' Hannah said. 'You're safe now. He won't hurt you any more.'

Molly looked up. 'Where's Long Meg?' she asked.

'I'm not sure. James said she'd hurt her arm. Maybe she'll be at breakfast.'

'I want Long Meg.'

For a second, Hannah was tempted to turn her back on Molly. She was such a horrid little thing. But she *was* just a child.

Hannah smiled brightly. 'Then let's go up to breakfast and see if we can find her.'

Molly sniffled a little, but she took Hannah's hand and they made their way down the corridor, to the ladder that led to the upper decks. The other women were still all in their beds. They watched Hannah and Molly silently. Sally clutched her infant and crossed herself.

'Aren't you coming up for breakfast?' Hannah asked.

Sally looked away and shook her head. 'Not today,' she said. 'We'm not allowed up.'

'What do you mean? What's happening?' asked Hannah.

Sally shrugged. The baby began to grizzle, and she jigged it up and down. 'We'm not allowed. There be biscuits in yon barrel.'

Molly's grip tightened on Hannah's hand. 'Why can't we go up?' she said in a very small voice.

'I don't know.' Hannah frowned. Was it something to do with Long Meg's disappearance? Perhaps they were punishing Dr Ullathorne now that he had been found out.

'I think we'd best stay down here for a while,' she said.

'Is Long Meg up there?' Molly asked. Hannah tried to smile. 'I'm sure we'll see her soon. Come on, let's go and play with your doll. You can make a bed for her out of my handkerchief.'

Molly allowed herself to be led back to their beds.

The wound on Molly's arm looked red and angry, and Hannah was afraid that the stagnant air of the cabin would make it worse. She traded her biscuit for a finger of gin, and carefully cleaned the wound. Molly yelped as the alcohol soaked into the cut, but clenched her teeth and said nothing. Hannah tore a strip off the hem of her dress, and bandaged Molly's arm.

Every now and then some sound came filtering down, the banging of wood, the sloshing of water, and once, a strange, high-pitched scream that didn't sound like it had come from a human. Hannah tried to act as if everything were normal. She didn't want Molly to be scared.

As the day went on, the cabin grew hot and stuffy. The women dozed and played cards. Noon came and went. Molly curled up in Hannah's bed and fell asleep. Hannah tried to fight off the drowsiness, but before long she slipped into an uneasy, restless sleep.

Hannah was woken by a screaming, shuddering noise.

Something enormous rushed and scraped down the side of the ship, hitting the water with a *thwack*. A few seconds later there was a faint boom. The screaming noise stopped and the ship lurched suddenly to one side. The women were all thrown out of their beds. Then, with a juddering groan of wood and water, the ship came to a complete stop.

The sudden stillness, after weeks of rolling and rocking from side to side, was strange. Hannah felt like every movement she made was magnified a hundred times. The women got to their feet and climbed back into their beds. Molly looked dazed. The light had grown dim. Hannah's mouth felt dry, and her head was spinning. She felt disoriented from sleeping during the day, and could not quite work out what time it was. Was it evening or morning?

A bell was ringing. There was a strange noise coming from above. Chanting and stamping. Molly's hand crept into Hannah's.

'What is it?' she asked. 'Is it Davy Jones?'

'Don't be silly,' said Hannah. 'I'm sure it's just...just the sailors singing. Or something.'

'Let's go and find Long Meg,' said Molly.

'I'm not sure we should go up there,' said Hannah.

Molly ignored her, and climbed off the bed.

'Come on,' she said, trotting down the aisle.

Hannah hesitated, then followed Molly down the corridor and up the stairs.

eighteen

**Scatterheart walked on until she found the house
of the west wind, and asked him if he knew where her
father's house was.
'Oh yes,' said the west wind. 'I'll blow you there.'
But he was just as tricksy as his brother, and blew the girl
into a vast and empty desert.**

As Hannah climbed up onto the upper deck, she was hit with
the stench of rotting fish.

The last streaks of light were sinking away below the
horizon, and stars twinkled overhead in the black sky.

The air was still and hot. Yellow lanterns hung from beams,
casting angular shadows. The deck and sails were festooned
with long strings of seaweed, draped like bunting. It looked

black and shiny in the strange yellow half-light.

A group of young sailors and officers stood by the port rail, shirtless and barefoot. Hannah noticed Robert Bracegirdle there with them. Without his shirt on, he looked even younger. He was just a skinny, rather nervous-looking little boy. The young men stamped their feet on the deck in a slow, monotonous rhythm, and chanted something over and over that Hannah could not quite make out. The bell was still ringing.

Molly was already standing on the deck, looking around at the decorations and the chanting men. 'Is it a party?' she asked Hannah.

Hannah shook her head. 'I don't think so.'

No one had noticed them yet, and Hannah led Molly into the shadow of the capstan. They crouched behind it, peering out at the men. Captain Gartside stood alone on the quarterdeck, watching.

The stamping grew faster and faster, until it was just a blur of sound. Then it stopped altogether. The chanting ceased. The bell stopped ringing. There was an eerie silence.

The young men looked around nervously. Bracegirdle was shivering.

Suddenly, there was a strange, animal-like cry, and three strange figures climbed over the starboard rail and dropped heavily onto the deck.

Molly whimpered.

They were monsters.

The tallest one was nearly twice the height of a man, and was some kind of merman, with the tall, pointed snout of a porpoise, a long, grey, shining fish-like body and strong, stout legs. Tall, branched horns spread from its head like antlers. Serpents twisted around its wrists. A rotting stench rolled off it in waves, and Hannah's stomach churned. It was crowned with a wreath of hemp, carried a tall, wicked-looking trident and wore a long cloak of plaited seaweed.

The second creature was smaller, and clad in a woman's ragged grey dress and green pelisse. The creature had thick golden curls of hair, studded with starfish and shells. The grey dress stretched awkwardly across the monster's body, and had torn in several places, revealing pale skin and fine black hairs.

The last monster wore a dark, hooded robe that covered its face and reached all the way to the ground. The creature's head whipped around, and Hannah felt it staring straight at her. She gasped as she saw a glowing red eye burning within the darkness of the hood, and saw blue smoke curling out from its nostrils.

'D–davy Jones…' breathed Molly, terrified.

'Behold!' boomed the porpoise-creature. 'We are Neptune, ruler of the Seven Seas, King of the Secret Currents, Lord of the Boundless Waves, Master of the Tides, High Constable of the Coral Caverns and Uttermost Recesses of the Deep. You, pathetic tadpoles, have crossed over into my land, this land where nothing is everything, where there is no latitude, this middle world. And you must be baptised by my queen, Amphitrite,' the monster in the dress sank into a low curtsey, 'in these waters, or else you will be consigned to the depths of the deepest oceans, to an endless existence in the gloom and darkness of Davy Jones's locker.'

The hooded creature bowed its head, its red eye glowing.

King Neptune raised his trident high in the air. 'Let the ancient and moistening rites of our aquatic court begin.'

Suddenly, the air was filled with high-pitched cries and whistles, as a horde of men swung themselves over the rail onto the deck.

Their faces were decorated with red swirls and strange patterns, and they wore wigs of seaweed and hemp.

King Neptune approached the quarterdeck.

'What payment do you offer in exchange for safe passage through these waters?' said Neptune.

Captain Gartside stepped forward. For the first time on the voyage, he was wearing his blue officer's coat and bicorn hat. Hannah was surprised to see him smiling.

'I, Ashton Gartside, captain of the *Derby Ram*, do offer you a hogshead of our very finest rum, with our great respects to His Majesty.'

King Neptune inclined his great antlered head. As he did so, the porpoise snout slipped to one side.

'See,' Hannah whispered to Molly. 'It's just the sailors. They're wearing costumes. It's Jemmy Griffin. He's wearing a porpoise skin.'

Molly was still rigid with terror. She shook her head. 'No,' she breathed. 'Davy Jones … the queen…'

'It's not really Davy Jones,' said Hannah. 'Just someone dressing up.'

Cheers burst from the painted men as bottles were handed down from the quarterdeck. One of them passed Neptune a large, leather-bound book. The great porpoise-king opened the book, and read out the names of the youngest sailors and officers. When he got to Bracegirdle's name, the boy lifted his head and tried to look brave.

'You tadpoles have never before crossed the Line. You must undergo baptism.'

The painted men cheered again, and ran about grabbing the young shirtless men. They tied their hands together with rope, and dunked them in barrels filled with bilge-water and effluent. They were then slopped with tar and dripping, and thrown overboard. This was accompanied with raucous shouts and laughter as the bottles were opened. The bedraggled young men were hauled back on deck. A wet and sticky Bracegirdle looked as if he were about to burst with pride.

Then Tam Chaunter produced his fiddle and the dancing began.

'Bring forth the women!' shouted King Neptune.

The women were ushered up to the deck, looking wide-eyed at the red-painted men and the seaweed bunting. But the drink flowed freely, and soon the air was full of laughter and song.

Hannah looked around for Long Meg, or James, but couldn't see either of them. More lanterns were lit, and in the brighter light, Hannah could see how crudely made the costumes were. But Molly still trembled, her eye fixed on Queen Amphitrite and Davy Jones.

'Molly,' said Hannah. 'It's all over. Now it's just a big party. Are you going to help me find Long Meg?'

Molly raised a shaking hand and pointed to Queen Amphitrite, who was twirling and dancing with another sailor. Her golden curls fell over her face, and Hannah couldn't see.

'No, silly,' said Hannah. 'That's just a sailor wearing a dress. It's not Long Meg.'

Molly looked at Hannah. For a moment, the giggling child who sang nursery rhymes and stole money vanished, and was replaced by a very serious little girl.

'It's Long Meg's dress,' she said. 'Her green coat.'

Hannah went cold.

The creature was wearing Meg's pelisse – Hannah's pelisse. It was so dirty and tattered that she hadn't recognised it. The fur trim had been torn off. And the golden curls weren't hair at all, they were curly wood-shavings, stuck together to make a wig.

Something roared in Hannah's head, and she felt dizzy. She ran over to the dancing queen, who had her back to Hannah, and grabbed her by the shoulder, spinning her around.

'Where did you get–' said Hannah, and then stopped.

It was James, his eyes sparkling with mirth, his mouth slack from rum.

'Hannah!' he shouted. 'Dance with me.'

He slipped an arm around her waist and whirled her in a circle, lifting her feet from the wooden deck.

'The dress...' said Hannah breathlessly. 'Why are you wearing Meg's dress? Where is she?'

James laughed. 'You worry to much, my sweet little Hannah.' He spun her around again. 'Meg is asleep in my cabin. She caught a chill the other night, and is resting alone where she will not be disturbed. She let me borrow her dress for the ceremony.'

Hannah nodded slowly, waiting for the feeling of relief to wash over her.

She remembered Long Meg winking at James down in the orlop deck. *You looks like you could use another dance with a short-heeled wench, mister.*

James swung her about, his seaweedy hair slapping her face, and his boozy breath making her feel ill. *Many thanks, ma'am, but I'm not really in the mood for dancing.*

She remembered the mocking look in his eyes. *People like her – they're like animals.*

She remembered what Long Meg had told her. *If there's one thing I can say for sure, it's that Lieutenant James Belforte is no gentleman.*

'I want to see her,' she said, trying to pull away.

James tightened his grip around her waist. 'Tomorrow,'

he said. 'You can see her tomorrow. Let her rest tonight. Let us dance. The stars are bright, we are young. You should be happy, Hannah!'

Hannah glanced up at the sky, looking for the burning eye of the Great Bear. She couldn't see it. She twisted her head, searching the skies.

'The bear…' she said. She was beginning to feel dizzy. 'I can't see it.'

James chuckled. 'The bear is gone,' he said. 'There are no bears in this half of the world.'

Hannah's vision began to blur as he continued to spin her in circles. 'How can it be gone? It's a star…'

'We just crossed the equator,' laughed James, clasping her close to him. He stank of rum and seaweed. 'The stars are different in the southern hemisphere. Haven't you noticed them changing?'

Hannah braced her feet on the deck and wrenched herself away from James. But she was so dizzy that the ship continued to spin around her, and she lost her balance and went tumbling to the deck.

She crawled away on her hands and knees, keeping her eyes tightly closed to stop the spinning. She bumped into someone, who hauled her to her feet.

She looked up and found herself staring up at Davy Jones, his head still cowled and his face still obscured. A cigar burned red in his mouth – the burning eye she had seen before, and gave off long plumes of blue smoke. He reached up and took the cigar out of his mouth and grinned at her. Hannah could make out a flash of teeth, stained with black saliva.

Molly was standing behind him, her face a blank mask of terror.

'Dr Fell,' she whimpered.

Hannah grabbed her hand, and they ran to the ladder that led to the lower deck, and clambered hastily down. They ran down the low-beamed wooden corridors until they reached James's cabin.

The door was shut, and Hannah stood outside staring at it, panting. She didn't want to open it, for fear of what she might find inside.

Molly squeezed her hand. Hannah reached out, turned the handle, and pushed the door open.

There was no one in the cabin. A shirt and a pair of breeches were neatly folded on the bed. Hannah closed her eyes for a moment. Then she looked at Molly.

'We have to go down and check,' she said.

Molly shook her head violently. 'I won't go back,' she said.

Hannah nodded. 'Then you go back to your bed and I'll meet you there soon. Be careful on your way back.'

Hannah took a deep breath, and made her way down the stairs to Dr Ullathorne's surgery.

When she found Long Meg, all feeling seemed to drain out of her.

She felt she should cry, or feel sick, or angry, or something. But she felt numb.

Meg's naked body was stretched out on the operating table, pale and lifeless. For a moment, Hannah stared at it, feeling only a vague fascination at Meg's full, soft breasts, and the tangle of dark hair between her legs.

Then she thought of James. *If there's one thing I can say for sure, it's that Lieutenant James Belforte is no gentleman.*

Meg's head was rolled to one side, her eyes staring unseeingly at the wall. The twin slashes on her cheeks had been joined by dozens of others, all over her white, cold body. Her hands lay limply at her sides. Her legs were turned slightly inwards, so her big toes touched. Black marks encircled her neck. Hannah thought of Dr Ullathorne's long white fingers. She thought of James's soft hands, his perfect white crescent-moon fingernails.

She stepped forward and ran her hands gently over Meg's stubbly head. She touched her grey lips, and closed her sightless eyes. She felt as if she should say something. But she was empty. It was like someone had dug out all her insides, and left her as an empty shell, or a china doll.

nineteen

Scatterheart wandered through the hot, baking sands of the desert, until she collapsed, dizzy and weary.

Two days after crossing the equator, and after three months at sea, the *Derby Ram* hit the doldrums.

The ship slowed to a crawl, and then stopped. There was no wind in this part of the ocean. Little breaths of air came from all directions, but they took the ship nowhere. The ship's crew sat around, hot and useless, waiting for a breeze that they could harness.

It was hot, hotter than Hannah had ever imagined. The heat pressed down on the ship like a damp woollen blanket, crushing and pounding and scorching. Faces turned red and raw. Lips cracked and blistered. The officers discarded their heavy woollen jackets and went around in shirtsleeves. The sailors who usually went shirtless and shoeless covered their backs and feet to protect them from the relentless sun.

The sails were slackened and hung limply from the masts. Little wavelets slapped against the hull, making the ship rock in a way that was sickening instead of bounding and rhythmic.

Hannah's stomach churned, and she cowered in her bed, racked with nausea. Her appetite left her, and any attempt to eat made her stomach clench in agony, as it twisted and heaved to expel the food.

Molly had taken to sleeping in Long Meg's bed. Every morning she would take out Long Meg's spoon and scratch another notch into the wood above the bed, then lie back down and watch Hannah, waiting for her to say something.

'Why won't you talk about Long Meg?' she asked one morning.

Hannah ignored her. She couldn't talk about her. If she spoke Meg's name, she knew that the numbness that had settled over her would vanish, and she would break in two. Molly's good eye was wide and bewildered.

'How come no one else is missing her?'

Hannah said nothing. Molly sighed, and wandered over to one of the bunks where Cathy was playing a half-hearted game of rummy with a sour-looking redhead called Patty, and Susan, a lumpy woman with a hare-lip.

'Don't you miss Long Meg?' Hannah heard her say.

Cathy turned to Molly.

'Shut your mouth,' she said, her eyes narrowing. 'She ain't comin' back.'

Molly frowned, the white shiny skin on her forehead crinkling like paper. 'I know that,' she said. 'But why aren't we talking about her? Remembering her?'

Patty scowled and put down her cards. 'So we don' end up like 'er.'

Hannah remembered how, early in the voyage, Long Meg had baited the officers. She would go running up to one, her face frozen in terror.

'Oh sir! Sir!' she would cry. 'Sir, help me! There be sommit followin' me! Sommit large and white! It is always behind me, wherever I goes!'

The officer would roll his eyes. 'What is it, Meg?'

Meg would suddenly drop her look of terror. 'It's my *arse*,' she'd say, and roar with laughter.

Hannah didn't speak to another soul for over a week.

The few times she left her bed to receive her meagre ration of water, she kept her head down, hoping that she wouldn't see James. She couldn't think about him. The image of his beautiful face, the feel of his soft hands, the cultured sound of his voice. These things were so far away from the image of Long Meg lying cold and still in Dr Ullathorne's surgery.

Surely James hadn't had anything to do with it. Surely. He was a gentleman.

But then she remembered James, laughing and wearing Meg's pelisse, his cheeks and neck flushed red from drink.

Hannah remembered her father bringing that pelisse home. It had come in a white box, wrapped in pale pink tissue paper, scented with rosewater.

After a week, the water rations dwindled to barely a trickle. Hannah's mouth became dry and tasted foul. Her tongue felt swollen and her gums ached. Sweat poured from her body every time she moved.

Everything was damp, and a layer of white mould crept over everything – fabric, leather, food. The metal bowls and spoons rusted, and after ten days, the men all sported beards as their razors became useless.

The ship floated limply in the stagnant water. A pool of effluent spread out around the ship, and the air hung thick with the smell of sewage, rotten food and damp. Strange milky-green seaweed grew everywhere, feeding on the filth in the water and growing larger, climbing up the hull of the ship.

The orlop deck was putrid. Filth seeped in from the water outside through cracks in the ship's hold, which had bulged awkwardly from the heat. The stomach-curdling smell of rotten flesh and blood suffused everything.

Hannah's knees and wrists ached constantly, and she developed black and blue marks on her skin. Sally told her that it was scurvy, and that she should see Dr Ullathorne, but

Hannah weakly shook her head.

Molten tar dripped from the seams of the deck above, down onto the convict women. Hannah's face and arms became spotted with black burns.

After Molly had scratched fifteen notches in the wood above Long Meg's bed, James came down to see her.

She turned away from him, but he put a gentle hand on her shoulder. A small part of her was glad he had come. She wondered why he hadn't come earlier.

'Hannah,' he said. 'Let me help you. You could die.'

She was too weak to protest. He helped her to her feet, and half-carried her up the stairs and onto the upper deck. He still smelled of violets and sandalwood, even though everything else smelled of rotting food and effluent.

Once outside, Hannah was temporarily blinded by the sun's glare on the sea. Pitch was boiling on the scorching bare boards of the deck.

James carefully tied some scraps of fabric around Hannah's feet so they would not burn on the roasting wood. He led her under a makeshift canvas awning, and sat her down.

Unlike all the other men on the ship, James was still clean-shaven. He held out a tin mug.

'Here,' he said. 'This will help.'

Hannah's thirst was unbearable. She took the mug and took an eager sip. She immediately spat it out again. The liquid sizzled on the deck. It burned her gums and tongue.

'It's vinegar,' said James. 'It will make you better.'

Hannah looked at the deck where she had spat the vinegar. It was red with blood from her mouth. Her gums felt spongy. She ran her swollen tongue over her teeth and something came loose. She spat again, and a white tooth hit the deck. It was followed by a long trail of bloody saliva which hung from Hannah's lower lip.

Out of the corner of her eye, she saw James wince. She closed her eyes in shame.

'Drink the vinegar, Hannah,' he said. 'Please.'

She lifted the cup to her lips and drank. The vinegar burned and stung, and her throat tried to close to stop her swallowing. She dropped the cup and bent over, retching. James pulled her hair back, and stroked her forehead. 'There, there,' he said. 'You'll be all right now. I'll look after you.'

Hannah dimly remembered the look on his face as he had whirled her around at the crossing of the line. She gingerly ran her tongue over her swollen gums. There was a gap between two of her upper teeth, on the left-hand side. She looked at the white tooth on the deck, surrounded by blood and saliva that was already drying in the heat.

'You lied to me,' she said, her voice hoarse and cracking. 'About Long Meg.'

'I did,' said James. 'I'm sorry. I tried to save her, but she was dead by the time I got there. There was nothing I could do. I didn't want to tell you ... I didn't want to upset you.'

He gently took her hand in his. 'I'd never do anything to hurt you, Hannah.'

Hannah blinked. The harsh brightness of the sun made her eyes ache. She felt the vinegar sloshing around in her empty stomach.

'You knew,' she coughed. 'You knew I'd find out before long. Everybody knows.'

James stroked her hand with his thumb. 'They think she died of an infection. It's better that way.'

The heat beat down hard. She felt claustrophobic, like it was crushing her beneath its terrible weight.

'Dr Ullathorne…' she started.

James sighed. 'What he did was wrong,' he said. 'But we need him, Hannah. He is the ship's surgeon. There are more than sixty people in the infirmary at the moment: convicts, sailors and officers. We won't survive this voyage without him.'

Hannah licked her lips, trying to moisten them.

'Hannah,' said James, then stopped. He squeezed her hand. 'I want to take care of you.'

'Why?' said Hannah. 'Why do you want to take care of me?'

'Because I love you.'

Hannah wondered if someone who could be so cruel, who did what James did to Long Meg, could really love. What had she done to make him feel like this about her?

'Why?' she said. 'Why do you love me?'

'I know who you are, Hannah,' he said. 'I know who your father was.'

Hannah frowned. 'He was a scoundrel,' she said.

'He was *Quality*,' said James. He squeezed her hand. 'I know I can make you happy.'

Hannah's head swam as she remembered Thomas Behr saying exactly those words to her. It seemed like another life.

Her heart began to ache, and she felt the numbness slip away. Misery welled up inside her. She clamped down on it, trying to hold onto the deadness that had blanketed her emotions for the past few days.

'Please, Hannah,' said James. 'Come up to my cabin. I'll look after you when we get to New South Wales. I'll marry you. We can go back to London and I'll buy us a house in Mayfair with forty servants and six carriages.'

Hannah stayed completely still. A rumble sounded from overhead. She opened her eyes, and looked at James. His uniform was crisp and unrumpled. There was no sheen of sweat on his brow. He was like an angel, floating above the ship while rest of them sweated and burned and festered.

She thought about Thomas Behr, and the way his shirtsleeves were always too short for his long arms. She thought about the great white bear, and a shadow passed over James's face, as if he could read her mind.

She knew he was lying about Long Meg.

He was just like her father. Hannah remembered how outraged Thomas Behr had been when Hannah told him that Arthur Cheshire had fired a serving maid because she made his cup rattle in its saucer. Hannah hadn't understood why

Thomas was so upset. Now she knew.

Her father hadn't cared about her. He'd *loved* her, but it wasn't the same thing. James didn't care about her either, but he would do anything to make her stay with him, even if it meant murdering every other convict on the ship.

Hannah had thought that James was a gentleman, like her father. A man of Quality. Long Meg had been right. James was not a gentleman, and not just because his father sold buttons.

But what choice did she have? James could offer her comfort and security. Otherwise, where would she end up? A servant in Sydney Town? Working in the factory? Hannah shuddered. James would look after her. Hannah bit her lip, and inside she apologised to Long Meg, and begged her forgiveness. Everything was going dark, like a curtain had been drawn over the sun.

She took a breath.

The sky opened up and hurled down water, so much that for a moment Hannah couldn't tell where the sea finished and the rain started. The tropical downpour was warm and made Hannah's dress cling to her body uncomfortably. The deck hissed and spat as the water hit it.

'Belforte!' called out a voice.

Hannah looked up and saw Captain Gartside, shirtless, with his hair hanging around his face in wet clumps. His face was cracked and red, his nose peeling. Water ran off his face in rivulets.

'In a moment, sir,' said James, not turning away from Hannah.

'Not in a moment, sir, now!' yelled Captain Gartside. 'The staghorn!'

James paused, looking at Hannah, then climbed to his feet and ran off into the rain.

The rain lasted for only a minute, and before long the baking sun had steamed away any water, and the deck was once more like a furnace.

James was still on the quarterdeck, giving orders to scurrying sailors. He still looked perfect, like the rain hadn't touched him. Captain Gartside was down on his knees, bracing himself against the main mast, hauling on a piece of rope. Sweat poured from his forehead.

Hannah sighed. She should wait for James. He would take her to his cabin and bring her water and real food. But the rain had washed something away from Hannah. Perhaps she deserved to be a servant in Sydney Town, or a factory girl.

Everything suddenly seemed too hard, too much. She didn't want to speak to James. She didn't want to think about Long Meg, or make any decisions. She just wanted to curl up on her bed and sleep. She wanted to sleep forever.

twenty

As Scatterheart lay on the sands of the desert, she thought longingly of the ice-garden and the white bear. She opened her eyes and was surprised to find herself in a lush green valley. She looked around and saw a castle before her. Scatterheart cried out with joy – it was the white bear's castle!

Hannah crawled back to her bed and collapsed there. The well of misery inside her overflowed, and hot tears appeared in her eyes. Everything was wrong. It had all turned out wrong.

She felt as if she were lying in hot soup. The air was thick with humidity and sweat. She lay on her back, staring into blackness. Her clothes were damp against her skin, and every part of her was hot and itchy. She tried to fan her face with her hand, but the air was so sluggish that it barely moved. She closed her eyes, hoping for sleep, but all she could see when she closed them were faces.

Her father's face, almost purple with fear.

Thomas's face as she had slammed the door.

Molly's one eye wide with terror as the doctor stood over her.

Long Meg's face, white and cold and empty as stone.

James's drunken face, laughing and dancing in Long Meg's dress while she lay dead in the infirmary.

She longed to turn her head and see Long Meg lying on her bunk. She would scratch the louse-bites on her stubbly head.

'The light troops are in full march,' she would say, looking over at Hannah.

Hannah sighed.

'What's wrong with you, Missy Lollpoop?' Long Meg asked.

Hannah's eyes ached, but she had no more tears. 'I miss you,' she said.

Meg rolled her eyes. 'You must be Josephus Rex.'

Hannah came to with a start. Had she been asleep? Something was different. She felt alert and awake, more so than she had felt for many days. Was she dreaming? She put out a hand and felt the reassuring rough wood of the ship's hull.

Something stirred.

For the briefest moment, Hannah felt the air around her move. She held her breath. The faintest breeze, a touch of cool on her brow. She clambered out of her bed and put out a hand to steady herself. She felt her way along the rough timbers, taking tentative steps in the blackness. When she reached the stairs that led to the upper decks she felt it again. A whisper of air tickling her cheek. She grasped the rail and pulled herself up.

The lower deck was silent. None of the sailors stirred. Hannah wondered if everyone else on the ship had died. She climbed onto the upper deck, and caught her breath.

The ship was covered in ice.

The deck glittered with frost, shining in the moonlight. The stars were bright and crisp. The ocean, still and flat as glass, stretched off into darkness, a great black slab.

There was no one to be seen. No watchmen, no sailors, no officers. Gooseflesh crept down Hannah's bare arms and she had never felt anything so wonderful. She inhaled deeply, the sweet, cold air filling her nose and mouth and throat and chest.

On the quarterdeck, she ran a hand across the glittering rail. The silver frost tinkled and fell to the deck. She closed her eyes and breathed deeply. A faint splash made her open them again. She peered out at the black water, and saw a flash of white.

The moon, she thought. Reflecting on the water. The white splotch was growing larger. She climbed another set of steps up onto the poop deck, the highest deck and a place where she had never been before. She tingled all over. Her hair felt as if it were standing on end. She watched, and waited.

It was a bear.

A great, white bear.

It walked over the surface of the ocean as if it were solid ice. It padded towards the ship. Hannah gripped the rail. More silver frost tinkled to her feet.

It came closer.

It was huge, almost a third of the size of the *Derby Ram*. It had a long, powerful body, elongated neck, and an angular, sloping head. It had small ears that stuck straight up, and small, black eyes that glittered in the moonlight. Its skin hung in loose folds, thick with coarse, white fur. It was nothing like the broken and dirty white bear that had fought the dogs at the Frost Fair.

As it came up to the stern of the *Derby Ram*, it reared up on its hind legs. Hannah started back in fear. With its hindquarters planted firmly on the frozen ocean, its head was level with hers.

She held her breath.

The bear placed its front paws against the stern and looked into Hannah's face. The black eyes glittered. Its breath was icy, and smelled of winter. The bear opened its mouth and roared.

An icy wind whipped Hannah's hair. She shrank from the sight of the huge yellow teeth, and the wet black mouth. The bear's muscles tensed, making its fur ripple and shake. Still looking into her eyes, it started to push.

The ship stirred sluggishly in the water. The bear strained. The timbers groaned, unused to movement. The bear continued to push. Hannah took a step towards it, and reached out a trembling hand. The ship inched forward, just a fraction.

She touched the bear's giant paw.

She felt the hard claws, the coarse, thick fur, the straining muscles. Then, like a creature awaking from a deep sleep, the *Derby Ram* began to move again, pushing slowly through the still water.

The bear let go. Hannah felt the fur and claws slip gently from beneath her fingers. The bear dropped back to all fours. Water fanned out from the ship, surrounding the bear with ripples.

It watched her as the ship slipped slowly out of the doldrums. When it had shrunk to the white splotch she had first seen, it winked out of sight. Hannah finally turned and made her way back to her bunk, where she fell instantly asleep.

twenty–
one

Inside the castle, a table was set for a grand feast, and at the head of the table sat the most handsome prince imaginable. She sat down and ate the feast, but the food tasted like ashes. The prince's tongue flickered in and out of his mouth like a snake's tongue.

Scatterheart shook her head.

'You're not my white bear,' she said, and left the castle.

Hannah woke to the familiar rocking sensation of the moving ship. Her hand was curled around Thomas's handkerchief.

Outside, women and men alike leaned over the railings to let the breeze ruffle their hair. The sails were taut and firm, and the *Derby Ram* cut through the warm waters like a knife. It was still hot, but the breeze brought relief from the crushing heat of the doldrums, and the general mood was one of festivity. Tam Chaunter brought out his fiddle, and Hopping Giles was singing.

'I dreamed a dream the other night,'

The other sailors joined in the chorus.

'Lowlands, lowlands away my John.'
'I dreamed a dream the other night,'
'Lowlands, my lowlands away.'

Hannah wove her way in and out of the crowd of convicts, sailors and officers, looking for Molly. She peered around the thick main mast, and came face-to-face with James.

'Looking for me?' he asked, smiling.

Hannah opened her mouth, but nothing came out. She thought of the white bear, and of Thomas's handkerchief.

James grabbed her hand and led her to the ship's railing. Sailors had cast lines over the side, and were hauling up silvery bonito fish. They would have fresh fish for dinner that night.

'I have good news,' James said. 'I've persuaded Captain Gartside to let me stay in New South Wales. They need more officers to administer the growing colony, and manage the convict labour. I'll buy us a nice house. You can have pretty new dresses. And after a few years you can apply to have your sentence revoked and we can go back to London.'

Hannah swallowed. A sailor heaved a wriggling fish onto the deck. It flapped and flailed on the wooden boards. The sailor tried to grab it, but it kept slipping out of his grasp. The sunlight glinted off its scales. The sailor finally caught the fish, and slammed its head against the side of the ship. The fish twitched, then stopped moving.

'I can't do this,' said Hannah, not looking at him. The sailor pulled out a knife and slit the fish's belly open. Red blood and grey-purple twists of entrails spilled out onto the deck.

'Don't worry, love,' he said, snaking an arm around her waist and pulling her tight. 'If you want us to be married then we shall. We can figure out something to tell people when we get back to England.'

Hannah pulled away from him. 'No,' she said.

His blue eyes turned to her, half smiling, half doubtful.

She shook her head. 'I don't love you, James.'

He looked genuinely puzzled. 'What do you mean?'

Hannah looked down at the water and said nothing.

James was silent for a moment. Hannah glanced up at him, and saw genuine hurt on his face. So he did love her, then.

'I'm sorry,' she said.

'Sorry?' said James. 'You should be grateful. Don't forget that you're a criminal. A convict.'

Hannah bit her lip. What did she have to be grateful for?

James gripped the rail, his knuckles white.

Hannah shifted uncomfortably. 'I'm sorry if I led you to believe … something that wasn't true.'

He laughed flatly. 'You're no better than that filthy bitch you were so fond of. Perhaps you'd be better off dead, too.'

Hannah went cold. 'Don't speak of Meg like that.'

'Like what? A bitch? A slut? A whore? You're all the same, you loose women. Crawl all over a man, making eyes and twirling your skirts around. Then you suck him dry, suck out the marrow from his bones and then, when there's nothing left of him but dry old bones, you spit him out again and move on to the next one. I know what you're like.'

The sailors and women close by pretended not to notice, although Hannah could tell they were all listening.

'I think I've had enough of this conversation,' said Hannah. 'I need to find Molly now.'

'Of course,' said James. 'How typical, that you should be drawn to such an ungodly wretch of a creature, an animal that was never touched by God's hand. Not me. You don't want me. I'm too polished. Too refined. You want the mutation, cursed to crawl in the darkest, most disgusting corners of the earth.' He grabbed her wrists, and pulled her against him, breathing heavily into her face. 'Would you rather spend your days with such a wretched monster, than with me?'

Hannah tried to free herself, but James's grip was too tight. She looked him dead in the eye, unflinching. 'I would rather spend all eternity in her company,' she said, 'than another second in yours.'

James stepped back, letting go of one of her wrists. Hannah wrenched her other wrist free, and was turning away when

James struck her on the temple. A flash of light exploded behind her eyes, and Hannah fell to the deck. Her head smacked hard on the wooden boards, and her wrist twisted painfully beneath her. James reached down and grabbed a handful of her hair, yanking her to her feet. Hannah felt dizzy and sick. Her head had started to throb, and her right eye felt tender and sore.

James pushed his face up against hers. 'If this is how you want it, then so be it,' he hissed. 'You will not get away with treating me like this. If you want to behave like an animal, you will be treated like one.'

He dragged her down the stairs to a small, barred enclosure, against the ship's hull. The brig. James shoved Hannah inside, slammed and bolted it shut.

'You can rot in here, for all I care.' She heard him spit, then leave.

Hannah slumped wearily onto the straw-covered floor. The cage stank of animals. She thought of the days that Long Meg had spent down here, and closed her eyes, trying to conjure up Meg's presence. There was nothing.

It was her own fault. If only she had listened to Molly from the beginning. If she hadn't left Meg with Dr Ullathorne. If she hadn't gone to James for help. If she hadn't trusted him when he said Meg was all right.

Long Meg was dead, and it was Hannah's fault.

twenty–two

Scatterheart walked on and on, until she came to the land of the south wind. She asked him if he knew of the land east o' the sun and west o' the moon.

'I have never blown over there,' said the south wind. 'But I'll take you to my brother, the north wind. He is the oldest and most powerful of us all. Climb on my back.'

For Hannah's thirteenth birthday, her father had taken her to Vauxhall Gardens. He had told her she could take a friend, but the only person she could think to bring was Thomas. Arthur Cheshire had not been impressed, but it was Hannah's birthday, and she had insisted.

After Arthur Cheshire had paid the three shillings and sixpence each for their admission, they were ushered into the gardens. High green hedges and tall trees towered overhead and stretched off before them in broad avenues.

Hannah could feel the scrunching of gravel through her thin slippers. The evening air was full of music and bright conversation. They listened to the orchestra play, raised on a pavilion lit up with shining lights. Thomas pointed out the statue of Georg Friedrich Handel, but Hannah was far too excited to be bothered with some long-dead musician.

They saw panoramas of the Arctic, Indian jugglers and a circus horse performing tricks. They ate slices of ham so thin you could see through them, and chocolate ices. Arthur Cheshire and Thomas drank port, Hannah had lemonade.

There was a loud bang, and everyone cried out in excitement. Coloured sparks showered down from the sky, pink and blue. Hannah held her breath as the fireworks soared and sprinkled overhead. It was like magic.

A tall tower was suddenly illuminated by a blaze of blue flame, and a delicate lady wearing a blue costume that sparkled with sequins and feathers tiptoed down a tightrope stretching from the tower across the gardens.

Hannah glanced at Thomas. His face was lit up with the pink and blue of the fireworks.

The bangs and whistles of the fireworks grew louder, as if they were coming closer and closer. A particularly loud one made Hannah jump, and she opened her eyes to the darkness of the orlop deck.

She had grown accustomed to the stench of the livestock

in the week that she had spent in the brig, but she still wasn't used to the darkness. Even the women's quarters had a dim half-light that filtered in from the hatches above. Hannah felt disgusting in her filthy dress, and was always thirsty. A deckhand came down every day to feed the cattle and slop some stew into a bowl for Hannah, but he wouldn't speak to her.

There was another loud bang from outside, and Hannah heard the wailing of a baby. There were other noises, the flapping of canvas and the scream of rope and metal, and then the whole ship felt as if it were falling over. The floor heaved beneath her, and she was thrown against the iron bars of her cage. She could hear the bosun's whistle up on deck, and men shouting. Feet pounded against wood. Then, everything was very still.

The ship had stopped.

Hannah pressed her face against the bars, straining to hear something that would tell her what was going on. Surely they could not have arrived? In New South Wales? Perhaps she had been locked in the brig for longer than she realised. Or had they returned to the doldrums?

There was a scraping noise down the side of the ship, and then a splash. More shouted commands. Was a boat being lowered into the water? Hannah felt dizzy and unstable now that the ship had stopped moving. She had grown so used to its constant motion – even in the doldrums it had been constantly rocking, the boards shifting beneath her bare feet.

Now it barely moved at all.

The air became heavy and still. In the animal pens close by, the cow shifted and mooed.

Hannah wasn't sure how long she spent pressed up against the bars, listening, but the ship finally grew quiet. She dimly heard the cries of gulls.

She tried to recite the kings of England to pass the time. She got stuck at Henry the Third. Did Henry the Fourth come straight after? Or was it an Edward? She knew it wasn't a George or a Charles.

The day dragged on. Hannah wondered what Long Meg had done to pass time in the brig.

'Oh you know,' she imagined Meg saying. 'I hold grand receptions and high teas. And there are *so* many gentleman callers.'

Hannah wondered if night had fallen. She thought of the Great Bear winking to life overhead, before remembering that it no longer appeared in these strange skies.

She was just drifting off to sleep when she heard a rustling in the straw. Probably a rat. The rustling came again, from behind one of the cows. There was a scurrying noise, which came closer and closer to Hannah's cage. She stiffened. It sounded like a very large rat.

'Hannah!' hissed a voice.

Hannah sighed with relief. 'Molly,' she said. 'What are you doing here? Why has the ship stopped?'

Molly came forward and Hannah felt her cool little fingers on hers.

'We're in a city. It has spiky hills and houses and people with brown skin and a big rock called the Table with a tablecloth made of clouds and ladies with no tops on.'

Hannah frowned. 'Are we in New South Wales?'

'No. Just stopped for new water and new animals.'

The mention of fresh water made Hannah's mouth sore. Molly wriggled a little, then pushed something into Hannah's hand.

'We got these,' she said. It was quite large, about the size of a large potato. It was smooth and oval shaped, with a rough point at one end. It felt cool and pleasant.

'What is it?' Hannah asked.

Molly laughed. 'It's heaven,' she said. 'Don't eat the skin.'

Then she was gone.

Hannah ran her hands over the smooth shape, wishing it was light so she could see. She lifted the object to her face and sniffed it.

It smelled like summer, sweet and fresh and fragrant. She dug a fingernail into the surface, and broke through the skin. Juice dribbled down her finger. She lifted the finger cautiously to her lips and tasted.

Molly was right. It tasted like heaven. Like warm nights and fireworks and lazy, sleepy afternoons in the sun. She peeled back the skin and licked the flesh inside. It was sticky and delicious. She took a bite. Juice dripped from her chin and splashed on her cheeks. Rough fibres stuck between her teeth. She licked and chewed until there was nothing left but the discarded skin and a small, flat oval stone that had lain at the fruit's centre.

Late the next afternoon, Hannah heard footsteps. A lantern burned in the darkness, and James emerged. His black hair was tousled, but he was still as beautiful as ever.

His eyes were unfocussed, his walk unsteady. Hannah hastily hid Thomas's handkerchief, and the stone and skin of the strange fruit underneath the straw. James slumped against the bars of the brig and slid to the ground. He reeked of alcohol and sweat. For a while, he said nothing, just stared at the bars of the cage. Then he looked at Hannah.

'We're in Cape Town,' he said.

Hannah said nothing. She wished she'd listened to Thomas's geography lessons more closely. Cape Town. Was that in Africa or South America?

'They have most excellent entertainment here.' James's voice was slurred. 'Fine food and drink. Friendly women.' He looked Hannah up and down. She drew her knees up to her chest and wrapped her arms around them.

James laughed. 'Don't play coy with me, slattern.'

Hannah remembered a time when James's laugh had made her feel warm inside.

'The women here are dark-skinned and bare-bellied. Any one of them would beg for me to take her with me and make her my wife. They would give anything. Anything.'

Hannah looked away.

James sighed. 'What is wrong with you? I acted the gentleman. I brought you toast.'

James made a choking noise, and Hannah realised he was crying. His mouth hung open, slack and wet. His eyes were watery, and white snot trailed from his nose. He must be very drunk.

'You should be begging me to marry you,' he said. 'You should be on your knees.'

Hannah closed her eyes and saw Thomas disappear into the London fog. Her heart ached. Where was he now? Was he thinking about her, too? Why hadn't she gone with him? She had been such a fool. James was still talking. Hannah tried not to listen.

'I could have any woman on this ship. Any woman in this town. In any town. But I want you. I hate that you do this to me.'

She imagined how the voyage would have been if she'd accepted Thomas's offer. She wondered why she had ever wanted a carriage and a house in Mayfair.

'Here,' mumbled James. 'I brought you a present.'

He held out a firm oval fruit. Its skin was orange, freckled with green and pink.

'It's a mango,' he said.

Hannah took the fruit. It was the same fruit that Molly had given her. She put it down on the straw.

'Go away, James,' she said.

James stared at her. His lower lip trembled, and his face was wet and blotchy.

'You'll change your mind,' he said. 'You'll be begging me to take you.'

Hannah said nothing. James got to his feet.

'Then you can die down here,' he said.

After he had gone, Hannah felt about in the darkness and picked up the mango. Almost without thinking, she dug her fingernails into the firm skin, and took a bite.

Then the swinging light returned, an arm reached into the cage and she was roughly jerked to her feet. The mango slipped from her hands and fell into the straw.

'I will not be treated this way,' hissed James, setting the lantern on the floor. 'You will not deny me again.'

He grabbed Hannah's dress through the steel bars of the cage, pulling her to him. Hannah's body hit the bars between them with a clang.

'Good enough to accept my gifts, but not good enough to marry, is that it?' he asked. His rum-soaked breath made Hannah gag. James pushed a finger into her open mouth.

'You will not take my gifts so easily,' he said. 'Spit it out.'

His finger twisted inside her mouth, trying to find the pieces of mango. Hannah tasted rum, sandalwood and tobacco.

She bit down hard.

Her mouth filled with something warm and wet that tasted like tarnished spoons. James screamed, pulling his finger out of her mouth and backing away. Red poured down over James's hand and wrist, dripping onto the floor. She spat his blood out and retched.

Shouts came from overhead, and footsteps approached.

'What's going on down here?' said a voice. Hannah peered into the gloom. It was Captain Gartside, flanked by two officers.

'Look what she's done to me!' cried James, brandishing his bloody hand.

Captain Gartside nodded to one of the officers. 'Take him to the infirmary.'

James was escorted away.

Captain Gartside turned to Hannah, and his eyebrows went up. Hannah realised what she must look like, dirty and unkempt, with James's blood and mango juice dripping from her chin.

'I thought you and Belforte were sweethearts,' the captain said. 'That's certainly the impression that he's given me.'

Hannah wiped her mouth with the back of her wrist. 'No, sir. We're not.'

Captain Gartside frowned. 'Then why has he been begging me to let him stay in New South Wales with you?'

'He says he loves me, sir.'

'He says you're a young lady of Quality, but I don't think you are.'

Hannah said nothing.

'It seems to me that if you were a young lady of Quality,

you wouldn't be nearly so interesting,' said Captain Gartside, with a slight smile. He put his hands behind his back. 'I hear that Lieutenant Belforte is very appealing to the ladies. It's not something I really understand – I come from a world where a man's worth is measured by how hard he works, instead of how much his coat cost.'

'Yes, sir.'

'It seems that you've discovered that the lieutenant is perhaps not so appealing.'

'Yes, sir.'

'I think it's best if you stay away from him,' said Captain Gartside. 'I cannot have my officers attacked by the prisoners. It just won't do. I should have you flogged, you know.'

'Yes, sir.' Hannah didn't know what else to say.

'That was a bad business, with your friend.'

She could still taste the blood in her mouth mingling with the sweetness of the mango.

Captain Gartside nodded. 'I'll tell Belforte to stay away from you, and I advise you to do likewise.' He turned to the other officer. 'Have her head shaved, and put her on half-rations.'

He turned and left the hold.

twenty-
three

The north wind was so fierce and cantankerous that he
blew cold gusts at them from a long way off.
Scatterheart asked if he had ever been to the castle that lay
east o' the sun and west o' the moon.
'Yes,' roared the north wind. 'Once I blew an aspen leaf
there, but afterwards I was so tired that I couldn't blow
a single gust for many days. I'll take you on my back and
blow you over there.'

Hannah climbed up onto the deck and breathed deeply. It
was late morning and a cool breeze blew, caressing Hannah's
newly-shaved head, and drying the tears that had fallen when
the officer had cut off her hair.

Most of the women were sitting on the forecastle. There

were few men to be seen, they having all gone to shore.

Hannah looked with amazement at the city that spread before them.

The *Derby Ram* had anchored in a broad sweeping harbour, the ocean spreading out behind them. Boats and ships bobbed side by side in the water. The city stretched along the shore, flat as flat, with clusters of squat buildings and white churches scattered here and there. The flatness of the city ended abruptly with steep, irregular hills that turned into jagged stone mountains. One of the mountains was completely flat on top, like a boiled egg with the top sliced off. A flat white curtain of cloud sat over it.

There was so much green. A rich, bright green that was unlike anything she had ever seen before. In London, trees were organised in straight lines. Grass was cropped short, and all plants were manicured into pleasing symmetrical shapes. The dark, wild green that crawled over the hills was a violent green, strangling and devouring. Instead of the city pushing back the vegetation, it was the other way around. The city seemed to be defending itself against the jungle.

'Hannah!' Molly came barrelling into her, wrapping her arms around Hannah's waist and burying her face in her chest. Hannah laughed. It was good to see her.

'Your *hair*!' cried Molly, open-mouthed. Hannah sat down on the deck and Molly ran her hands over Hannah's scalp.

'You look like Long Meg did,' said Molly, then bit her lip. Hannah smiled.

'I do, don't I?' she said. 'It feels so strange, like I've lost a limb but discovered there was another one there all along. Now sit down, there's something I need to tell you.'

Molly sat down next to her, holding Hannah's hand. She looked up at Hannah, her good eye the same colour as the ocean. The strange, melted skin that had once so revolted Hannah now seemed smooth and unique.

'I want to tell you a story,' she said.

'What kind of story?' asked Molly.

Hannah remembered snuggling up in the chintz armchair in her house in London. 'It's a story that someone used to tell me. His name is Thomas Behr, and the story is about a girl called Scatterheart.'

Molly frowned. 'That's a silly name,' she said.

'Well, she was called Scatterheart because she was fickle. She gave her heart away too easily, and too often. Like she was scattering it on the ground.'

'But isn't love a good thing to give away?'

'I suppose it is,' said Hannah. 'But not when you give it to people who don't deserve it.'

'Like presents. If you give a present to everyone, then it doesn't really mean anything. If you only give a present to one person, it makes them special.'

Hannah thought about the earrings that her father had brought her. Molly was looking down at the boards of the deck, running her fingers along the wood grain. Hannah wondered if she had ever gotten a present, ever felt special.

The *Derby Ram*'s launch boat was pulling up alongside the ship. It was towing a floating platform loaded with brown wooden barrels. Ropes were lowered and men heaved and pulled.

The barrels were hauled up onto the upper deck, and the bosun cracked the first one open. It was full of fresh water.

'All right then, ladies.' The bosun winked. 'Time for you to practice your trade.'

Hannah stared at him, puzzled, but most of the other women seemed to know what he meant. The few sailors that had returned with the water melted away, until there were only women on the upper deck. The door to the mess was opened, the barrels rolled in, and water poured into the giant copper kettle over the fire.

More barrels were opened, and the women drank their fill. The water was cool and smooth and sweet, like the finest lemonade from Vauxhall. Hannah drank and drank until she thought she might burst. Molly's stomach swelled as she swallowed so fast she got the hiccups.

'So what happens?' asked Molly. 'In the story?'

Hannah told her about Scatterheart and her father. She told her about the white bear that asked to marry Scatterheart, and their long journey to the castle. Molly's eye went wide when she heard about the ice-castle and the white silk sheets, and the feast upon the table.

'What did she eat?' she asked eagerly.

'Oh, everything,' said Hannah. 'Roast beef and chickens

no bigger than a sparrow. Whitebait and parsnips, pheasant pie, potted sturgeon, currants and candied orange flowers.'

'And mangos?' asked Molly.

Hannah laughed. 'Definitely mangos.'

More women appeared from the lower decks of the ship, bearing armfuls of dirty clothes, hammocks and countless other scraps and pieces of fabric. They were filthy and stiff, having only been washed in sea-water over the past few months. A small mountain of clothing grew on the upper deck. The smell of damp and sour sweat filled the air.

As the water boiled, clothes were dumped into the kettle, stirred around with a poker, and then hauled out, dripping and steaming, and handed to the waiting women, who took the wet fabric to a spare stretch of decking and began to beat it against the wooden boards.

Hannah was tossed a wet linen shirt, and she copied the other women, bringing it down against the boards with a satisfying *thwack* that sent a spray of hot water into the air, splashing her face and arms. Rivers of brown water ran from the deck and over the side of the ship as the women scrubbed and boiled and beat the clothing clean.

As they worked, Hannah told Molly about the garden, and the little white door that Scatterheart wasn't to open.

'Does she open it?' asked Molly, wringing out a linen shirt.

'Of course,' said Hannah. 'They always do, in stories.'

She told Molly about how Scatterheart ate the blue fruit,

and how the white bear was cursed and banished to the castle in the land east o' the sun and west o' the moon.

'So he isn't really a bear?' asked Molly.

'No,' said Hannah. 'He's really a handsome prince.'

'Who cursed him?'

'A witch.'

'Why?'

Hannah shrugged. 'I suppose she didn't like him,' she said. 'Perhaps he refused to marry her.'

Molly nodded. 'So does Scatterheart go to rescue him?'

'No,' said Hannah. 'Not at first.'

'Why not?'

'Because she is fickle. She doesn't really care about anyone apart from herself.' Hannah felt a hot lump of shame rise in her throat, and she bit her lip. 'She tries to go home to her father, but she gets lost.'

They worked for hours, stopping in the afternoon for fresh bread and cheese brought to them on a tiny rowboat by a strange little boy with skin the colour of chocolate. He wore only short trousers and nothing else, and his arms and legs were stick-thin. Hannah looked at the bread and cheese, remembering that she was on half-rations. But the bosun winked again and let her have a full share.

Molly listened intently as Hannah told her about the old sawdust-woman with the copper acorn, and the glass-woman with the silver acorn. When Hannah got to the part about the wax-child with the golden acorn, Molly wriggled.

'That's me,' she said proudly.

She told Molly about the tricksy east wind, and his brother the west wind. Hannah told her about how Scatterheart nearly died in the desert, but at the last moment stumbled upon the green valley where the white bear's castle was.

'Is the bear inside?' asked Molly.

'Well, inside is a table with a huge feast on it, and at the head of the table, there is a handsome prince.'

'Is it him? Is the curse broken?'

'No,' said Hannah. 'Scatterheart thinks it is, but then she realises that it's all just a trick.'

'Who is it then?' asked Molly.

Hannah sighed. 'No one important.'

She told Molly about the south wind, and the north wind, and how the north wind promised to take Hannah to the land east o' the sun and west o' the moon. Then the meal was over, and they got up again to finish the washing.

The mood was festive. Molly wriggled in and around the women, who passed her the clean, wet clothes to hang from the ship's rigging to dry. One of the women began to sing one of the sailors' shanties, and the other women joined in, thwacking the wet clothes against the deck in rhythm to the song:

'Where it's wave over wave, sea over bow
I'm as happy a man as the sea will allow
There's no other life for a sailor like me

But to sail the salt sea, oh! sail on the sea
There's no other life but to sail the salt sea.'

Hannah sang too, feeling her troubles wash away with the dirty water.

Everything would be all right now. She would stay away from James, and soon they would arrive in New South Wales. Thomas would be waiting there for her, in the harbour. He would see her and blush and take off his glasses and stammer, and she would take his hand in hers and look into his eyes and they wouldn't have to say anything. As he held her close, she would feel something pressing against her chest. Examining him more closely, she would notice the front of his officer's uniform was pinned with medals. Thomas had distinguished himself in the marines, showing unbelievable courage and resourcefulness against pirates and shipwreck and sea-monsters. He had won a very handsome reward. He would take her back to London and her hair would grow back. They wouldn't have the big house in Mayfair that Hannah had dreamed of, but they would be happy and comfortable. They would still be respectable, and go to garden parties and Vauxhall Gardens to see the fireworks.

Molly came running up to her, skidding and laughing on the wet deck. The sun was sinking into the green hills, and the sky was a deep purple.

'We should ask the north wind to blow our laundry dry,' she said, panting.

Hannah looked at her shining eye and her melted face. What would happen to Molly when they reached New South Wales? Hannah tried to imagine her in the comfortable little house in London with Thomas, but couldn't. She couldn't see her at the garden parties. If Hannah took her to Vauxhall Gardens to see the fireworks and the tightrope walker, people might think she was part of the entertainment.

'What happens to her?' asked Molly.

Hannah stared at her blankly, trying to figure out where Molly would fit in.

'To Scatterheart,' said Molly. 'Does she find the land?'

'She does,' said Hannah.

'And is the bear there?'

Hannah shook her head. 'There is a huge lake, and a field of spikes, and a mountain made of glass–' she paused.

'Then what? Does she find the bear?'

Hannah said nothing. She looked down at her hands, white and wrinkled from the water, out at the ocean which was turning inky black as night came. She looked up to the unfamiliar stars overhead, searching in vain for the Great Bear.

'Hannah?' asked Molly. 'Does she find him?'

Hannah looked back to Molly, a frown creasing her forehead.

'I– I don't remember. I don't remember what happens next.'

twenty–
four

As Scatterheart and the north wind flew over the ocean,
the north wind became more and more weary. His wings
drooped lower and lower until at last he sank so low that
the tops of the waves splashed over his heels.
'Are you afraid?' asked the north wind.
No, she wasn't.

They stayed in Cape Town for a week.

By the time they left, the ship, which had felt so huge and
empty for months, was crammed full of sacks, barrels and
crates. The orlop deck was a chorus of squawks, bleats and
the lowing of confused cattle. They kept the women awake at
night with their mournful noises until, after a week back at
sea, they seemed to settle down in the stuffy darkness.

Hannah tried to avoid James, but he was everywhere.

One afternoon, she was sitting with Cathy, Patty and Sally, picking oakum. Sally's baby lay on the deck nearby, swaddled in a rough wool blanket.

Hannah's fingernails were sore and red. Sweat dripped from her forehead into her eyes. She wiped it away, but one of the coarse hempen fibres wriggled its way into her eye and made it itch and sting. She rubbed at it.

'Cryin' over the loss of your beau?' asked Cathy, smirking.

'No,' Hannah said. 'I have something in my eye.'

Cathy and the other women laughed.

'You is jealous,' said Cathy. 'Jealous that you ain't the favourite anymore.'

She pointed to the forecastle, where James was leaning against the railing, talking to one of the convict women. Hannah squinted in the sunlight. It was Sarah, an Irish girl who had rosy cheeks and an ample bosom. She saw Sarah laugh, and James stroke her cheek. Hannah shuddered, imagining James stroking Long Meg's cold, white cheek.

The women all laughed again when they saw her reaction.

'See how she pines for her sweetheart!'

'Think of the long, cold nights to come.'

'Let's face it, girls, who wouldn't be upset if the handsome lieutenant didn't want us no more.'

Cathy made an appreciative noise. 'We is lucky that he still stands up with us for the featherbed jig.'

Hannah turned on them. 'How can you talk like that?'

The women looked at her, surprised.

'After what he did to Long Meg,' said Hannah. 'He killed her. You know that, don't you? And here you are twittering on about how handsome he is.'

'Don't be slappin' your morals down on us, miss,' said Cathy. 'We does what we does to survive. And that's more than as can be said for Long Meg.'

'Long Meg was trying to protect Molly,' said Hannah. 'That's why she died.'

'No,' said Cathy, standing up. 'She died because you didn't save her. You was the one who had the power over the lieutenant. You was the one who was there. You could of saved her. So stop pretendin' that you is one of us. You isn't. You never was. You never will be.'

The days wore on, and the southern ocean slipped by beneath them. Molly's notches above Long Meg's bed grew crowded, until there were over a hundred of them. The weather grew colder, and Molly huddled up to Hannah at night to keep warm.

Hannah could not remember the end of Thomas Behr's story.

'Surely she finds him,' said Molly as they sat together on the forecastle.

'I suppose so,' said Hannah.

Molly stood up and leaned over the railing, watching the

ocean rush by beneath them. 'Is he in a cave? Or a castle? Or at the bottom of the ocean, in Davy Jones's locker?'

'I don't know. Maybe Thomas will be able to tell us when we get to New South Wales. He'll remember.'

Molly asked her about Thomas, and Hannah smiled.

'When I was younger, I called him Mr Bear,' she said. 'He knew so many stories.'

'Is he a convict like us? Or a sailor?'

'He's an officer. He's very brave and strong.'

'Has he fought a shark?' asked Molly.

'Oh, probably,' said Hannah.

'And a tiger? Has he fought a tiger?'

'Of course,' said Hannah. 'He fought a tiger in India.'

The sea grew ferocious, and the women were no longer allowed onto the upper deck for fear of falling overboard in the rough swell. The wind howled and screamed in the rigging, and sea-spray was constantly soaking the upper decks and dripping through to the lower and orlop decks.

The women were allowed up onto the lower deck once a day for their dinner, which they clutched with cold hands, trying to soak up what little warmth there was.

The sailors were edgy and nervous, muttering stories of terrible storms and shipwrecks. Molly listened, her good eye wide, as Jemmy Griffin told her about the wreck of the *Flying Dutchman*.

'D–did they all die?' Molly's voice was barely a whisper.

Jemmy Griffin nodded. 'But they says the ghost of the ship still sails these waters, with the dead sailors working every hour of the day in complete silence.'

Molly's mouth was open.

'Keep an eye out for the *Dutchman*, missy,' said Jemmy. 'You'll know her for her ragged black sails, and the ghostly figures that appear on her decks.'

Molly looked out the porthole, and Jemmy Griffin chuckled. 'Not yet,' he said. 'The storm ain't fierce enough. Wait another two weeks. Then you'll see her.'

As Jemmy had predicted, after two weeks the storm intensified. Waves as tall as mountains crashed over the *Derby Ram*, sending rivers of water pouring through the grate in the ceiling and soaking the women. Men worked the ship's pumps constantly, but she took in gallons of water which sloshed and rolled around the orlop deck and the hold.

One large wave washed through the mess and put out the stove in the galley. There was no dry wood or coal anywhere to be found in the ship, and so everyone ate stale biscuits and cold salt pork. The temperature continued to drop. In the few moments of stillness when the ship was not being battered and pounded by water, frost formed along the ropes and the rails of the ship.

Captain Gartside ordered extra rations of grog for everyone on board the ship. Hannah hated the taste of the sailors' rum, but she gulped it down anyway, savouring the few moments of warmth it brought before another wave crashed against the ship and drenched her once more.

The storm continued for a fortnight. Nearly a month after leaving Cape Town, Hannah sat on her bed, huddled against the ship's hull, her damp blanket pulled up around her and her cold, stiff fingers clutching Thomas's handkerchief. The now familiar aching in her abdomen had returned, and was all the worse for the cold. Hannah got up and went over to the chest where the clean rags were kept.

The dragging pain intensified, and Hannah bent over slightly as she made her way back to her bed. As she curled up under her wet blanket, she wished that Long Meg was there to make fun of her.

Don't be such a layabout, she'd say. *If a woman kept to her bed every time she had brambles in the strawberry patch, Rome would've never been builded, and King George'd have holes in his socks.*

Molly scratched another notch in the wood above Long Meg's bed. They'd been at sea now for four months.

'Can't we go outside?' Molly asked, putting down the spoon.

'Not in this weather,' said Hannah. 'We're not allowed.'

'Why not?'

Hannah sighed. 'We just can't.'

She closed her eyes and pictured what was now a familiar scene. The ship sailed regally into Port Jackson. The harbour was crowded with onlookers waving handkerchiefs and cheering. A long, angled gangplank was lowered, and the convict women descended. Hannah was last. Her hair had grown into a short, fashionable style, and she had sewn herself a new dress and pelisse. She was weary, but her cheeks were pink and her eyes sparkled. The crowd parted before her to reveal Thomas standing at the back.

She opened her eyes again. Molly was gone. She was not in any of the other beds. Surely she couldn't have gone on deck in this weather?

With a sigh, Hannah climbed out of her own bed and made her way along the aisle to the stairs. Water sloshed around her feet. Her legs were stiff and aching from the cold. She pulled herself up the stairs, and made her way onto the lower deck.

The ship was groaning, her timbers shrieking as they were battered by the wind and the rain and the sea. Hannah got down on her hands and knees to climb the flight of stairs to the upper deck. The hatch was closed, and she struggled with the catch. It finally clicked open. The weather rushed in at her, buffeting her from all sides. Molly couldn't be up here.

There were no sailors on deck. The sails had been rolled up, and every rope and piece of canvas had been secured. Hannah couldn't see Molly anywhere. She was reaching out to lower the hatch again, when she heard a scream. She peered through the rain again and could just make out a dark shape on the forecastle.

She crawled out onto the deck, and made her way over

to the stairs on her hands and knees. The wind was howling and screeching in the rigging. She looked up to the forecastle deck, and saw a figure in black standing between the guns. It was too tall and broad to be Molly.

A roar made her turn around, and she screamed. An enormous wave towered above the ship, higher than Hannah had thought possible. It surged and boiled up over them, and then hung there, suspended for a moment. The figure on deck had turned when Hannah had screamed, and in the instant before the wave came crashing down, Hannah saw his face.

It was Dr Ullathorne.

When the wave hit, Hannah was slammed against the deck. The air was crushed out of her lungs and she hit her head hard. Her mouth and nostrils filled with salt water and she felt dragged towards the ocean as the water poured off the side of the ship. Somehow her numb fingers managed to hold onto the rail, and she gasped for air.

Dr Ullathorne was leaning over the railing, yelling something into the wind. Hannah blinked water from her eyes, and saw another face.

It was Molly, clinging to the rigging on the bowsprit, her white face full of terror. Hannah pulled herself upright and began to climb the stairs.

Then, they were falling. The *Derby Ram* rushed and tumbled down into the trough created by the monster wave. The ship tilted forward dramatically and Hannah found the stairs suddenly sloping downwards as the ship was sucked, nose-first into the trough. Molly screamed again, high and piercing. Hannah went skidding across the forecastle deck. The deck was almost vertical as the ship plunged downwards. Hannah caught a glimpse of Molly, dangling from a rope and screaming.

The ship smacked down into the bottom of the trough with a booming crash. The timbers shuddered and screamed with the effort of staying together. Hannah felt the boards beneath her buckle and shift, and for a moment she thought the *Derby Ram* was being crushed to splinters. But the ship immediately righted itself in the water, and the deck was horizontal once more. Hannah pulled herself upwards. The doctor didn't look at her, just stared out at Molly, his face blank.

Molly was frozen against the bowsprit. Below her, the ocean churned.

Hannah leaned over the rail. 'Molly!' she screamed. 'Grab my hand!'

But Molly was too far away. Hannah turned to Dr Ullathorne.

'Help me!' she said. 'Get help!'

Dr Ullathorne didn't take his eyes off Molly.

Hannah glanced down at the thrashing waters below, and gritted her teeth. She swung one leg over the forecastle rail, and then the other. Gripping the rail behind her with one hand, she reached out to grab a rope. She leaned forward, letting go of the rail to reach out for Molly.

There was a crack, as another wave hit the side of the ship.

Water hit Hannah with a smack, and she lost her hold on the rope. She fell down onto the lower-front part of the forecastle deck and grabbed one of the knightheads to stop herself from being washed overboard. She looked up. Molly still clung to the bowsprit, where it angled up and out over the ocean.

'Molly!' cried Hannah. 'Can you climb down to me?'

Molly turned her enormous frightened eye to Hannah.

'It's all right,' Hannah yelled. 'I'll catch you if you fall. You just need to move over the lower deck, in away from the water!'

Molly closed her eye, and after what seemed like an age, she began to move. She inched down along the bowsprit, eye tightly squeezed shut. The ship juddered as it rushed into another trough, and Molly lost her grip. She slipped and tumbled along the bowsprit and slammed against the stern of the ship, falling to the lower part of the deck with a thump.

Hannah rushed over and helped her up. She was still conscious, but looked very dazed. Hannah dragged her over to the tiny door which led to the upper-deck cabins. There was no handle; it only opened from the inside. She pushed and kicked and yelled, but the noise was sucked away by the roar of the storm.

Water pounded down on them from all around, and Hannah felt the ocean trying to suck her and Molly in and down into Davy Jones's locker. Her limbs felt heavy, her sopping dress dragging on her.

The doctor was standing on the forecastle deck, leaning

over the rail and staring at them.

'Help us, damn you!' screamed Hannah.

He didn't move, just stared. Hannah thought she saw a flicker of a smile play around his crumbling face. He looked terrible. His nose had completely collapsed in on itself, and his sunken cheeks were streaked with thick black lines where Meg has slashed him with the knife. One of his eyes was red and weeping, the other clouded over with a black film. His lips were covered in white pustules which swelled them to five times their original size, exposing rotten teeth and strings of black saliva.

She looked him in the eye. 'I'll repay you, I promise. Anything.'

Molly gripped Hannah's arm. 'He followed me, Hannah. I just wanted to go out to the air and see the stars and look for the *Flying Dutchman*. But he followed me and I runned away until I couldn't run any more and then I climbed.'

Hannah didn't look away from him. 'Anything.'

For a moment, Hannah thought he was going to walk away. Then he was lying on the forecastle deck on his stomach, leaning over the edge and reaching down to them.

Hannah stretched out one arm, wrapped the other around Molly and jumped. Dr Ullathorne caught her arm and hauled, just as another great wave came crashing down on top of them. His grip didn't slacken as he heaved them up onto the forecastle deck.

Hannah looked down and saw water surging over the small

platform where they had stood before, sucking and drawing back out to sea. Hannah shuddered, imagining her and Molly being sucked with it, down to the bottom of the ocean.

Hannah clung to the deck for a moment, panting and trying not to cry, then she pulled herself upright to face the doctor. Even through the storm, she could smell his rotting flesh. He had helped Molly to her feet, and stood with his hand clamped on her shoulder.

'Thank you,' said Hannah.

The doctor smiled. His lips were so swollen he couldn't close his mouth. 'No need,' he said.

He turned to Molly. 'Come along, my dear.'

Molly turned to Hannah, shocked. The driving wind and rain whipped wet ropes of hair against her face.

Hannah reached out. 'Molly, come with me.'

'I don't think so,' said Dr Ullathorne.

Hannah stared at him. 'What do you mean?'

'You said "anything". I want her. With no more... interventions. No more late night visits from your friends. There's only so many excuses I can make to Gartside.'

Molly tried to run to Hannah, but Dr Ullathorne tightened his grip on her shoulder.

'Why?' asked Hannah. 'What can you possibly want with her?'

'Study,' he hissed. 'If I can cure her deformity, then I can find the cure to my own sickness.'

Hannah tasted bile.

'You'll kill her,' she said.

'A small price to pay,' he said quietly, then another giant wave pounded the ship with gallons of rushing water.

They were all knocked down, grasping for something to hold onto. Hannah clambered to her feet, and managed to put herself between Molly and Dr Ullathorne. The doctor struggled to stand, slipping on the wet deck.

The ship seemed to hang in the air for a moment, as it reached the crest of another mountainous wave. Dr Ullathorne leapt at Hannah and Molly, his fingers extended like claws. Hannah lashed out at him, pushing him away. He staggered backwards, falling heavily against the rail.

The ship tilted forwards as it began to rush down the wave into the next trough. It hit the bottom of the trough so hard that Hannah imagined they had tumbled all the way to the bottom of the ocean, and were smacking against the seabed. Dr Ullathorne was thrown back again, and the rail behind him snapped. He teetered, trying to find some balance or handhold.

Hannah hesitated. He reached out towards her. 'I saved you,' he said.

Hannah wished that Thomas was there to tell her what to do. Or Long Meg. Meg would want him to die. *Send him over arsey yarsey!* she'd yell.

But Long Meg wasn't there. There was no one else. Just Hannah. She looked upwards into the storm. The rain stung her eyes.

'I'm sorry, Meg,' she said.

The doctor slumped in relief, and held out his other hand.

Hannah took a step forward, and looked into his eyes. She grabbed his wrists. The ship tilted again.

'I'm sorry I didn't do this earlier,' she said, and pushed.

Dr Ullathorne screamed, but the sound was snatched away by the wind. Then he was gone. There was a rumble of thunder and a crack of lightning, as if the storm were devouring him. In the sudden brightness of the lightning, Hannah thought she could see another figure, over on the poop deck, silhouetted against the raging storm. But the lightning flickered out, and the figure vanished.

twenty–
five

**The north wind had just enough strength to toss
Scatterheart onto a deserted beach on a far-off shore.**

Once Hannah and Molly had made their way back to the
orlop deck, Hannah's composure left her, and she began to
shake with cold and terror. The expression on the doctor's
face as he was snatched overboard appeared every time she
closed her eyes. She imagined the water filling his mouth and
nostrils and sucking him down.

Molly was quiet, clinging to Hannah. They waited for the
cry to go up when it was discovered that the doctor was no
longer on board. Had they been seen on the forecastle? Had
there really been someone watching from the poop deck? She
would probably be hanged for killing an officer. She trembled,

until finally her body gave in to its exhaustion and she slipped into a troubled sleep.

Hannah woke the next morning to a strange stillness. The ship was almost motionless. It was quiet. The other women were muttering to each other, their faces serious. Molly was standing with them, but when she saw that Hannah was awake, she came over.

'One of the officers is dead,' she said. 'The little one who is smaller than me.'

'Bracegirdle?' said Hannah.

Molly nodded. 'Something wasn't tied up that was supposed to be. It rolled across the deck in the storm and squished him.'

'What about Dr Ullathorne?' said Hannah, quietly. 'Has anyone mentioned him?'

Molly nodded again. 'Someone went down to get a bandage and he wasn't there. They're sayin' he fell overboard.'

Hannah closed her eyes. It was over. He was gone.

'We have to go upstairs,' said Molly. 'For the funeral.'

All the ship's inhabitants assembled on the upper deck before breakfast. The officers wore their formal uniforms, and the sailors had all donned hats. Captain Gartside stood by the starboard rail, holding a Bible. He was wearing his full captain's uniform. Next to him, two wooden planks were suspended over the ocean, each end held a sailor.

One plank bore the body of Bracegirdle, sewn into his

hammock. Hannah heard Patty say that the final stitch was through the dead sailor's nose, to make sure he was really dead. The canvas hammock was weighted down with two cannonballs, so that the body would sink. A red ensign flag was draped over the canvas parcel.

The second plank bore a hemp wreath, as Dr Ullathorne's body had not been recovered from the ocean. Another red flag was folded on top of it.

The ship had been stopped, and bobbed gently in the water. The red and blue flags all flew at half-mast.

Captain Gartside nodded at the bosun, who cupped a hand around his mouth to yell.

'Ship's company, *off* hats!'

The officers and sailors removed their hats. The women bowed their heads and clasped their hands.

Captain Gartside looked down at the Bible and started to read aloud.

'I will take heed to my ways,' he said. 'That I offend not in my tongue. I will keep my mouth as it were with a bridle. I held my tongue, and spake nothing. My heart was hot within me, and while I was thus musing, the fire kindled.'

James was standing to the left of Captain Gartside. He was staring at her. He flashed a glance down to the hemp wreath, and then smiled strangely at Hannah.

Did he know? She looked down at her hands, feeling panic rise.

'For man walketh in a vain shadow, and disquiets himself

in vain. He has heaped up riches, but cannot tell who should gather them.'

Hannah closed her eyes and wished to be transported to wherever Thomas was. She remembered how terribly she had treated him in London. She had been no better than James, really. She glanced back up at him. He was still staring at her.

'As it was in the beginning, is now, and ever shall be: world without end. Amen.'

Captain Gartside shut the Bible and turned to look at the ocean. Everyone waited for him to speak again.

Hannah felt tears rising. Why hadn't Long Meg had a funeral? Why hadn't the sailors taken their hats off and bowed their heads to her?

Hannah wondered what had happened to her body. She imagined Dr Ullathorne and James dumping it over the side of the ship in the middle of the night.

Captain Gartside sighed, and turned back to the crowd.

'We therefore commit their bodies to the deep, to be turned into corruption, looking for the resurrection of the body, when the sea shall give up her dead. Ashes to ashes, dust to dust. The Lord bless them and keep them.'

'Amen,' muttered the assembled men and women.

'Amen,' said Hannah fiercely, remembering Long Meg.

The four sailors holding the planks tipped their ends upwards, holding onto the corners of the red flags. The canvas-wrapped body and the hemp wreath slid from the planks and fell into the water with a splash. The wreath bobbed on the surface, but the body was pulled under immediately.

Three days later, Hannah was awoken by the sound of shouting. Men were yelling on the upper deck. She could hear the pounding of feet on the boards above.

She strained her ears to try and hear what the men were yelling. The other women were awake as well, sitting up and listening. Susan, who slept closest to the stairs to the gun deck, gave out a hoarse cry.

'Land ahoy,' she said. 'That's what they're sayin'. *Land ahoy.*'

Like the bursting of a dam, the women poured up the ladder and onto the decks. Hannah pushed through the crowd of women and sailors and scrambled up onto the forecastle, Molly hot on her heels. She averted her eyes from the place where the doctor had fallen. She leaned as far as she dared over the side of the rail, and looked.

There was a dark shadow on the horizon. Hannah burst into tears.

The smudge on the horizon was not Port Jackson. It was Van Diemen's Land, the very bottom point of the southern continent. Port Jackson, Navigator Dollard told them, was another three weeks sailing. But the smudge meant that they had crossed the Atlantic Ocean and the Southern Ocean. They were in Parts Beyond the Seas.

Hannah was haunted by Dr Ullathorne's white face in her dreams. She tried to put it out of her mind, and concentrated on imagining their arrival in Port Jackson, and her reunion with Thomas. By this stage, her tales of Mr Bear's adventures had become so wild and fantastic, that she was half-imagining Thomas greeting her at the harbour astride a white elephant, his head wreathed with garlands of flowers bestowed on him by grateful natives, after having saved their village from marauding bandits.

'What did Mr Bear do after he left the savages' village?' asked Molly, as they sat on their beds late one night.

Hannah yawned. 'Oh, something to do with a volcano,' she said.

'What?'

'He, er, had a treasure map that led to an amazing hoard of treasure in a volcano.'

'And was he all right?'

'Of course,' said Hannah. 'Not so much as a singed hair.'

'So when did he meet the witch?'

'What witch?'

'The witch,' said Molly. 'The one who turned him into a bear and sent him to the land east o' the sun and west o' the moon.'

Hannah shook her head. 'That's a different story. A different bear.'

'No it isn't,' said Molly. 'It's Mr Bear. In both.'

It took three weeks for the smudge on the horizon to become

land. Hannah counted the notches above Long Meg's bed – they had been at sea for five months.

All the convicts were on the upper decks, leaning over the railing or out gunholes. They clutched rolls of fabric containing their blankets, and their few meagre possessions. Hannah had left her blanket in the orlop deck. She wouldn't need it, Thomas would have a proper one for her.

All she carried was his handkerchief, neatly folded. It was a drab, tattered square of fabric, but Hannah held it gently and carefully.

The sun was bright and warm, though the wind still carried a chill. The salty, fresh smell of the ocean mingled with something else, something green and sharp and tangy. The convicts cheered and wept. Hannah held Molly's hand so tightly she yelped and wriggled.

The sun sparkled on the sea so blue and bright that it hurt Hannah's eyes. Green hills dripped down to the water, a low, twisted, greyish green that made Hannah think of wild, impenetrable brambles and sleeping princesses. Strange trees rose over the green tangle, smooth and twisted, with pink, flesh-like bark. Their trunks had bulges and crevices that looked like human body parts. Some of them looked like they were flinging out their arms and waving in welcome. Others twisted in to each other, their cracks and wrinkles somehow intimate and obscene.

Sailors pushed through the women as commands were shouted. The bosun's whistle shrilled. Ropes were slackened.

The ship's wheel was spun around and around, and slowly, the *Derby Ram* turned towards the rise of grey-green.

The ocean pressed up against the land and pushed in, until it became a river. It wriggled into the land like a snake, poking its nose into each white sandy cove and green inlet before moving on, pushing deep into the earth towards the rise of blue-green mountains to the west.

Molly was leaning out over the rail as far as she dared, her bundle of bedding lying on the deck behind her.

'Look, Hannah!' she cried. 'It's like paradise.'

Hundreds of pink and grey birds perched in the twisted trees. As the ship neared them, they launched themselves into the air, moving like a single creature. As they rose, they made a raucous squawking noise.

Hannah laughed. 'I don't think birds in Paradise would sound like that,' she said.

Molly giggled.

Hannah felt an overwhelming sense of peace come over her. This was it. Thomas would be waiting for her, and then everything would be alright.

Molly smiled at her. 'We made it,' she said. 'East o' the sun, west o' the moon.'

Hannah craned her neck eagerly, trying to get a glimpse of Sydney Cove. Thomas would be there, wearing his uniform. She'd spot him instantly in the crowd of cheering onlookers. He would be able to explain the mistake about her arrest. She would be made free.

They approached a headland, smooth and green with manicured lawns and neatly cropped bushes and trees. A woman dressed in a sophisticated if somewhat old-fashioned gown and pelisse sat on a stone seat on the headland, shading herself from the sun with a parasol.

Hannah's heart was beating so loudly in her chest that she thought the woman must be able to hear it.

As they rounded the headland, Hannah saw Sydney Cove spread out before them. It was not much of a city: a sprawl of yellow stone buildings, surrounded by fields and, beyond it, forest. A river divided the tiny city.

Hannah could barely stand still. She smoothed her grey serge dress and pinched her cheeks. Her hair had started to grow back, and was now a few inches long. She tried to tuck it behind her ears, wishing she had a proper looking-glass and some ribbon.

As the ship neared the wharf, Hannah looked for Thomas. The cheering crowds she had imagined weren't there. There were a few bored-looking officers waiting for them, and a handful of dock-hands waiting to help with disembarking.

She couldn't see Thomas.

There were shouts and splashes, then a screaming noise as the anchor was lowered with a splash. A gangplank was lowered to the wharf, and Captain Gartside descended, flanked by a few other officers. They spoke briefly to the men awaiting them on the wharf, then Captain Gartside turned and signalled to the remaining officers on the *Derby Ram*.

'All right then, ladies,' shouted the bosun. 'Form an orderly line. No pushing.'

They shuffled down the gangplank. Hannah and Molly were towards the back of the line. Hannah stepped onto the wharf and looked around.

He wasn't there.

The wooden boards of the wharf seemed to buckle and sway beneath her. Her head felt fuzzy and her eyes blurred. The detailed scene she had imagined, of her and Thomas flying into each other's arms, weeping and laughing with joy, repeated over and over again in her mind, mocking her.

He wasn't there.

Molly tugged on her hand. 'Perhaps he's running late,' she said.

Hannah nodded and swallowed. She balled up the handkerchief in her hand.

For a moment, she felt a surge of panic as she tried to remember her conversation with Thomas. Had he really said he was coming to New South Wales? What if he wasn't there at all? What if he had stayed in London? What if he was in France fighting Napoleon? What if he had been sent to Africa, or China?

'Come on,' said Molly, pulling on her hand.

Hannah took a step forward, her mind whirling. The wharf seemed to disappear beneath her, and her foot fell forward into blank space. She toppled after it, falling face-down on the deck.

Strong hands lifted her up from behind.

'You need to get your land-legs back,' said a voice. Hannah remembered being carried on to the *Derby Ram* by those arms, spoken to with that voice. She turned around.

It was James, smiling gently and sweetly at her, as if no bad words had ever passed between them. Hannah noticed the fresh white scar on his finger where she had bitten him. She felt hot tears burning in her eyes, and squeezed them tightly closed. A lump of misery lodged in her throat. He wasn't here. He hadn't come.

She stumbled forward, James's hand on her back, as the ground rocked and swayed beneath her.

Through a haze of tears, she made out wide, unpaved streets fringed by sand-coloured stone buildings. Horse-drawn carts and buggies rumbled along the dusty streets. On the fringes of the tiny city, the golden buildings were replaced by wattle-and-daub huts, and Hannah could see some crude lean-to's snuggling into the grey rocks that hung over the hillside. Children ran barefoot amongst the rocks. They looked wild and savage. Hannah thought of the ragged children she had seen playing hussle-cap back in London, and thought that they seemed like well-behaved children of Quality compared to these fierce creatures. The light was bright and harsh, everything looked too clear and crisp. Hannah's head ached with the brilliance of everything.

A man leaned against a building, wearing nothing but a scrap of cloth around his loins and some kind of animal-skin cloak. His skin was as black as the bottom of a coal-scuttle. He looked at Hannah, and she was startled to see the whites of his eyes standing out so drastically against his dark face. He grinned at her; a challenging, threatening grin. His teeth were white also, whiter than any teeth Hannah had seen before.

All around them rose gentle sloping hills, covered in grey-green that looked curly and dense, like the fleece on a sheep's back. The air smelled of something tangy and earthy.

A part of Hannah was expecting Thomas suddenly to appear from behind a building, or come galloping up on a sweaty horse. But another part of her knew that he wasn't coming. She stopped, unable to walk any further.

The ground pitched beneath her. The lump of misery in her throat swelled, until she couldn't breathe.

'It's all right, Hannah,' said James. 'I'm here. You're just land-sick.'

She turned to look at him. He was as handsome as he had ever been. His eyes were still large and gentle, his skin still white as snow. He smiled at her.

'Hannah?' he said gently.

The lump in Hannah's throat cut off her breathing entirely, and she coughed violently, vomiting bile onto the dusty brown earth beneath them. A sour, bitter smell rose hotly in the air. Hannah felt it overwhelm her.

She staggered after the other women, who were being loaded in groups onto flat-bottomed barge at the other end of the wharf.

'Where are we going?' asked Molly in a quiet, frightened voice. 'Aren't we there already?'

'No,' said James. 'They're sending you up the river to a town called Parramatta. It's where all the unmarried women go.' He gripped Hannah's arm. 'Hannah, it doesn't have to be like this. It's not too late.'

She twisted her arm free, and scrambled onto the barge, and then leaned down to help Molly up.

'I'll come for you, Hannah,' said James. 'Don't worry.'

She didn't look back as the barge cast off and drifted slowly away from Sydney Town.

The river glinted silver, reflecting the tangle of greys and greens and browns that crowded greedily around its banks. Farmland stretched off into the distance, brown and gold, dotted with the occasional sheep. Birds rose from the trees in rainbow-coloured fluttering clouds, screeching and calling. But to Hannah, everything was bitter, tainted by the taste of bile in the back of her throat.

PART III:

East o' the sun,
west o' the moon

twenty–
six

The north wind whisked away, dropping a single acorn on the beach next to Scatterheart. She picked it up and put it in her pocket with the other three.

Late that night, the barge pulled up in Parramatta. A few dim orange lights burned in the windows of the huts clustered on the riverbank. The darkness otherwise was absolute, and Hannah shivered, imagining what might be lurking just beyond the ring of light cast by the boatman's lamp. She remembered the challenge in the face of the native in Sydney Town. She held Molly's hand tightly.

They were lined up along the waterfront, on a rickety wooden pier. A handful of men and women huddled together, watching. Some looked like farmers, with coarse hands and broad hats. Others were clearly people of higher rank, women in long skirts and bonnets, and men wearing top hats and carrying canes.

A man in an officer's uniform, carrying a lamp, paraded up and down in front of them. He examined each of the women, looked at their teeth and into their eyes, asked their names and the crime that had sent them to New South Wales.

Some of the women he assigned to the people waiting on the pier, others he left standing. When he reached Molly, he bent down to look her in the eye.

'What's your name, little miss?'

'M–molly,' she answered.

'What's your last name, Molly?'

'Just Molly.'

'Well, Just Molly, how old are you?'

Molly shrugged, relaxing a little. 'Seven, eight, nine. Not sure.'

He nodded, and waved at a woman waiting in the crowd.

'Take her to the orphanage,' he said. 'She's too young for the factory.'

Molly gripped Hannah's hand as the woman came for her.

'Wait,' said Hannah. 'She's … she's my sister.'

The officer shrugged. 'Makes no difference if she's your own child. She's to the orphanage.'

The woman tried to take Molly by the hand, but Molly hissed and spat at her.

'I ain't no orphing!' she said. 'I want to stay with Hannah.'

The woman grabbed Molly around the waist and picked her up. Molly kicked and bit and yelled, but the woman was strong. She carried Molly away.

'Hannah!' Molly cried, her voice shrill. 'Don't let them take me.'

Hannah caught a glimpse of Molly's face, pale and frightened.

'It'll be all right, Molly,' said Hannah helplessly.

As the woman and Molly disappeared into the darkness, Hannah heard a wailing cry that tugged at her, somewhere deep inside.

The officer turned to her.

'Name?' he asked.

'Hannah Cheshire,' said Hannah.

'Age?'

'I'm fourteen,' said Hannah, and then realised that it wasn't true. She had turned fifteen somewhere during the voyage and not realised.

'Crime?'

Hannah frowned. 'I committed no crime,' she said. 'I'm here by mistake.'

The officer raised an eyebrow. 'Aren't you all?' he said.

He grabbed her by the chin, and forced open her mouth, looking at her teeth. Hannah felt humiliated, like a horse being examined by a prospective buyer. She thought of the tooth she had spat onto the deck of the *Derby Ram*. The officer glanced at her short hair.

'Got punished on the voyage, did we?' he asked. 'What did you do?'

'I haven't done anything wrong,' she said. For a moment she saw Dr Ullathorne's face as he tumbled into the ocean. 'I need to find Thomas Behr. He's an officer.'

The man looked sharply at her. 'Thomas Behr, you say?'

Hannah's heart leapt. 'Yes, do you know him? Is he here?'

The man paused, considering her. Then he shook his head. 'There is no one here by that name,' he said. 'You're too saucy for service. Off to the factory.'

The Female Factory was a wretched loft above a gaol that was not much bigger than their room in the orlop deck, but filled with nearly twice as many women.

Hannah crowded in with the rest of the new arrivals, and stared around in horror. The building seemed barely to hold together. The wind whistled through gaps between the roof and walls, and the floorboards were so buckled that Hannah could fit her fingers through the gaps.

She spent the first night shivering in the draughty room, wishing she had not left her blanket on board the ship. They were not given any bedding, or clean clothes. Shortly before dawn, it started to rain. The roof leaked, and cold water spattered and dripped onto Hannah.

The women who lived in the factory were the ones who weren't selected to serve in the houses of the Sydney and Parramatta residents, or on neighbouring farms. They were the worst of the convict women; the evil, the sick, and the elderly.

Hannah wasn't sure why she'd been sent there, instead of being assigned to a family. When she arrived, the factory superintendent raised his eyebrows. The officer escorting her leaned over and muttered something in his ear. Hannah started. Had the man said Thomas Behr's name? She swallowed nervously. What was going on? Why did the superintendent narrow his eyes at her and purse his lips? Where was Thomas?

Hannah hated it in the factory. Men were allowed in at all hours of the day and night, and were always to be found in corners with women who would do just about anything for a couple of copper coins. *Buttock-and-twang*, they called it, leering and simpering at the men. Convicts, officers and free men arrived in a constant stream, clutching a handful of coins in their grubby fists.

Each Thursday, about a dozen of the convict women would dance the mermaid dance. They were stripped naked, and bright blue numbers were painted on their backs. Then someone would play a fiddle or a flute, and the women would dance. The men called out the numbers of their favourites, bidding against each other. They stamped and clapped and whistled. The women would dance harder – trying to outdo each other in wantonness and vulgarity. When the dancing was finished, the highest bidder would pay his money and slip away with his prize.

The first week, Hannah was afraid that she would be forced to join the mermaid dancers. But it turned out that the women volunteered, and the superintendent split the money. Hannah was disgusted that the women could be so obscene, just for a few copper coins. Then she remembered what Long Meg had said about protection. What was it that Cathy had said to her? *We does what we does to survive.*

There were few familiar faces in the factory. A handful of women from the *Derby Ram* were there, including Tabby, who, on arrival, burrowed into a greasy and filthy pile of raw wool and rarely emerged.

The women were set to work each day, carding and spinning wool gathered from a nearby sheep farm. Other, more skilled women wove the coarse yarn into a rough, scratchy fabric that clothed the convicts in winter. Women who misbehaved in the factory were sent out to do manual labour. They were fitted with spiked iron collars and marched out of the factory by red-coated marines who whipped them to the beat of a drum as they hauled buckets of earth and rubble around for building works. If they paused or were insubordinate in any way, they were given the 'Botany Bay dozen' – twenty-five lashes, or twelve if the woman agreed to receive them naked.

The superintendent of the Female Factory was a man called Green, and he appeared at infrequent and random intervals to toss them a sloppy bucket of 'smiggins' – a watery soup made from barley. He despised the women, referred to them as nothing other than 'filthy whores', and looked disgusted every time he had to touch them. At all other times, they were left to themselves.

Hannah asked everyone she could find if they had seen Thomas Behr. She barely noticed the stinking smell of the greasy sheep's wool, or how sore her fingers became after only a few hours of carding. She didn't care that the food was much worse than it had been on the *Derby Ram*, and was distributed much less often. She was far too eager to find out any news of Thomas.

The women shook their heads and shrugged. Hannah felt a terrible sinking feeling inside. What if he had never come to New South Wales in the first place? What if he'd decided not to become a marine after all?

But there was the strange look that the officer at the pier had given her when she mentioned his name. He had to know something. Maybe Thomas had been sent back to England.

One night, Hannah was curled up in her corner, her stomach grumbling even though they'd just been served dinner. A woman with frizzy brown hair came up to Hannah, introduced herself as Bess, and sat down.

'I heard you was looking for a gentleman,' she said.

Hannah's heart pounded. 'His name's Thomas Behr. Do you know of him?'

Bess shook her head. 'I don't know no names. But I heard

a story in Sydney Town, afore there were some ill feelings between my mistress and me and I got sent here.'

'What story?'

Bess scratched a red rash on her arm. 'An officer got in trouble. Sommit about a woman. He killed a woman? Sommit like that. Then he ran away. That could be your man.'

Hannah shook her head. 'Thomas would never kill someone. It isn't him.'

Bess shrugged and stood up. 'Men do all sorts of things when there's a lass involved.'

She shuffled off.

Tabby was peering at Hannah from her pile of wool. 'Ye seek grace at a graceless face,' she said.

'That woman knew something,' said Hannah.

Tabby shrugged. 'Ain swallow makes no summer.'

Hannah sighed.

'Need makes naked men spar, and sorrow makes websters spin,' said Tabby.

Hannah looked at her, uncomprehending.

'Kings and bears oft worry their keepers,' said Tabby.

Hannah grabbed her thin, bony arm. 'Do you know something? Did you hear something?'

Tabby shook her head. 'Puddings and paramours would be hotly handled.'

Hannah released her.

'It is na time to stop when the head is off,' said Tabby, chuckling, and burrowed back down into her fleece.

Three days later, a new woman arrived from Sydney Town. She had a large purple bruise on her cheek, and her right eye was swollen nearly shut. When Superintendent Green came in with a servant bearing their meagre evening meal, Hannah hastened over to speak to her.

'Behr?' asked the woman, narrowing her eyes.

'Have you heard of him?' asked Hannah.

The woman shook her head. 'I don't think so,' she said.

Hannah grabbed the woman's wrist. 'Please, think,' she said. 'You haven't ever heard of anyone called Behr?'

Bess wandered over. 'I thought it might have been that officer,' she said to the new woman. 'You know, the one who killed that woman.'

The woman shook her head. 'That was a bad business,' she said.

Hannah released the woman's wrist. 'Never mind,' she said, turning to leave.

'Wait,' said the new woman. 'That officer, he had a German name. It might have been Behr.'

'It couldn't have been,' said Hannah. 'Thomas isn't a murderer.'

The woman closed her eyes, trying to remember. 'I heard my master talking about it,' she touched the bruise on her cheek and winced. 'My *old* master, I should say. He said some German officer fell in love with a convict woman. Then something happened to get him into trouble, and he disappeared.'

Another woman with a shaved head looked up. 'Are you talking about that officer who killed his superior? In cold blood, they say.'

'I heard he killed the woman,' said Bess.

'No,' said the woman with the shaved head. 'The superior killed the woman, and *he* killed the superior. He was hanged two months ago.'

Bess shook her head. 'I heard he was sent back to England.'

'You're both wrong,' said the woman with the black eye. 'He was sent to Van Diemen's Land, to work in a chain gang.'

'It doesn't matter,' said Hannah. 'It isn't him.'

Superintendent Green banged his cane against a wall.

'All right, you worthless whores,' he yelled. 'Back to work.'

The other women went back over to the looms. Hannah remained sitting on the floor. What was the point in moving? He was gone. He probably never left England. She was alone in this horrible hell at the end of the world. Even Molly had been taken away from her.

'You!' Superintendent Green barked, towering over Hannah. 'Laziness will not be tolerated!'

He brought his cane down hard on Hannah's back. The thin wood sliced through her dress and bit deep into her skin, but Hannah didn't move. The pain exploded again as Superintendent Green brought the cane down a second time.

Hannah struggled to her feet and made her way over to the piles of greasy wool where women sat cross-legged on the floor, carding wool.

The blood dried into her dress and her back became stiff and painful. But it didn't matter. Nothing mattered any more.

On Sundays, the women of the Female Factory were lined up along the front of the building, and the single men of the colony were invited to come and inspect them. Some preened and simpered, others scowled and scuffed their shoes in the dirt.

Men shuffled along in front of the women. When a man found a woman he liked the look of, he would drop his handkerchief in front of her. If the woman liked the look of the man, she would pick up his handkerchief, and go home with him.

Hannah quite enjoyed the fresh air, but made a sullen face whenever a man passed her. They never dropped their handkerchief for her. A part of her was vaguely insulted – wasn't she beautiful anymore? Back in London, these dirty and rough men would have given anything to be able to just look at her, to stand close to her. Now they were too good for her.

Hannah's third Sunday outside the factory was overcast and gloomy, the clouds threatening rain. Tabby stood hunched next to her, chewing on something black and pungent.

Hannah felt for the pocket she had sewn into her grey serge dress. Thomas's handkerchief was still there, a wretched little shred of cloth, like the tattered fragment of hope that she clung to. She ignored the men shuffling past, their skin cracked and orange from the sun. She stared steadfastly down at her feet, trying to look as invisible as she could. Tabby spat, a stream of black sputum.

Something white fluttered to the ground in front of her. She looked up, shocked, into the blue eyes of James. He looked embarrassed to be there, amongst such lowly men and vulgar women. But he smiled at Hannah and glanced down at his handkerchief, which had settled into the dust at Hannah's feet.

'A broken ship is come to land,' muttered Tabby.

'Go home, James,' said Hannah.

'Hannah,' he said. 'I need to talk to you. I got my inheritance. There was a clause that said I could have it if I got married. So I'm marrying you.'

Hannah shook her head in disbelief.

'I've bought some land near here – a hundred acres – and ten convicts to work as servants. There's a big house. You'll love it. There's white china and chintz armchairs and velvet curtains. That's why I took so long to come for you. I wanted to make sure everything was perfect.'

She ignored him. He reached out and grabbed her wrist. 'I know you love me, deep down.'

Hannah tried to pull away, but his grip tightened. 'Things

could be much worse for you than they are now,' he said, his voice taking on a dark tone. 'I know what you did.'

Hannah closed her eyes and pictured Thomas looking up at the ceiling-rose in her sitting room, laughing as she told him stories about the plaster bears that were hiding behind the white plaster leaves and flowers.

'I saw you, on the night of the storm. With Ullathorne. I saw you push him.' James's voice was hushed so no one else would hear.

Hannah opened her eyes, and laughed a mirthless laugh. 'Go on,' she said. 'Tell the superintendent what I did. Tell Captain Gartside. You can tell Governor Macquarie for all I care. I will only leave here with one man.'

'He's dead,' said James.

'Stop it. I won't go with you.'

'Your precious Behr. He's dead.'

Hannah shook her head.

'He went crazy,' said James. 'He disobeyed orders and then murdered a superior officer in a drunken rage. He was hanged.'

'I don't believe you,' said Hannah.

James shrugged, and pressed something into her hand, something cold and hard. Then he bent down to pick up his handkerchief.

'I'll be back next week,' he said, and walked away.

'Rotten toad,' said Tabby. 'He that shames shall be shemt.'

Hannah looked down at what he had placed in her hand. It was a pair of round, silver rimmed spectacles. One of the lenses was missing, and the other was smudged and cracked. The arms were bent out of shape. Thomas's spectacles.

For a moment, Hannah felt Superintendent Green's cane strike her a thousand times.

For a moment, she shattered into a million pieces and was blown away by the wind.

But just for a moment. Then there was nothing.

That night, Tabby burrowed down into her greasy wool bed and never got up again. Hannah found her the next morning, her black-bird-eyes clouded and sightless. Her right hand was curled into a claw. Her left clutched a black feather. Hannah felt the last sliver of warmth leave her body. Everyone had left her. Her mother, her father, Long Meg, Molly, Thomas Behr. Even crazy old Tabby.

The next Sunday, when James dropped his handkerchief at her feet, Hannah bent down and picked it up.

twenty-
seven

Scatterheart left the beach, and travelled on alone.

James took her home that very day, in a buggy that he drove himself.

Hannah had no possessions to collect – Thomas's handkerchief was tucked into her dress. She pulled it out and wrapped the broken spectacles in it.

James spoke briefly to the superintendent, signed a form and then escorted Hannah to the buggy.

She felt like a cow or a sheep bought at market. She thought that James would be much happier with this arrangement than actually marrying her. This way it was more of a business transaction.

James's house lay about six miles from Parramatta. He told

her that he had bought it from a rich couple who had come to
New South Wales to develop a new breed of sheep, but had
then returned to England.

It was a squat, imposing square, made from rough yellow
stone. Hannah could see the vertical marks in the stone where
the convicts had hewn it into blocks, and she imagined that
the occasional dark discoloured patch of stone was stained
with their blood. The big house looked lonely and strange,
surrounded by flat earth, sprouting prickly yellow-and-brown
grass, and the occasional bedraggled eucalypt.

'We'll have a garden soon,' said James. 'I've put in an order
for a convict with landscaping experience.'

Due to his new-found fortune, and his officer status, James
could pick the very best of the convicts to form his staff.
There was a cook, a porter and a butler. Hannah had a lady's
maid, and James a manservant. The remaining five convicts
worked on the land, preparing it for crops and cattle. James
had ordered cattle from England – 'None of these pathetic
local breeds', he said – and with them would come another
fifteen convicts to work on his estate.

Inside, the house was well-furnished and comfortable.
As James had promised, there was a full white china dining-
service, with silver cutlery. Maroon velvet curtains hung from
the tall windows. The floorboards were newly polished. The
sitting room contained three green chintz armchairs and a
matching chaise longue. The walls were painted a crisp white,
as wallpaper was hard to come by in the colony. No pictures

hung on the walls, although James had said on the way home that he was thinking of getting a portrait commissioned.

Hannah hated the house immediately. Harsh white light flooded each room, exposing every crack, every smudge, every speck of dust. The velvet curtains looked gaudy and cheap, the furniture oversized and unreal, like Hannah was living in a doll's house.

James led Hannah up to her room – hung with pink and white lace, with a soft, comfortable-looking bed. A hip-bath stood in a corner, steam rising from the water. Hannah forgot that she hated the house for a moment, and let out a soft cry. How long had it been since she had had a hot bath?

James smiled. 'I'll leave you to bathe,' he said, and left the room, closing the door behind him.

Hannah hesitated only for a moment. She peeled off her grey-serge dress and tossed it in a corner. Then she stepped into the bath and sighed with pleasure.

There was an assortment of oils and soaps on a small table next to the bath, along with a soft-bristled scrubbing brush. Hannah used them all, scrubbing and splashing until the bath water had turned brown from months of accumulated filth.

When the water finally grew cold, she climbed out and dried herself. Her skin felt as soft as rose-petals.

She padded over to the large mahogany wardrobe and opened the doors. Inside was a large collection of dresses, bonnets, coats and shoes, all exquisitely tailored.

She put on a pale pink muslin dress with delicate white trim, and pulled on some white kid-leather shoes. It felt strange to be wearing shoes again.

On a dressing-table were cosmetics and perfumes – all imported from London or Paris. Hannah picked up one of the little bottles with a happy sigh, and removed the cork. The smell of lavender reminded her so strongly of her father that for a brief moment she thought she was in her bedroom back in London.

She looked up and saw her reflection in the mirror of the dressing-table. For a moment she didn't recognise the brown, freckled face that looked back at her. Her hair was still spiky and uneven – too short for even the most daring of London fashions. She had a small scar above her right eyebrow, from when James had hit her. The pink dress she wore, with its lace collar and pearl buttons, looked wrong against her dishevelled hair and tanned skin. *Mutton dressed as lamb*, Long Meg would have said.

She put the bottle back down, her hand trembling. She didn't want this. She didn't want lace and expensive scents. What did any of it matter anyway, if Thomas was dead?

That night she sat opposite James, eating a pie which the cook assured her was lamb, but Hannah suspected was really kangaroo. She could barely swallow. The food tasted like ashes, and stuck in her throat like the toast James had brought her on the *Derby Ram*.

'Did you enjoy your bath?' asked James.

'Yes,' said Hannah. 'Thank you,' she added, after a pause.

The only noise for a while was the scraping of cutlery on china.

'You'll be happy here,' said James. It wasn't a question, so Hannah didn't bother to reply.

'Your new life will take some getting used to,' said James. 'And I am quite happy for you to sleep in your own room, for now.'

For now. The words hung heavy in the air.

Hannah looked at the white china plates and silver forks and spoons, the crisp white tablecloth and the elegant mahogany chairs. She hated them. She hated the silver toast-rack, the delicate pink china cups and saucers, the dresses that James bought her, and the tiny satin slippers that were already coated in a thick layer of yellow dust. Everything reminded her of her old life in London, and she knew that the one thing she truly wanted from that old life, she couldn't have.

'You must be exhausted,' said James.

'Yes,' said Hannah.

'You've been through a lot.'

'Yes.'

James nodded. 'You may go to bed early tonight,' he said. 'I shan't ask you to stay up with me.'

Hannah rose and left the table, feeling like a little girl again.

James had taken up an administrative position in Parramatta, overseeing the distribution of convict labour to the free settlers. Hannah was left on her own for most of the day. Occasionally, James's work would take him to Sydney for a few days, and then Hannah would see no one other than the shy girl who dressed her and brought her cups of tea in the morning, and the butler when he came to serve the evening meal.

Every Thursday, James would stay out until the small hours of the morning. Hannah would wake to the first pale light appearing, and hear James swearing and stumbling up the hallway, his voice thick with drink.

The first few times, she shrank into her bedclothes, terrified that he would burst into her room and demand that she offer herself to him. But he never did, and Hannah remembered the women at the factory dancing the mermaid dance, blue numbers daubed on their backs, paint dripping down over their buttocks and thighs.

She imagined James standing in the ring of clapping, jeering men. He wouldn't come into her room. He was already getting his fill.

Hannah spent her days wandering around the house and surrounds, and staring out the window over the flat farmland towards the looming blue-grey mountains to the west and thinking about Thomas.

She remembered when she had first met him. She had been only eleven years old. He seemed so much bigger, so old and grown up, although Hannah now realised he couldn't have been more than sixteen.

Hannah's father had let her nurse go. 'Rag-mannered blue-stocking', he called her, scowling heavily under perfectly shaped eyebrows. 'And you're getting too old for a nurse anyway,' he had added. 'I'll hire you a tutor. Someone who's been to Oxford.'

Hannah had loved her nurse, and cried and pleaded with her father to reinstate her, but he was adamant.

'Only the best for my little princess,' he said.

Hannah had resolved to hate her new tutor.

He had arrived at their front door, hat in hand, a parcel of books tucked under one arm, just as he always did for the next three years. He was a large man, and he hunched over self-consciously when he went to shake Arthur Cheshire's hand. Hannah took one look at him – his unkempt pale hair like straw, his silver-rimmed spectacles – and burst into tears, fleeing up to her bedroom where she refused to come out.

He had followed her and tapped on the door.

'Go away!' Hannah had said. 'I want my nurse!'

Hannah heard a sliding noise and a soft thump, as Mr Behr had sat down in the corridor outside her bedroom door.

'Do you like stories?' he asked.

Hannah had paused mid-sob. 'What kind of stories?'

'Oh, all sorts,' Mr Behr had said. 'Princesses and trolls and witches and castles.'

He had paused.

'Go on,' said Hannah, sniffing.

She heard Mr Behr chuckle.

'Well,' he had said. 'My favourite is a story about a girl called Scatterheart, who was very beautiful, but selfish and vain. Her heart was as fickle as the changing winds...'

Hannah stared out the thick glass window. She tried once more to remember how Scatterheart's story ended, but her mind was still a blank. Perhaps there would never be a happy ending.

The convict butler discreetly entered the room and placed another log on the fire. Hannah turned to look at him. He looked about forty, with thinning hair and a slight limp.

'What's your name?' she asked.

The butler looked at his shoes. 'Pete, madam,' he said. 'Pete Levine.'

'Nice to meet you, Pete,' said Hannah. 'I'm Hannah.'

'Yes, madam,' said Pete.

'What did you do?' asked Hannah. 'To get here?'

Pete looked uncomfortable. 'Please be excusin' me, madam, but Lieutenant Belforte told us we weren't to talk to you.'

Hannah blushed. 'Oh.'

Pete let himself out of the room without a word. Hannah stared out the window. The only colour between the grey skies and the brown earth was the stripe of blue-grey that was the westerly mountains.

Hannah wondered what was on the other side, and dimly remembered James saying something about an expedition to cross them, and a new road.

She closed her eyes. After Mr Behr had finished telling her Scatterheart's story that first time, she had opened her door and come out into the corridor. Her eyes had been red from crying, and she was still sniffling. But her mind whirled with the story of Scatterheart and the white bear. She had shyly taken Mr Behr's hand, and he had led her downstairs to the sitting room, where they had talked about history and geography and stories.

His hand had been so large, it had engulfed hers entirely. It was a soft hand, soft as velvet. His eyes had sparkled as he talked about stars and discoveries and adventures. His enthusiasm was infectious, and Hannah clasped her hands together and leaned forward in her chair with her mouth open, eager to hear about far-off lands and enchanted castles. When the grandfather clock in the hallway had chimed twelve, he stood up to leave. Hannah couldn't wait for their next lesson. She had already completely forgotten her nurse.

Hannah heard the scraping of feet, and turned to look out another window. A native was shuffling down the road that led to Parramatta, dragging his feet in the dirt. Hannah held her breath. She had heard stories about the natives from the women in the factory. They were cannibals, violent and unpredictable. Lured the children away from the town with their singing and dancing, and then...

Hannah shuddered. The native's head snapped up and looked in her direction, showing the bright whites of his eyes. Hannah shrank back into her chair.

'Savages,' James had called them. 'Stay away from them, they're animals.'

His words had made Hannah think of Long Meg and Molly. She wondered where Molly was, and hoped that she had found a good home where she would be loved and looked after. On their way back from the Female Factory, Hannah had asked James if Molly could come and live with them.

'The freak?' James had said, his face twisting. 'I don't think so.'

The native shuffled off, and Hannah relaxed. A wave of weariness swept over her, and she climbed the stairs to her room and crawled into her bed. It was still morning, but already the day had dragged on too long.

She felt under her pillow – a feather-pillow that James had gone into Sydney Town to buy for her – and drew out a little bundle of ragged cloth.

Unwrapping Thomas's handkerchief, she looked down at the broken and twisted frames of his spectacles. She waited for the grief to come, the tears, the sobbing. But nothing happened. With a sigh, she curled up on her bed.

She slept fitfully, dreaming that she awoke to James returning home.

'I have brought you a bridal gift,' he said, dumping a bulky paper package on the dining table.

Hannah opened the package to reveal a thick, white bearskin rug. The bear's head, stuffed and lifeless, stared at her with mournful glass eyes.

Hannah awoke with a start and looked around the room. How long had she been asleep? A minute? An hour?

The front door banged. 'Hannah!' James was home.

He called her name again, and Hannah sighed and slid off the bed.

He was standing at the bottom of the stairs, waiting for her. Her heart caught a little to see him, still so handsome. She wished she could go back to the happy, ignorant days on the *Derby Ram* where she had believed him to be a true gentleman, her handsome prince. If she could still believe that, how happy she would be now.

'I have to make a short trip into Sydney,' he said. 'I thought perhaps you would like to accompany me.'

He paused, clearly waiting for the gratitude that he felt this statement deserved. Hannah just nodded, and returned to her room.

They took a small private boat down the river to Sydney the next morning.

It felt good to be on the water again, the familiar rocking of a boat, the gentle lapping of small waves against the hull. Hannah said so to James, who raised his eyebrows.

'I thought you would be keen to forget that particular experience,' he said.

Hannah thought about it. She had certainly experienced some terrible things on board the *Derby Ram*. But she also remembered the sun shining on her face, and the wind whispering through her hair. She remembered joking with Long Meg. She remembered how sweet the water had tasted when they stopped in Cape Town.

'What about you?' she said. 'Don't you want to go back to London? Play piquet and drink brandy at White's?'

James shrugged. 'I like it here,' he added. 'I like the idea of taming the wilderness. Making it civilised.'

Hannah looked down the river, at the twisted low grey and green trees and thick snarls of undergrowth. She didn't think it could ever be tamed.

As the countryside slipped slowly by, Hannah found herself relaxing. The rhythm of the water was soothing, and the sun made her sleepy. She was on the point of drifting off when she heard a rustling of leaves on the bank. Hannah started as a native appeared on the riverbank.

It was a woman – as brown as mahogany. She wore a sort of string belt which had a number of animal skins hanging from it, covering her private areas. Her breasts hung low and bare, reaching almost to her belly.

Hannah stared. She thought of Long Meg, grey and cold and naked on Dr Ullathorne's operating table. This woman looked so *alive*. She moved like she was made from water, graceful and flowing. The sun gleamed on her dark skin. Her hair was a mass of wild black fuzz.

She looked at James, Hannah and the convict boatman, and a vague look of contempt passed over her face. There was another rustle, and a small child stepped out of the bushes behind her. He was completely naked. The woman said something to him, and the child burst out laughing, flashing his white teeth. Hannah thought of Molly, laughing at Long Meg, or a Mr Bear story.

James turned at the noise, and saw the natives. He reached out a hand and covered Hannah's eyes.

'Don't look at them,' he said.

Hannah pushed James's hand away and looked back at the natives as the boat continued on down the river. She thought that the woman had found *them* disgusting, too.

'Hannah!' James said sharply. 'You should not look at such a vulgar display of...' he paused, searching for a word that could appropriately convey his revulsion, 'savageness.'

James shook his head. 'Damn murkies,' he said. 'Can't even put them to work,' he said. 'They're worse than convicts.'

Late that afternoon, the boat anchored on the outskirts of Sydney Town. A few ramshackle wooden huts stood near the tiny wharf, and Hannah could smell animal manure. A dirty goat was tethered to a post, bleating plaintively. A carriage was waiting to convey Hannah and James to their hotel. A few scrawny children danced around the carriage horse – horses were rare in the colony, and only the rich could afford them for anything other than ploughing and farm-work.

James offered Hannah his hand to help her into the carriage, but she ignored it and climbed up on her own. James followed her, and rapped sharply on the roof. The groom uttered a sharp command to the horse and the carriage rumbled off.

Hannah peered out the window of the carriage, looking around the growing town with interest. She had barely glimpsed it on arrival. The streets were wide – mostly unpaved, but some paved in yellow sandstone, and some in what looked like blocks of wood. The buildings were simple yet elegant, either made of the yellow stone that seemed to be everywhere, or whitewashed timber. Cottages stood in neat rows, with shady verandahs and immaculate kitchen gardens, trimmed with geranium hedges.

They passed an elegant three-storey house made of sandstone. A delicate verandah sloped over the street. An immaculately dressed man sat underneath it on a cane chair, sipping at a tall glass. He was very handsome, and winked at Hannah as she stared from the window of the carriage.

'Filth.' James scowled.

Hannah was surprised. 'Isn't he a gentleman?'

'A gentleman! That's Simeon Lord. He is an ex-convict. Made a fortune through *trade*.'

James said the word as if it were an oath.

'Oh,' said Hannah, looking back at the grand house as the carriage rumbled past. It looked much more stylish than James's ugly squat house.

'You must learn, Hannah,' said James, 'that money is no indication of Quality. It doesn't matter how fancy your house is. Once convict scum, always convict scum.'

Hannah said nothing, but thought of James's father, rich from selling buttons.

James pointed from the window of the carriage. 'See there? Those ladies sitting on that verandah? They may wear fine dresses and have silk slippers, but look at their hands and faces. As filthy as pigs.'

He pointed again. 'And that young dandy crossing the road ahead of us. He must have a dozen rings on his fingers. His shirt-pins are bejewelled, and his pocket-watch is solid gold. Yet he wears no stockings or socks on his feet. For heaven's sake, you can see his ankles.'

The disgust in his voice was plain, and Hannah miserably thought of her father's well-tailored coats and gleaming hessians. Then she thought of Thomas's ill-fitting hand-me-downs and battered spectacles and sighed.

The carriage rumbled on, through a busy market that stank of fish and rotting fruit. Caged many-coloured birds screeched and flapped.

There were men in cages too, skin pulled tautly over their hungry bones. One man had no skin at all on his chest or back, just angry-looking flesh, shiny like the burn on Molly's face. His collar bones rose from the twisted flesh, white and shining like the top of Hannah's father's walking stick. Hannah looked away, feeling ill.

'What happened to that man?' she asked.

'Two hundred lashes is called a "feeler",' he said. 'When they've had too many, the skin doesn't grow back.'

Hannah looked back at the man. A thick, savage scar slashed diagonally across his face from his left temple, down over his left eye, his nose, and dividing his lips before disappearing under his jawbone.

'Disgusting,' said James.

Market stalls were piled high with brightly-coloured fruits that Hannah didn't recognise. They shone and glowed red, green and yellow. Hannah thought of the mangos she had eaten in Cape Town, and remembered the sharp metallic taste of blood when she had bitten James.

She realised absently that he was talking to her again.

'Hmm?' she said.

He frowned. 'I was asking whether there is anything you desire me to buy you while we are here.'

Hannah hesitated. She was loathe to ask, but she was getting desperate. 'Do you think,' she said, summoning up her courage. 'Do you think I could perhaps have a small number of books?'

The frown on James's face deepened. 'What do you want books for?'

'To read,' said Hannah. Wasn't that obvious?

James shook his head. 'I don't think it's appropriate for young ladies to be filling their heads with nonsense from novels and romances,' he said.

'You sound like my father,' she said.

'Your father was a sensible man,' said James.

The carriage rumbled to a halt outside a large yellow building. Two skinny little boys wearing short pants and no shoes came running up to take their bags inside.

James climbed down from the carriage and Hannah followed, once again ignoring his offered arm.

They entered the hotel. The lobby was cool and quiet. The floor was marble, and the brass railings on the staircase gleamed. James looked around and sniffed.

'Very cramped,' he said. 'But it's the only respectable hotel in town.'

Hannah thought it looked nice. The two little boys deposited the last of their bags, and stood grinning at Hannah and James. One took off his hat and held it in his grubby hands.

'Thank you, boys,' said Hannah, smiling at them both.

'Pleasure, miss,' said the boy holding his hat. He had a cheerful round face that was smudged with dirt. She wondered if Molly was wandering the streets of Sydney, carrying bags for rich people.

She turned to James. 'Do you have a penny or two for these boys?'

'No,' he said, and turned to climb the stairs. 'I don't give money to convicts.'

Hannah blushed and smiled apologetically at the boys. The round-faced boy scowled at her. The other one just shrugged,

and they turned and left the hotel. Hannah began to follow
James up the stairs, but stopped halfway.

'Aren't *I* one of those filthy convicts?' she said.

James turned and looked at her sharply.

'No,' he said, firm. 'You are not. You are a young lady of
Quality. Your father was a well-respected London gentleman.
You will tell *no one* how you came to be here.'

They had a small set of rooms on the third floor of the hotel,
looking out over Sydney harbour.

'A maid will be up shortly to help you dress,' he said. 'I'll
be back later to escort you to dinner.'

Hannah didn't wonder where he was going. She didn't
really care.

The suite comprised of a dressing room, sitting room and
bedroom. Hannah eyed the large bed with its embroidered
damask quilt with suspicion. She was not sharing a bed with
James, not for anything. Not even for books.

She looked around the rooms, opening the empty drawers
and cupboards. A porter came in and delivered their bags.

Hannah sat down in a brown velvet armchair, then stood
up again. What was she supposed to *do*? It was worse than
James's house. At least there Hannah could walk about the
property.

She got up and went to the window. A large ship was
anchored near the wharf. Hannah wondered if it was another
convict transport. Two young women were strolling down the

street below her, chatting animatedly, arms linked. Even from three storeys up, Hannah could tell that they were not ladies of Quality – their bonnets were obviously home-made, their voices broad and uncultured. They were probably native-born children of ex-convicts. *Currency lasses*, James called them, his words usually accompanied by a sneer. *Vulgarity descends*, James said. *It's in their blood.* Hannah didn't think these girls looked particularly like criminals.

One of them said something in a hushed voice, and the other burst out laughing. Hannah felt a sharp stab of jealousy. She had never really had any friends of her own age in London. Only Thomas Behr. Then Long Meg and Molly on the *Derby Ram*. She wondered where Molly was now.

There was a soft tap on the door, and a young woman wearing a maid's cap entered. She bobbed a curtsey.

'Evening, madam,' she said. Her voice had the same strange broadness as the girls on the street. 'Lieutenant Belforte sent me up to help you change.'

Hannah nodded, and the girl bent over the cases, opening them and unpacking them into drawers and shelves. She pulled out Hannah's pink muslin dress.

'This is a fine gown,' she said. 'Shall you wear it to dinner tonight?'

Hannah shrugged. 'I suppose so,' she said.

The girl smoothed the dress, and hung it up to air. Hannah looked at the girl with interest. Her skin was honey-coloured from the sun, her hair a flaxy yellow. Freckles dusted her nose

and cheeks, and her eyes sparkled blue. She looked strong
and healthy. Hannah knew that she was supposed to find
sun-browned skin vulgar – dark like a savage – but on this
girl it looked beautiful. The maid saw Hannah looking, and
Hannah blushed.

'I'm sorry,' she said. 'It's just … Have you always lived in
Sydney?'

The girl nodded. 'My papa is a merchant. He imports
fabric from London and Paris for the exclusives.'

Hannah frowned. 'Exclusives?'

The girl looked embarrassed. 'Yes, madam. Exclusives.
Sterlings. Like yourself. Free-settlers.'

'I see,' said Hannah. 'So your father was a convict?'

The girl nodded. 'And my mama. Third fleet.'

'Then you're a currency lass,' said Hannah.

'We prefer "natives",' said the girl, a note of pride creeping
into her voice.

'But I thought natives were – the savages.'

'Oh no, madam!' said the girl, looking scandalized. 'We
are native-born. Our parents are emancipists. The free-settlers
are the exclusives. The savages are blackies, or murkies, or
boongs.'

Hannah was confused. The girl ushered Hannah into the
dressing room, and expertly began to remove her travelling-
dress. Hannah felt vaguely embarrassed – this girl was so pretty
and confident – and Hannah was just a convict. Shouldn't *she*
be waiting on the girl?

'Is this your first time to Sydney Town, madam?' asked the girl, selecting a clean corselette from the trunk.

'Yes,' said Hannah. 'Except for when – when I arrived.'

'It's a beautiful city, isn't it?'

Hannah thought of the stench of the market, the men in cages, the scrawny, filthy children.

The girl laced Hannah's corselet like an expert, and held out a petticoat for Hannah to step into.

'I think it must be the most beautiful city in the world,' she said, oblivious to Hannah's demurring.

Hannah thought it was hardly a city. She could probably walk from one side to the other in an hour. 'But you've never been anywhere else,' she said.

'I don't need to, madam.'

'Really? You don't want to go to London one day?'

The girl made a face. 'London, madam? Not a chance. Papa says it is always dark and dirty, and that the sun never shines.'

She gestured out a window at the ocean. The sun was sinking behind Sydney Town, turning the yellow houses gold and pink. The ocean sparkled blue and white, deepening into a rich indigo as it stretched out to the darkening horizon. Grey-green hills sloped down to the water, tangled and wild. Hannah blinked. It *was* beautiful. She remembered the wonder she had felt as the *Derby Ram* had sailed into the harbour. Perhaps it was the most beautiful city in the world.

'But what do you *do* here?' said Hannah, thinking of her

constant boredom. 'In London, there are always parties and picnics and balls–'

She stopped herself. What was she talking about? She had never been to a ball or a party. She had been just as bored in London, except when she had had her lessons with Thomas.

The girl laughed. 'We have all those things too,' she said. 'And we also go horse-riding and hunting and fishing. But we spend most of our time at the beach.'

'The beach?' Hannah had never been to Brighton, but had heard that the sea air was excessively good for the lungs.

The girl sighed, her eyes dreamy. 'I do love the beach,' she said. 'The water is often very cold, but once you get in it's beautiful.'

'You *swim*? In *public*?'

The girl managed to look embarrassed and defiant at the same time. 'Of course you *exclusives* don't do it, madam.'

Hannah blushed.

'But madam, it is the best feeling in the world! The water is so cold and fresh, and it swirls around you like champagne. It's like you're as light as a feather. It's like flying.'

Hannah smiled. It *did* sound nice.

'And then afterwards the sand is so warm from the sun. It's like heaven.'

Hannah raised her arms as the girl lowered the pink muslin dress over her head. She did up the buttons with deft fingers, and then bade Hannah sit at the dressing-table while she did something about Hannah's hair.

Hannah looked in the mirror and saw her messy crop of short hair.

'It's very fashionable in London at the moment,' she said, blushing.

The door to the suite opened and James stood in the doorway.

'Are you ready?' he said, without a glance at the maid. 'We are dining with the Gormans.'

'Who?' said Hannah. The maid bobbed a curtsey as she left the room. James made no attempt to move from the open door, so she had to squeeze past him. He stared openly at her cleavage.

'The Gormans. A very well-respected family from Castle Hill.'

Hannah rose reluctantly from her dressing-table. James came and took her arm. He smelled of whiskey and cigars.

As they passed through the hotel lounge, they met a stout, ginger-haired man of middle age.

'Good evening, lieutenant,' said the man.

'Dr Redfern,' said James. 'This is Hannah, whom I told you about before.'

The man bowed. 'Lovely to meet you,' he said.

'Dr Redfern is Assistant Surgeon to the colony,' James told Hannah. 'He delivered Governor Macquarie's first son earlier this year.'

Hannah bobbed a rather stiff curtsey, remembering her

last encounter with a doctor. There was an uncomfortable pause, and Dr Redfern raised his eyebrows at James.

'Ah,' said James, patting his coat pockets rather theatrically. 'I've left my snuffbox upstairs.'

The doctor smiled. 'I'll look after her until you get back.'

James nodded and left.

'The lieutenant tells me you have been ill,' said Dr Redfern.

'No,' said Hannah. 'I'm not sick.'

He nodded. 'This is a harsh country,' he said. 'It is difficult for delicate women to thrive here.'

Hannah tried to smile. She thought of the hotel maid that had dressed her. *She* certainly seemed as if she were thriving.

'You know, Lieutenant Belforte wants nothing more than your happiness,' said Dr Redfern. 'And of course, he is very eager for you to bear him a son.'

Hannah felt suddenly dizzy. 'Oh,' she said. 'So that's what all this is about.'

'How old are you?' asked the doctor.

'Fifteen,' said Hannah.

'A little young yet, for childbirth,' he said. 'But it will come sooner than you expect.'

'Not if I have anything to do with it,' said Hannah darkly.

Dr Redfern considered her, his head tilted on one side. 'You're not happy here,' he observed.

Hannah shrugged. 'No. But I'm not sure if I could be happy anywhere.'

'You don't love Lieutenant Belforte.' It wasn't a question.

'No,' said Hannah. 'I never will.'

'Then why are you here with him?'

Hannah smiled bitterly. 'I'm not sure I have a choice.'

'You could have waited out your sentence,' said the doctor. 'Gone back to London.'

'There's nothing for me there,' said Hannah. 'I have no family left. No friends. Nothing.'

Dr Redfern bit his lip. 'Have you told Lieutenant Belforte how you feel?'

'There's no point. And anyway, he doesn't want to hear about the problems of a convict.'

'I see,' said Dr Redfern. His forehead was creased with concerned lines.

'I'm sorry to waste your time,' said Hannah. 'But I think I'm a lost cause.'

The doctor hesitated, then reached into a pocket. 'Here is my card,' he said, handing over a white rectangle of paper. 'If you ever need anything,' he said. 'Anything at all. Even just to talk.'

Hannah took it dubiously.

Dr Redfern seemed to hesitate for a moment. 'You *do* know that I'm a convict too, don't you?'

Hannah looked up. 'You?'

'Yes,' said the doctor. 'At least I was.'

Hannah stared at him. He seemed so gentlemanly. And he was so well-respected in the colony.

James came back into the room. Hannah wondered if he knew that Dr Redfern was a convict.

The dining room was furnished with dark mahogany tables and chairs, with oil-lamps burning on the walls and candles on the tables. The Gormans were already seated. Mr Gorman was a thin, grey-haired man with a monocle. He wore an old-fashioned but well-tailored jacket and breeches. Mrs Gorman was a brash woman dressed in a loud orange taffeta gown, with a large matching turban. Hannah disliked them both immediately.

James bowed as they approached the table. 'Mr and Mrs Gorman, I'd like to present my wife, Hannah.'

Hannah froze, and stared at James. His *wife*?

'Behave yourself,' muttered James, as he pushed her forward to shake hands with Mrs Gorman.

'Mrs Belforte, how do you do?' said Mrs Gorman. Her hand was clammy, putting Hannah in mind of Mr Harris in London. She smiled woodenly, her jaws aching, and sat down.

The dinner was interminable. Mrs Gorman drank heavily, speaking only of the latest London fashions, and of the poor quality of servants in the colony. Once or twice, Hannah tried to turn their conversation towards literature, or art, but Mrs Gorman would not be drawn in.

Hannah could not say or do anything right. Over the first course of dried cod, Hannah mentioned her surprise at the lack of fresh fish available in the colony.

'We are almost surrounded by water,' she said. 'Yet I have had nothing but dried herring and smoked salmon since I got here!'

Mr and Mrs Gorman exchanged glances. Hannah looked at James, who had pursed his lips in disapproval.

'Did I say something wrong?' said Hannah.

James tried to smile, but the smile was so forced that it turned into a sneer. 'Dearest,' he said. 'Only the *convicts* eat native fish. We don't want to be like them, do we?'

Mr Gorman cleared his throat. 'Nothing like a good English fish, is what I say. Nothing like it in the world.'

'Indeed,' agreed Mrs Gorman.

Hannah glared at her, thinking she looked like a fat, pink pig in an orange dress. There was an uncomfortable pause.

'Have you heard any progress on the new road through the mountains?' Mr Gorman asked James.

James shrugged. 'It is continuing on schedule,' he said. 'Governor Macquarie expects that it will be complete by the middle of next year.'

'I should be terrified to travel through those mountains,' declared Mrs Gorman. 'Full of murkies and wild animals.'

'Nonsense, Mary,' said Mr Gorman. 'The road will be quite safe.'

Mrs Gorman shook her head as she motioned for the waiter to refill her glass. 'Not at all, my dear,' she said. 'Haven't you heard about the wild man?'

Mr Gorman snorted.

'I'm sure it's of no great matter,' said James, with a strange glance at Hannah.

'It's true!' protested Mrs Gorman. 'Why, they say that officer is hiding in the mountains, living like a murky. You know, the one who murdered–'

'Mrs Gorman, how do you find the roast lamb?' interrupted James, his expression cold and furious.

Hannah stared at him. Had Mrs Gorman been talking about Thomas? Her heart was pounding. Mrs Gorman hadn't noticed James's abrupt tone, and was bemoaning the lack of any *real* mustard.

'I believe you,' said Hannah suddenly. Everyone turned to look at her. James's face was black with anger.

'I believe you, Mrs Gorman,' Hannah repeated. 'About the wild man in the mountains. Tell me more about him.'

'This is hardly appropriate, Hannah,' said James.

'Oh, don't be so stuffy, lieutenant,' said Mrs Gorman. She turned to Hannah.

'They say he fell in love with a convict woman and murdered a superior officer who caught them … *you* know.'

'That's enough,' said James.

'I think it's *terribly* romantic,' Mrs Gorman sighed.

'I said enough,' James repeated. 'Mrs Gorman, a respectable woman like yourself should know better than to listen to vulgar gossip.'

Mrs Gorman looked startled, and shut her mouth with

a snap. Mr Gorman busied himself with a tureen of green beans. James turned to Hannah.

'That officer was hanged for his offences,' he said. 'Only convicts are saying otherwise, and who would believe them?'

Hannah swallowed. Was he lying to her again? Could Thomas be alive?

'Perhaps I *should* believe it, then,' she said slowly. 'After all, James, I *am* a convict.'

She turned to Mr and Mrs Gorman. Mrs Gorman's mouth had dropped open again in surprise.

'Didn't my *husband* mention that?' said Hannah, feigning surprise. 'Dear me.'

James said nothing, but Hannah could see his skin had turned mottled-red, and veins stood out in his neck.

A waiter appeared to remove the second course. Bowls of fruit and sweetmeats were placed in front of them. Nobody spoke. Hannah stood up, tossing her napkin onto the table.

'I'm afraid I have a headache,' she said. 'I beg you to excuse me.'

James didn't return to their suite until very late. Hannah was sitting by the window, looking out at the few burning yellow lights of Sydney Town and the surrounding black abyss. Stars twinkled overhead, but there was still no Great Bear. He closed the door behind him and stood staring at Hannah.

'You will learn to respect me,' he said. His voice was slurred, and he swayed on his feet.

'I don't see why I should,' she said. 'After all, I'm a filthy, vulgar convict. And it's not like we're married.'

'We are,' he said. 'You are my wife.'

Hannah felt bitterness flood through her. 'Am I?' she said. 'I'm sorry, I don't remember our wedding day. Was my gown beautiful? Who performed the ceremony? Did my father walk me down the aisle?'

'Things work differently here,' he said.

'Not that differently,' she replied. 'I would *never* consent to be your wife.'

James laughed. 'What did you think you were doing when you picked up my handkerchief at the factory?'

She stared at him, thunderstruck.

He sighed. 'I'm tired of fighting with you, Hannah. I just want you to be happy.'

Hannah frowned. 'No, you don't. You want me to fit your idea of a perfect wife. You don't care how I feel. I'm just an acquisition to you, like a new horse or a set of cufflinks. Your ticket to *Quality*.'

James pulled off his necktie with a savage yank.

'I've been very patient with you, Hannah,' said James, his lips a thin line. 'But I won't wait much longer. You humiliated me tonight. Mr and Mrs Gorman are good people.'

Hannah screwed up her face. 'They are everything that is hateful,' she said. 'They are shallow and heartless and selfish. You think convicts are vulgar? The Gormans are a *study* in vulgar.'

'They are people of Quality,' said James.

'If being a person of Quality means being like them,' said Hannah, 'then I am glad to be a convict.'

James stepped towards her and grabbed her wrist.

'You are *not* a convict,' he said, his lips white with anger. 'You didn't commit a crime. You are a young lady of Quality, so act like it.'

'I didn't steal anything,' said Hannah, 'But I let my father sack a servant because she made the cup rattle in its saucer. I was hurtful and cruel to the one man who has ever truly loved me. And I killed Dr Ullathorne.' She shrugged. 'I've committed crimes,' she said. 'And I am happy to pay my penance.'

'What penance?' said James, his voice rising. 'You have *everything*. You have pretty dresses and a big house with lots of servants. You have a handsome husband. You have money. What is your penance?'

'You,' said Hannah. 'Having to spend the rest of my life with you is my penance.'

He hit her, hard. Hannah went reeling back and crashed into the sideboard. She put a hand to her cheek, and winced in pain.

'Is this how you think men of Quality behave?' she asked softly.

James left early the next morning, after instructing Hannah that she was not to leave the hotel. Hannah dressed slowly, and made her way down to the lounge for breakfast.

Dr Redfern was there, sitting alone reading a newspaper and drinking tea with lemon.

'Mrs Belforte,' he said, smiling. His eyes flickered over the rising bruise on Hannah's cheek, but he made no comment. 'What can I do for you?'

Hannah swallowed, nervously. 'Doctor,' she said. 'Have you heard … do you know anything about a man named Thomas Behr?'

Dr Redfern looked startled. 'Ensign Behr?' he shook his head. 'Mrs Belforte, you'd best not worry yourself about him. It was a bad business. Very bad.'

'But you know of him!' Hannah felt tears begin to spill over her cheeks. 'Please, I must know what happened. Is he really dead?'

Dr Redfern sighed. 'This place can break the spirits of even the very best of men,' he said, standing up and folding his newspaper. 'You should forget about Behr.'

twenty-
eight

**As Scatterheart walked through the strange lands, she felt
her spirits lift. She would find the white bear.**

After the visit to Sydney, James spent even less time at the
house. He would barely exchange more than a sentence with
Hannah for days on end. That suited Hannah fine, although
her boredom didn't dissipate. She took to spending her
days in a half-conscious doze, lying draped across the chaise
longue, a handkerchief draped over her eyes to shield them
from the sun.

On one such morning, she was having a daydream about
swimming with Thomas. The sun would soak into her skin
like honey, filling her with warmth. The ocean would swirl
around them, wrapping them in a cocoon of sparkling blue.

Hannah was jerked from her dream by a rustling sound from outside. Someone was approaching the house. Hannah frowned, pulling the handkerchief from her face. James was in Sydney again, not due to return for at least another day. The convict farm-workers were all off erecting a new fence in the southern field, and besides, they never came to the house. The house-servants were all accounted for – Hannah had sent most of them away for the day, and her maid was upstairs lying down with a headache.

She thought of the savage she had seen before with his white eyes and teeth, and reached out to grab the poker.

The shuffling grew nearer. Hannah's heart beat loud in her chest. Whoever it was, was right outside the sitting room window.

When the knocking came, Hannah let out a little scream, and retreated to the other side of the room. She held her breath.

'Hannah?' said a voice.

Hannah let out the breath sharply. 'Molly?' she said.

'Hannah, let me in!'

Molly looked exhausted, and even thinner than she had done on the *Derby Ram*. She wore a new dress of brown flannel and sturdy leather boots, but her face and hands were dirty and smudged.

'Molly, what are you doing here?' asked Hannah, sinking into one of the armchairs as Molly investigated the remains of Hannah's breakfast.

Molly attacked a piece of cold toast. 'I 'scaped,' she said proudly with her mouth full. 'I didn't like being a orphing.'

'But didn't you get to go to a new home?'

Molly snorted, reaching for the jam. 'Orphings like me don't get a new home. We just gets made hungry and sad and cold. An listenin' to the old man read from the big book about hell and sin. Bah!' She sprayed breadcrumbs across the room. 'I isn't no orphing.'

'But you can't stay here,' said Hannah. 'James will send you back.'

Molly frowned at her. 'No he won't, because we won't be here.'

'What do you mean?'

Molly rolled her eye. 'We have to go and rescue Mr Bear, silly! Have you forgot? He's trapped in the castle!'

Hannah bit her lip. 'That's just a story.'

'Mr Bear isn't no story. He's real. He needs bein' rescued.' She reached over the table and grabbed Hannah's sleeve. 'Thomas needs bein' rescued.'

Hannah looked down at the table. 'Thomas is dead,' she said. It was easier to say than she had thought it would be. She thought about what Mrs Gorman had said in Sydney about the wild man. *They say he fell in love with a convict woman, and murdered a superior officer who caught them ... you know.* Even if he wasn't dead, he didn't love her any more.

'No he ain't.'

Hannah stood up. 'He is,' she said woodenly. 'He's dead.

He fell in love with a convict woman and murdered an officer. They hanged him.'

'No,' said Molly.

'Yes,' said Hannah. 'He was hanged. Not wrestling a tiger, or exploring a volcano, or escaping from Davy Jones's locker. He murdered someone.'

Molly groaned. 'You ain't listenin',' she said. 'He ain't dead.'

Hannah closed her eyes. 'I think you should go.'

'Listen!' Molly banged her hand down on the table. 'I met a boy who saw him. Something terrible happened, and Mr Bear runned away. He's hiding. If he comes back, then they'll kill him.'

'What about the woman? The one he fell in love with?'

'There ain't no woman, and he's not dead. But he needs rescuin'.' Molly stood up. 'Don't you want to know how the story ends?' she asked.

Hannah finally raised her head and looked at Molly. Her melted face was paler than usual, her eye hard with determination. Her little hands were clenched into fists. Hannah thought about Scatterheart, walking through strange lands on her own. Scatterheart didn't have someone fierce like Molly around to help her.

'Well?' said Molly. 'Are you coming?'

Hannah paused. 'Where is he?' she asked.

Molly smiled triumphantly and turned. 'There.' She pointed out the window, towards the blue-green mountains.

'The boy I met is working on the new road through the mountains. He saw Mr Bear head up there, four weeks ago.'

Hannah looked up at the mountains that lurked just above the horizon. They looked like a good place for a white bear to hide. The fuzziness that had clouded her mind for weeks suddenly lifted. He was alive. Something seemed to catch on fire inside her, filling her with heat and energy.

She grinned. 'The cook will be back in a few hours,' she said. 'We'd better go and stock up on food now.'

Molly crowed with delight.

twenty-
nine

Soon Scatterheart came to a great lake, too wide to walk around. She cracked open the copper acorn, and found a pair of copper slippers. She put on the slippers, and walked across the water of the lake without sinking.

They stayed off the main road, trudging through fields and scrambling over crude fences.

Hannah carried a canvas bag containing a woollen blanket, three small loaves of bread, a hunk of cheese, some currant-cake and six apples.

She had wished for a bit of cured ham or salt-pork, but the exclusives dined only on fresh meat – dried meat was convict-fare. Hannah had also filled an empty glass bottle with water for them to drink.

In her dress pocket, Thomas's glasses, wrapped in his handkerchief, snuggled next to a leather purse containing a handful of coins she had stolen from James's bureau. The colony didn't have its own currency, and the coins were a jumble of British pennies and shillings, four silver Dutch guilders, and some little copper coins that Hannah suspected were Portuguese.

They trudged west towards the mountains, climbing over the rough fences that separated properties.

There was no wilderness in this part of the country. Hannah was glad. The thick knots of bushes and twisted trees she had seen crowding the banks of the river seemed hostile and secretive.

This countryside was mostly farmland, cleared of trees and scrub. Some fields were planted with neat rows of crops, while others had just a scratchy yellow grass that sheep and cows picked at.

As the afternoon wore on, the gentle rise of Prospect Hill appeared before them. Hannah thought of the map. The mountains were still a long way away. They turned south to skirt around the hill, and as night fell, they crept up to a barn near Prospect Creek.

The farmhouse was further south. Hannah could just make out a light burning in a far-off window. The barn was full of hay, warm and dry, smelling like summer. They snuggled down into it.

The straw reminded Hannah of her mattress on the *Derby*

Ram, and she thought of the long days and nights spent talking with Long Meg. She sighed.

'Have you ever been in love?' Hannah had asked her one night as they lay on their bunks.

'Sure I has,' said Long Meg. 'I is in love almost every night.'

'No,' said Hannah. '*Really* in love. With one person. A person who's not a customer.'

Long Meg had looked away. 'Maybe,' she said. 'Maybe once.'

'Tell me.'

'His name was Jimmy. He was as bluff as bull beef. We was a team, I'd reel in the rich coves and he'd land 'em.' She sighed. 'But he was born under a threepenny halfpenny planet. So he was never worth a groat.'

'What happened?' asked Hannah. 'Did you want to marry him?'

'Shut your bone-box,' said Long Meg. 'I is telling this story.'

She picked at a piece of straw poking through her mattress. Hannah waited.

'One day I found him lying bread-and-butter fashion with another lass.'

'Oh,' said Hannah. 'I'm sorry.'

'When he noticed me, he looked so feared.' She snorted. 'He certainly made a coffee house of Miss Brown.'

'A coffee house?'

'He went in but spent nothing.'

Hannah made a face.

'He made some mighty pretty speeches then, but I don' dally with men with fingers in more'n one pie.'

She saw Hannah's expression. 'That's different,' she said. 'That's business.'

'What happened to Jimmy?' asked Hannah.

Long Meg shrugged. 'Got caught with his fingers in someone's pockets. A week later, he danced on nothin' and died of hempen fever.'

Hannah rolled over in the straw and looked at Molly. She was asleep, her breathing slow and steady. Hannah wriggled a little against the scratchy straw. She wondered what Thomas was doing now – where he was, what he was thinking. Was he thinking of her, too? Had there really been another woman? Hannah thought of the way Thomas had looked at her when he had asked her to marry him, and decided that it was impossible.

The smell of the straw was sweetly overpowering. Hannah closed her eyes, and wondered how the story would finish. What would she do, after she had found Thomas? Would they go back to Sydney? To London? The thought occurred to Hannah that if Thomas *had* killed someone, it would make things very difficult, but she pushed it from her mind. There was no room for niggling worries in Hannah's happily-ever-after.

When she awoke the next morning, Hannah found Molly sitting cross-legged in front of her, a steaming slice of apple and rhubarb pie in her hand.

'Where on earth did you get that from?' asked Hannah, looking around.

Molly snickered. 'King's pictures, miss!'

'You *stole* it?'

Molly nodded, her mouth full. She held out a chunk to Hannah, who accepted it gratefully. It was so fresh that the apple burned Hannah's tongue. The pastry was soft and crumbly. It was the best thing Hannah had ever eaten. The rhubarb was just tart enough, mixing perfectly with the sugary sweetness of the apple. Hannah thought about the long evenings at the dining table with James, and how the tasteless food had stuck in her throat. She licked crumbs off her fingers and smiled at Molly.

'Time to go,' she said.

They splashed over Prospect Creek, Hannah's boots filling with water. Spread out before them were brown fields. The clouds rumbled overhead. Everything looked grey and drab. A few scraggly sheep raised their heads as Hannah and Molly approached, but turned away, uninterested.

They walked on and on, speaking rarely. They stopped to rest for a while by the bank of another stream, and Hannah shared out some bread and cheese. Then they forded the stream and continued on. As the light faded it began to rain steadily. They marched on, trying to find somewhere to shelter. Darkness closed in around them, and Hannah thought they might have to sleep out in the rain. She was afraid they would get turned around in the dark, and end up walking back to Parramatta. Molly's teeth were chattering.

Through the curtain of rain, Hannah could make out a dim glow. She made for it, praying that it wouldn't be a constable come to send her back to James.

The house where the light was burning was little more than a shack, barely a few feet square. It had no windows, and was made from a very crude wattle-and-daub. A thin light shone from the cracks in the walls, and from underneath the door. A drizzle of smoke came from the chimney.

Hannah rapped on the door. There was no catch or handle, and the door swung inwards under her hands. She pushed it all the way open and peered in.

The shack was smoky and dim. The only light came from the crude fireplace, which was just a pit dug in the dirt floor. In the corner, on a bundle of sacking, huddled a man, a woman and four small children, the smallest still a baby. They looked at Hannah and Molly with wide, untrusting eyes. The man held a knife, and was crouched protectively over his wife and children.

He was filthy – they all were. Dirt caked everything, and Hannah could smell rotting meat and faeces. She was reminded of the orlop deck on the *Derby Ram* and shuddered.

'I'm terribly sorry to barge in on you,' she said. 'But we

were wondering if we could shelter here until the rain stops. My friend here is very cold.'

She saw the man's eyes flick to Molly, and widen as he saw her melted face and missing eye. The woman muttered something and made the sign of the cross.

'Please,' said Hannah. 'I can pay you.'

She held out a shilling, and the man's eyes gleamed in the firelight. He nodded slowly.

'Ye can stay until dawn,' he said.

There was no room on the sacking, so Hannah and Molly crouched in the dirt, near to the fire. The smoke made Hannah's eyes water. The children eyed them both curiously. They were very thin. Hannah could see their bones jutting out under their skin.

'Where are ye headed?' asked the man.

Hannah paused. 'The mountains,' she said, finally. 'We're looking for someone.'

The man looked uninterested. 'Yer sweetheart's workin' on the road, I expect,' he said.

'The road?'

He jerked his head to the west. 'They's buildin' a road to cross the mountains.'

Hannah stiffened. She hoped they would not run into too many people on their way to find Thomas. She swallowed. One of the children started to cough.

'What's on the other side?' she asked. 'Of the mountains?'

The man shrugged. 'Dunno,' he said. 'Some says that if you cross the mountains, you gets to China. Others says there's an ocean. Or a desert.'

Molly smiled. 'I'd like to see China,' she said.

'I wouldn't go too far into those mountains, if I was you,' said the man. 'Too many savages. Eat yer brains and stick yer head on a stick. Soon as look at ye.'

The coughing child had woken the baby, who started to cry. The woman jiggled it half-heartedly. The baby looked pale and sickly. Hannah looked around the hut. There was no furniture, just a scuffed tea-chest and the pile of sacking.

'Have you been here long?'

The man spat into the fire, which hissed. 'Stopped countin' at ten years.'

When at last dawn came, Hannah was relieved to leave the hut. She stood, stiff and cold, her clothes still damp from the rain. It was still drizzling outside.

They trudged through wet fields that stank of rotting wheat. Occasionally they approached another dilapidated hut, but they skirted around, not wanting to meet any more of the hungry farmers barely scratching a living from the inhospitable land. The fields were separated by rough cairns of rock, and the occasional wood and wire fence to keep sheep penned in.

As they passed one such fence, Molly squeaked suddenly, and pinched herself. Hannah followed her gaze to where a large black-and-white bird sat perched on a fence-post.

'Good morning, Mr Magpie, where's your wife?' muttered Molly, pinching herself again. The bird ignored her, hunching up its shoulders in the rain.

'Why are you doing that?' asked Hannah.

'One magpie is bad luck,' said Molly. 'One for sorrow, two for mirth. Three for a wedding, four for a birth. Five for rich, six for poor. Seven for a witch, I can tell you no more.'

Hannah laughed at her. 'It's just a bird,' she said. 'And a fairly ugly one at that. Look at its wicked beak!'

The bird had black, glossy feathers, with a white collar just under its head. More white feathers showed under the bird's folded wings. Its beak was white, its eyes like shiny black stones.

Molly shook her head, not taking her eye off the magpie. 'It carries a drop of the devil's blood under its tongue,' she said.

Hannah shook her head. 'Maybe that's why this one's so quiet. Usually magpies are such chattery things.'

The magpie, as if it had heard her, opened his beak and let out a full-throated, melodic warble. It was like no birdsong Hannah had ever heard before. It was beautiful, yet full of longing. Hannah felt tears rise.

Molly saluted the magpie respectfully. 'This is no ordinary chatterpie,' she said. 'It must be a magic one.'

The magpie turned its glittering eye upon them, and Hannah had to agree.

'What did one magpie mean again?' she asked Molly.

'One for sorrow,' said Molly.

Hannah looked around at the grey and brown landscape and shivered. The land stretched out as far as she could see all around her, brown spiky grass broken only occasionally by a crude fence or scraggled stand of trees. She felt very small.

The magpie launched itself from the post, flapping up into the grey sky.

The rain stopped mid-morning, and by midday the skies had cleared. The wet earth steamed in the sunlight, and strange, unfamiliar birds swooped and sang overhead. The mountains looked close enough to touch, and Hannah's spirits rose. A thick tangle of trees and bushes lay before them – the only thing that lay between them and the mountains.

As they pushed through the twisty branches and dense green undergrowth, Hannah thought she saw something sparkling ahead. She pushed further, and then let out a little cry of dismay.

They stood on the banks of a river. The previous night's rain had swollen it beyond its banks, and it was seeping into the grass on either bank. It was far too wide and deep to wade across.

Hannah sank onto the ground with a sigh. 'We'll have to follow it,' she said dismally. 'Until we can find a shallower place to cross.'

Molly coughed, and Hannah looked at her sharply. 'Don't you go catching a cold. I have enough to worry about.'

Molly stifled her cough. 'Just swallowed a fly,' she said.

Hannah raised her eyebrows. 'We may as well eat something, while we're here,' she said, pulling out the bread and cheese.

As they ate their meal, they watched the debris being carried down the river – logs, branches, the occasional floating corpse of a creature too unfortunate to escape the storm.

'Ho, there!' said a voice, making both Hannah and Molly jump.

A man sat in a small wooden boat in the middle of the river. He was working his oars back and forth furiously to keep himself stationary.

'Can I be offerin' any assistance, my ladies?' he asked, a mocking tone in his voice. He was a wiry, pointy-looking man with a hooked nose and grey stubble on his chin. His skin was sallow, his eyes squinting.

Hannah scrambled to her feet. 'Do you think you could row us across this river?' she asked.

The man looked at her. 'And why would two such pretty little misses want to cross the ole Nepean River?' he asked. 'There ain't nothin' on the other side but trees and savages.'

'My– my husband is working on the road through the mountains,' improvised Hannah. 'We're going to him.'

The man laughed. 'Oh, aye,' he said. 'Your husband. Then how could I refuse?'

Hannah started towards the riverbank eagerly.

'Wait,' he said. 'You'll have to make it worth my while.'

'Of course,' said Hannah. 'I can pay you. How much?'

The man considered it. 'A shilling,' he said.

'A shilling?' said Hannah incredulously.

The man grinned. 'How bad do you want to see your…
husband?'

Hannah sighed. 'Fine. A shilling.'

He rowed his boat to the riverbank, his arms straining to keep the boat steady in the fast current. Hannah handed over her shilling, then she and Molly clambered into the boat, which rocked alarmingly and sunk low into the water under their weight. Hannah sat down on the wooden plank that acted as a seat, while Molly crouched in the stern. The man pushed off the bank with an oar.

Halfway across, the man bent forward and strained against the oars. The boat came to a stop. The water rushed around them. He looked at Hannah expectantly.

'What?' she asked him. His beady eyes were roaming all over her body.

'I'm waiting for my payment, little miss.'

'I already paid you,' said Hannah, unsettled. 'A shilling.'

The man scratched his head. 'Well now, little miss. I can't say as I remember that.'

'What do you mean?' said Hannah, looking to the shore and wondering if they would be able to swim.

'You didn't give me no shilling, little miss. I needs my payment.' He grinned, revealing four rotten teeth, sprouting in otherwise bare, yellowing gums.

Molly whimpered. Hannah sighed, and reached for her purse. 'How much do you want?'

'How much do you got?'

'You're not having it all! That's robbery!'

The man shrugged. 'Maybe it is. I'm not a bad man. I'll make you a deal. Either you give me what's in there,' he nodded towards her purse. 'Or you give me what's under *there.*' He tweaked her skirt.

Hannah went cold. 'Take us to the shore,' she said, trying to keep her voice steady. 'I'll give you all our money when we're there.'

The man winked at her and dipped his oar in the water. Once they had reached solid ground, Hannah handed over the purse, and the man put his fingers to his forehead in a lazy salute and pushed the boat back onto the river.

'Give my regards to yer husband, missy.'

thirty

On the other side of the lake, Scatterheart found herself in a great wilderness. She saw sights of great beauty, and once or twice came perilously close to death. But on she walked.

The foothills rose before them. Looking south, down the Nepean, Hannah could just make out some kind of excavation, and some temporary-looking buildings.

'That must be where they're building the road,' she said.

Molly nodded. 'Maybe they've seen Mr Bear,' she said.

Hannah considered it. If they went downriver to the road, they might learn more about where Thomas was hiding. However they also might get turned in to the authorities and sent back to Parramatta. But who knew how far the mountains went on? She had no map, there was no path. She didn't even know where to start looking. She might never find him.

'Right then,' she said. 'We'll go down to the road. But we have to be careful no one sees us, until we're sure we can trust them.'

'Right,' said Molly. 'I ain't goin' back to bein' a orphing.'

They kept to the undergrowth, staying away from clearings and the exposed riverbank. The forest was thin here, the soil was dry, and trees found little purchase on the steep hillside. The ground was covered by a thick, rough grass that scratched at Hannah's ankles.

After only a few minutes, they were both out of breath. They paused to sip at the water bottle. Hannah drew a deep breath, her chest already sore and aching. Molly was coughing again. Hannah smiled brightly.

'Shall we have a story?' she said.

Molly nodded.

'Well then,' said Hannah, as she pushed through some low branches. 'This is a story about another great forest. A forest full of tangles and thorns, with a sleeping princess at its heart…'

They walked and walked, until Hannah had run out of breath to tell the story with. By late afternoon, they reached a weatherboard shack, with no windows and large hinged double doors securely bolted shut. A somewhat faded sign was stencilled onto the doors:

Blue Mountains Western Road
Storage

Molly looked at Hannah. 'No one's around,' she said.

'I suppose they're up in the mountains, working on the road,' said Hannah.

'Want me to break open that lock?' Molly's eye gleamed.

Hannah shook her head. 'No,' she said. 'It'll just be shovels and rope and things in there. We don't need any of that.'

Molly looked disappointed.

The road seemed deserted, just a churned dirt and rubble strip that carved through the scrub and curved up the slope of the foothills. It was about twelve feet wide, with trees and bushes cleared a further four feet on either side. Another sign was painted on wooden boards, and banged into the ground.

Blue Mountains Western Road

Tresspassing FORBIDDEN

Persons not carrying a pass signed by the Governor will be harshly prosecuted.

Hannah listened for the sound of voices, but heard nothing other than the faint gurgling of the river behind them.

She looked at Molly and shrugged. 'I suppose it can't hurt to walk on the road,' she said. 'It'll be much easier than pushing through the forest. We'll just have to be careful we don't run into anyone.'

Hannah glanced up at the sky. The sun had disappeared behind the looming bulk of the mountains, but she guessed there was still a few hours before it got dark. They started to trudge up the slope.

It wasn't much of a road. It was wide, and cleared of

vegetation, but there were large stones and branches littered across it, making for stubbed toes and twisted ankles.

When they reached the summit of the first foothill, they turned to see how far they had come. The mountains cast long shadows over the flat golden fields of Emu Plains. The river was a dark brown ribbon that snaked across the land from the north to the south, fringed with green. Hannah could see the lump of Prospect Hill, and the cluster of yellow buildings that was Parramatta. She wondered if James had returned yet, and noticed her gone. Further east, she could just make out Sydney Town, and beyond it, the blue sparkle of the ocean.

They sheltered that night just off the road, under a tall, straight-trunked tree, with rough, scratchy bark like cracked clay. It was cold, but they huddled close together under their blanket.

The next day, they continued along the road through the foothills. The trees on either side of them grew taller and broader, and the undergrowth grew thicker and greener, into a rough snarl of shrubs and creepers that bordered the road like a solid wall. The sharp, tangy smell of the forest grew stronger as they trudged over hills and down valleys.

Hannah went through every story Thomas had ever told her – the cat who wore boots, the girl who wore a donkey's skin, Bluebeard and his seven dead wives.

Molly listened attentively, but she spoke little. Her face was pale, and she often lagged behind Hannah.

On the third day, Hannah finished the story of Cendrillon and her glass slipper, and thought of Thomas. She pictured him sitting by a fire, maybe whittling something from a stick. He would hear them approach, and grip his knife more firmly, rising to a crouch. Hannah would appear from the undergrowth, and the knife would fall to the ground.

She was so caught up in her daydream that she didn't hear the sound of a human whistle, or make out the regular tramp of footsteps. When the man came around a bend in the road, he stopped short and stared at them.

Hannah threw a desperate glance to either side, wondering if they could run and hide, but this part of the road seemed unusually wide and bare. Molly edged behind Hannah, making a quiet frightened noise.

The man was tall and broad-shouldered. He had a scraggly beard and a cracked, sun-burned face. His clothes looked reasonably new and sturdy, but were caked with dirt. He carried a sack on his shoulder. He raised his eyebrows, and Hannah thought that the sight of a short-haired girl in an expensive dress, and a half-faced child must be very odd indeed.

'I don't suppose it's worth asking if you has a pass,' he said. His voice didn't have the broad twang that the currency lads and lasses had – he sounded like an English farmer.

Hannah bit her lip and shook her head. She wondered if he would try and arrest them, and if they could fight him off. He looked awfully strong.

'Convicts?' said the man.

'Yes,' said Hannah.

He nodded. 'Me too, at least for now. They tells us if we works hard on this road we'll get our freedom.'

He didn't *look* like he was going to arrest them.

'Why are you coming back?' asked Hannah.

The man made a rueful face and held up his hand. It was roughly bandaged with a strip of linen.

'Got me a mean splinter,' he said. 'Infected. I got to go back and get fixed up. But I should be back in a day or two. I'm Will. Will Appledore.'

Hannah smiled. 'I'm Hannah. This is Molly.'

Molly shrank further behind Hannah.

'So, Hannah,' he said, his eyes twinkling, 'where are you running away from?'

Molly stepped forward. 'We're looking for someone,' she said.

He looked at Molly, and a flash of pity crossed his face when he saw her missing eye. Hannah decided they could trust him.

'We're looking for a ... a friend,' she said. 'Thomas Behr.'

Appledore shrugged. 'He ain't working on the road,' he said. 'I knows everyone in the gang.'

'He's not working on the road,' said Hannah. 'He's hiding. In the mountains.'

Appledore stared at her silently for a moment. 'There be a few people hiding in these mountains,' he said.

'He was an officer,' said Hannah. 'He ran away.'

'Could be anywhere,' said Appledore, shaking his head. 'Could be dead.'

'He's not dead,' said Hannah. 'I'm sure of it. Can't you tell us anything?'

'Sorry, miss,' he said. 'I'd help you if I could. But I got a family, and Superintendent Cox says if we works well on the road, we'll get our freedom, and some land into the bargain. It's not worth my while to be breaking the law, helping a fugitive.'

'So you *do* know something,' said Hannah. 'You must.'

Appledore hesitated, then shook his head. 'Sorry,' he said.

Hannah inwardly cursed the river-man who had taken all her money.

'I– I don't have any more money. I don't have anything I can give you.'

As she said this, she knew it wasn't true. The man with the boat had given her two options for payment. She gulped, and felt sick inside. But she'd already come so far.

'I could…' she stammered, blushing and looking away.

Appledore raised his eyebrows. 'I got a daughter your age,' he said, and sighed. 'This place turns the very best of men and women into thieves and whores.'

Hannah felt a strange mixture of disappointment and relief. How would she find him now?

'Look,' said Appledore. 'I hasn't seen you, if anyone asks.

And you hasn't seen me. We saw someone, when we were working on the road. I don't know if it's who you're looking for, but I know where you can find him.'

Hannah felt the spark of hope again.

'If you walk along this road for about three days,' said Appledore, 'you'll reach a place called Weatherboard. You'll know it, because there is a weatherboard storage hut, like the one back at the river. There's a rough track that leads from the hut to the river, about a mile away. We used to go swimming there. Follow the river downstream until you reach the waterfall, and wait until it gets dark. Then stand on the cliff and look out over the valley. That's how you'll find him.'

Molly darted forward and grabbed Appledore's hand. 'Thank you,' she said.

He blushed. 'Remember,' he said. 'I hasn't seen you, and you hasn't seen me.'

Gradually, the foothills turned into mountains. The terrain grew rocky and tangled, coarse and spiky on the ridges, and green and moist in the valleys. Stone culverts had been constructed over chattering little streams, but the road often became boggy, and Hannah's skirt was soon caked with thick brown mud. The water in the streams was stained brownish-yellow, like tea. It was ice-cold, and tasted like rich earth and sharp, tangy eucalypts. Hannah thought it was delicious.

She measured out their food carefully, keeping an eye out for a tree that bore fruit – apples or pears or something. There were no familiar trees – not that she would know an apple tree if she saw one, unless it was bearing fruit. There were no berries or nuts, and the mushrooms looked so strange and wild, and came in such strange colours, that Hannah was afraid to even touch them.

On the morning of the fourth day, Hannah began to look eagerly for the weatherboard hut. It was a beautiful day. The sun was bright and hot – there was not a cloud to be seen.

'What did Will Appledore mean about finding Mr Bear at the waterfall, Hannah?' asked Molly.

'I'm not sure,' said Hannah. 'It might not be him at all.'

'It is,' said Molly. 'I'm sure.'

The walked on for a while in silence, before Molly turned to Hannah again.

'How will we be able to see him at night, when it's dark?'

Hannah shrugged. 'Maybe he comes to the waterfall to get fresh water,' she said.

Molly looked up at the blue sky above them. 'Maybe the stars will show us the way,' she said dreamily.

Hannah smiled, but worry was beginning to eat at her. They had been walking for four days – why hadn't they reached the hut? Had they passed it and not noticed? Had the workers come back and dismantled it? Had Will Appledore lied to them? What if it wasn't Thomas at all?

When they finally clambered to the top of a crest, late that afternoon, Hannah could have cried with happiness. It was there. Nestled in the foliage by the side of the road, stood a simple, square wooden hut. Molly clapped her hands and danced about with happiness.

'We're coming, Mr Bear!' she yelled.

'Hush,' said Hannah. 'There might be more workers nearby.'

Molly hushed. Hannah walked around the hut, praying to find the track to the waterfall and not a soldier lying in wait for them. But there it was, a rough beaten track through the undergrowth. Hannah was surprised. Was it really this easy?

'Come on,' she said to Molly. 'We can make it to the waterfall before it gets dark.'

They pushed their way along the track. It looked like it had been unused for several months, and vines and spiky grass pulled and scratched at them.

They could hear the waterfall long before they saw it – a dull roaring sound which reminded Hannah of being on the *Derby Ram* during the storm where she had pushed Dr Ullathorne overboard.

Hannah walked on, her lungs burning. The air seemed very thin, and she struggled to draw a breath. She heard Molly singing to herself up ahead.

She tried to concentrate on putting one foot in front of the other. Sweat poured from her brow, her heart pounded in her throat and her breath came in short, painful rasps.

Would they really find Thomas at the waterfall? She imagined him crouching over a fast-flowing river, collecting water, or washing a shirt. He would look up when he saw her, and his face would be stunned. Then he would smile, and come running over and catch her up in his arms …

Up ahead, Molly stopped singing abruptly. Hannah couldn't see her.

'Molly?' she called. There was no answer. Hannah scrambled up the slope and broke through the last of the tangle of branches.

Molly was standing on the edge of a rocky precipice. A river, thick and furious, rushed to the edge of the sandy rock and was hurled over the edge, sending up a great sheet of white spray. Beyond the waterfall were mountains. Mountains after mountains after mountains. Stretching out before them, above them, around them. Mountains wreathed in dull bluish-green, with the occasional rough wall or pinnacle of yellow rock.

Molly had her mouth open. Without looking back at Hannah, she reached her hand back. Hannah grasped it tightly and squeezed.

'It goes on forever,' whispered Molly.

And it did. Ridges and surges of land stretched on as far as they could see, peaks and valleys that eventually disappeared into the blue haze that hung over everything.

Hannah had never imagined that the world could be so big. Even after they had come so far on the *Derby Ram*, she could not bring herself to believe that such a distance could exist. It yawned out above and below her. It filled her with a gaping emptiness.

The late afternoon sun bathed the mountains in yellow light and dramatic blue shadows. Hannah looked down, and her stomach lurched. Far, far down in the valley below, she could see where the river was finally reunited with the earth, etching a great curved line into the scrub. It wound away out of sight between two soaring peaks.

The emptiness inside Hannah swallowed her heart. She felt like she wanted to cry, but couldn't. How could they find one person hidden in all that vastness?

'We'll never find him,' she whispered. 'Never.'

Molly looked back at her and smiled, then turned back to the view, drinking in the vastness of the world. 'We already have,' she said. 'This is it. We found it. This is the land that lies east o' the sun and west o' the moon.'

And perhaps it was. Hannah realised she had been wrong when she had said it was Port Jackson. It was beautiful there, but not like these mountains. Port Jackson seemed tame compared to the mountains.

'This place is beautiful and terrible ... like...' she stopped, trying to find the right word.

'Like the white bear,' said Molly softly.

Hannah nodded.

They sat on the rocky precipice beside the waterfall and watched the sun go down, and the mountains and valleys around them disappear into the blue haze. The last rays of sunlight turned the spray from the waterfall into a dancing cloud of rainbows.

Had Will Appledore been joking when he said that they'd find him once the sun had gone down?

Molly was staring dreamily out at the view. 'It looks like the ocean,' she said. 'Like big frozen waves.'

For a moment, Hannah pictured a castle, made entirely of ice, its white turrets and battlements gleaming in the pink and orange rays of the setting sun.

'Molly!' she gasped. But the castle was gone. Hannah shook her head. 'I thought I'd remembered the rest of the story,' she said. 'But I haven't.'

There was a rustling above them, and Hannah looked up to see a strange white bird perched on a branch above them. Molly looked up too and squeaked.

It was a large bird, pure white, except for its black beak and eyes, and a mane of bright yellow that sat on the very top of its head. Hannah stared at it, open-mouthed.

'Is it magic?' asked Molly.

'I don't know,' said Hannah. 'It might be.'

The bird bobbed its head up and down, and its yellow mane opened out into a golden fan of feathers.

'It's beautiful!' Molly exclaimed.

The bird looked at her with a beady black eye, and then opened its beak and made the most terrible noise Hannah had ever heard. It was simultaneously high-pitched and raucous, like the scream of a dying man. Molly clapped her hands over her ears.

'It looked so beautiful,' she said, appalled.

'Nothing is as it seems in this place,' said Hannah, not taking her eyes off the bird. 'The magpie looked foul and sounded beautiful. This bird looks beautiful but sounds foul.'

The bird let out the raucous, screeching cry again, and then flapped its wings and soared off into the darkening sky. Hannah watched it go, winging its way across the valley to a yellow rocky outcrop.

'It's showing us the way to go!' said Molly, pointing after it. 'That's what Will Appledore meant. He knew that the bird would come and show us how to find Mr Bear.'

Hannah smiled and shook her head. 'I think maybe Will Appledore was having a joke on us,' she said sadly.

A yellow star appeared in the direction where the bird had flown, low and large on the horizon. Another joined it, burning red, further up in the sky. Then a green one, and suddenly the whole sky was peppered with stars, so many that there was barely any black left.

'Beautiful,' murmured Molly.

But there was no Great Bear to guide them. Hannah sighed, and reached into their pack for the blanket and one of the wrinkled apples. Molly curled up in the hollow of one of the rocks.

'Wake me up when Mr Bear gets here,' she said sleepily.

Hannah covered her with the blanket, and stared out over the blackness. She sat still for what felt like hours, watching the stars move.

Suddenly, she could see a white sliver appear on the horizon, shining brightly. For a moment, her heart leaped. It was the White Bear, come to rescue them! But it was only the moon, drifting slowly upwards into the night sky. As it rose, Hannah began to make out the shapes of the mountains.

As the moon escaped the horizon and sailed fully into the sky, it shone a strange, pale light over the cliff-top and the waterfall. Hannah stared at the bright yellow star that burned just below the horizon.

'Molly,' she said softly.

She stared at the star. It seemed to flicker.

'Molly!' she said again, shaking her awake.

'Did Mr Bear come?' Molly asked sleepily.

'No,' said Hannah. 'But I know where he is.'

She pointed to the yellow star.

'It's not a star at all,' she said. 'It's a campfire.'

thirty-
one

**Soon Scatterheart reached a field of great sharp spikes.
She cracked open the silver acorn, and inside it were two
silver slippers. She put them on, and walked across the
spikes without injury.**

When the sun rose the next morning, Hannah looked towards the place where the fire had been. There were three crumbling peaks of yellow rock high on the mountain across the valley.

'That's where we're going,' said Hannah.

Molly clapped her hands and leapt to her feet, but swayed a little and had to sit down again.

'Molly?' said Hannah. 'Are you all right?'

'Just hungry,' said Molly. 'What's for breakfast?'

After Hannah had shared out their small portions of stale

bread and cheese, they set off.

To the left of the waterfall, the cliff angled downwards until it merged with the slope of the mountain. They made for that, and when the cliff-face ended, Hannah took one last look at the three yellow rocks where she had seen the campfire, and plunged into the forest.

It was hard going, and after an hour Hannah found herself longing for the rough muddy road that they had left behind. There was no path, and the creepers and shrubs seemed to be trying to push them back to Parramatta. Hannah wished she had a knife or something to cut away at the undergrowth and clear their way, but she had to duck and weave and tear at the vines with her bare hands. Her forearms and ankles were soon scratched and itchy. Flies and mosquitoes buzzed and feasted, and as they descended, a canopy of green closed over their heads and blocked out the sun.

It became colder as they descended into the valley. The layer of sweat that Hannah had built up struggling with the undergrowth now made her shiver. She felt very enclosed. The noise of birds and insects seemed magnified and up close.

A mosquito was buzzing by her ear. She slapped at it, hitting herself in the head. When she looked at her hand, she saw a smear of black insect and red blood.

By midday, Hannah had no idea if they were heading in the right direction. They were now walking uphill, but she couldn't see the three yellow rocks at all. She thought of Thomas's story of the sleeping princess in the castle, and the giant forest of thorns that had grown around it.

'Hannah! Hannah!'

Hannah looked around. Molly sounded hysterical.

'Hannah! Hurry!'

The forest was so strange. The closeness of the vegetation made sounds dart all over the place, and turned Hannah around so she kept going in quite the opposite direction to the one she intended. Hannah pushed through a thick tangle of green branches, and saw Molly. She was crouched down on the ground, her whole body shaking.

'Molly?' said Hannah. 'Are you all right?'

Molly turned, and Hannah was surprised to see that she was laughing.

'Come here,' she said.

Hannah crouched down too. Half-hidden in the scrub was the most peculiar creature Hannah had ever seen.

It was about the size of a large rabbit, or a small dog. It was shaped like an upside-down teacup, just a dome-shaped lump huddled against the forest floor. It had a long, thin black snout and two beady little eyes. But by far the strangest thing about it was its coat of thick yellow and brown spikes.

'Is it a giant hedgehog?' asked Molly.

Hannah shook her head. 'I don't know.'

The creature turned its head and sniffed the air with its long nose. Molly giggled. It raised itself onto four stubby legs finished with long claws, and, with a shudder of spikes, waddled off into the foliage.

Hannah and Molly both laughed to see the comical little creature move.

'Well, that was easy,' said Molly.

'What was?'

'The second challenge.'

Hannah looked blank.

Molly smiled. 'The field of spikes. In Mr Bear's story. He must be the field of spikes that Scatterheart has to pass.'

Hannah started to laugh. 'Come on, then,' she said. 'We'll stop for a rest at the top of this hill.'

They continued to climb, their spirits buoyed by the laughter. But after only a few minutes, Molly stiffened.

'What is it?' asked Hannah.

'Can't you smell it? Like cinders and death.'

Hannah shook her head. 'I can't smell anything,' she said.

Molly fell behind Hannah, looking uncomfortable. After some time, Hannah realised that she *could* smell something. Something sharp and black, like burnt toast.

'Can't we go another way?' asked Molly.

'I don't know if there *is* another way.'

The smell grew stronger. A thin haze of smoke clouded Hannah's vision. A faint breeze made the trees above whisper and rustle. Something drifted down from the sky.

'Snow!' cried Molly. 'It's snowing!'

Sure enough, white fragments were whirling down towards them. Hannah held out a hand to catch one. It was not cold, like snow. It was like a thin scrap of paper. Hannah touched it with a cautious finger, and it smudged away into nothing.

'It isn't snow,' she said. 'It's ashes.'

They pushed through a curtain of scrub, and found themselves standing before a field of blackness.

As far as they could see, there was black. The grass and plants had all been burned away, leaving scorched earth and the bare, charred remains of trees.

'Let's go back,' said Molly softly.

Hannah took her hand and smiled encouragingly. 'Look,' she said. 'Look at those burnt tree-trunks. Maybe *this* is the field of spikes. Come on.'

'We'll be burned,' said Molly, putting a hand to her melted face.

Hannah took her hand. 'No, we won't. We have good strong boots. We'll be careful.'

They picked their way through the field of black earth, past the dark skeletons of trees. Soon they were surrounded by the black forest. At the stumps of some trees, orange glowed faintly as fire still consumed the life within. Occasionally they came across the charred carcasses of animals.

The bitter smell of the smoke stung Hannah's eyes, and made Molly cough.

The black forest was eerily silent. No birds screeched overhead. There was no rustling of leaves as the breeze drifted through the dead trees.

Ashes floated down silently, settling on the ground until another breath of wind stirred them up again. Every now and then, the silence would be penetrated by a sharp *crack*, as a charred branch became too weak to cling to its tree-trunk, and fell to the ground, dislodging another cloud of white ash.

As they reached the bottom of the hill, green began to creep back into the landscape. Soon, the trees were only blackened on one side, and the undergrowth surged back into life. The bottom of the hill widened into a long, green gully, with a trickle of water flowing through it. They drank gladly from the stream, and washed the ash and soot from their faces.

'We may as well follow this stream, while we can,' said Hannah as she refilled the water bottle.

Her stomach rumbled, but the sourness of the smoke made her feel sick and a little dizzy. They could eat later.

The smell of smoke still pervaded the air, so they didn't notice the campsite until they stumbled through a thick copse of young trees, and found themselves in the middle of it.

They were in a clearing, surrounded by five or six crude little huts made from strips of bark propped up with tree branches.

Twenty or thirty men, women and children, sprawled around a crackling fire. A scrawny yellow dog lay stretched out by one of the men, eyes closed. It didn't seem to notice their intrusion.

They were all completely naked, save for long cloaks made of grey-brown fur hides, sewn together with some kind of thick, yellow twine. Their hair was long, black and matted, and all the men had thick black beards. One of the women held an infant to her bare breast.

An old man lay on a reddish-grey fur hide by the fire – his grizzled face sporting deep lines and a white, straggled whiskers. A younger man bent over him, holding a shallow brown dish of what appeared to be water.

Four men stood, and approached Hannah and Molly.

They had painted white lines on their arms and legs, and across their noses, as if they wore their bones outside their flesh. One had a necklace of animal teeth around his neck, another a white shard of bone pierced through his nose. Their skin was covered in patterned scars – a sickle-shape over the left eyebrow, a cross on the fleshy part of the arm. They all held spears, tall, straight and deadly. Their arms and legs were thin, but sinewy and muscled. They were clearly very strong.

Hannah felt her cheeks burn when she saw their blatant nakedness, but Molly stared openly, fascinated.

'Please,' said Hannah. 'We mean you no harm.' The ludicrousness of her words, combined with her rising sense of panic, made hysterical laughter bubble up inside her.

The man with the animal necklace said something to the other three. Their language sounded completely alien to Hannah – it may well have been the barking of the yellow dog by the fire, or the sound of the wind in the *Derby Ram*'s rigging.

One of the men reached out and gently touched Hannah's head. Her hair was perhaps three inches long now, matted and greasy. The man seemed curious at her shorn hair, and rubbed her head with the palm of his hand. Hannah was surprised to see that the blackness of them didn't extend to their palms, which were as pink as her own.

The man grinned suddenly, baring his startlingly-white teeth, and said something to his companions, who all burst out laughing. Hannah tried to smile, hoping that their laughter was a good sign.

'What do they want?' asked Molly in a whisper.

As she spoke, the four warrior men turned their attention to her. Their eyes widened in surprise when they saw her melted-wax face, and they started chattering excitedly to each other. They touched her face curiously, running their fingers over her skin. The other men and women approached also, crowding around to see Molly and touch her face.

Molly stood stock-still, her face even whiter than usual, her one eye glancing warily at the sharp spears which the warrior men still held.

One of the warrior men put down his spear, and, gently but firmly, took Hannah's bag from her.

'Hey!' said Molly indignantly. 'That's ours!'

'Shh!' said Hannah. 'Let them take it.'

The man rummaged through the bag. He sniffed the bread curiously, but laid it aside, not seeming to recognise it as food.

He brought forth a hunk of the cheese, but tossed it into the dirt in disgust when he smelled it, wiping his fingers on the ground and grimacing hideously.

He ran his hands over the cool hardness of the water bottle, and held it up to see the light shining through it, but cast it aside also.

He seemed uninterested in their damp woollen blanket. Hannah held her breath as the man reached into the bag once more. He pulled out a pathetic brown lump of fabric, torn and ragged. He pulled it away, discarding it in the dirt with their other belongings, and looked at what it had revealed.

Thomas's spectacles.

The man held them up to the firelight, and smiled as the silver rims sparkled in the orange glow.

'No,' whispered Hannah.

The man grinned, and placed the spectacles around his throat like a necklace, the arms reaching around behind his neck.

He said something to the other men and women, who turned away from Molly and Hannah and returned to the warmth of their fire.

One of the women brought over a haunch of the animal that had been roasting over the fire, and gave it to Hannah. The man replaced the food, blanket and water bottle in the canvas bag, stood up, and presented it to Hannah.

'Not Mr Bear's spectacles,' said Molly.

'We have to leave them,' said Hannah.

The man stepped back, picking up his spear, and made a gesture which seemed to indicate they should leave.

Hannah bobbed a curtsey to the man. 'Thank you, sir.'

The man laughed again, and mimicked her.

Molly darted forward behind the warrior man, and bent down to pick something up from the dirt.

'Molly!' hissed Hannah.

The man tensed, gripping his spear.

Molly scurried back behind Hannah, clutching something in her hand.

Hannah grabbed her other hand, and they ran from the clearing, not stopping until they had put some considerable distance between themselves and the campsite. Hannah sank to the ground, her heart still pounding, and her hands still shaking.

'Here,' said Molly, panting.

She held out the scrap of brown fabric that Thomas's spectacles had been wrapped in.

'It's Mr Bear's handkerchief,' she said.

Hannah took it, rubbing the tattered fabric between her thumb and forefinger. 'Thank you,' she said.

'Why were they so interested in me?' asked Molly.

Hannah shrugged. 'I suppose because … because you look different.'

'No one ever did that before,' said Molly. 'Just *looked*. Most people look away and get all embarrassed.'

Hannah glanced over at her, and took her hand impulsively. 'Most people are stupid,' she said.

thirty–
two

Scatterheart walked on and on, until she came to a great glass mountain that was so slippery she could not climb it. She cracked open the golden acorn, and found a pair of golden slippers. She put on the slippers, and climbed the mountain with ease.

They sheltered under the overhang of a large yellowish rock that night. Hannah shared out some of the meat that the savages had offered them. It was tough and stringy, but Hannah was glad to have a change from stale bread and cheese.

There was barely any food left in her canvas bag. Only enough for one or two more small, pathetic meals. Hannah's stomach rumbled hungrily, and she wondered if she could pick some nuts or mushrooms or something.

There were trees sporting strange grey and brown fruits that were rough and hard to touch, and could not be broken open to reveal any edible flesh. Molly found a crop of bright blue berries, but Hannah shuddered, remembering the blue fruit that Scatterheart had eaten in the ice-garden, and forbade Molly to touch them.

'Knowing this place,' she said, 'anything that looked at all edible would be filled with deadly poison.'

Molly cheered weakly when night fell and they could make out the yellow glow of the campfire high above them on the mountain.

'It still seems so far,' said Hannah.

'We're definitely closer,' replied Molly.

Hannah huddled next to Molly and closed her eyes. The few scraps of the savages' meat had done little to fill her stomach.

Molly was coughing again, her little body shaking with spasms. Hannah wriggled around, trying to find a more comfortable place to sleep, but every way she moved, rocks and tree roots poked into her.

Molly was quiet the next day. Hannah tried to tell her the story of Little Red-Cap, visiting her grandmother in the forest, but Molly was distant and vague.

The terrain began to rise again. Strange trees twisted and curled around other trees, like they were trying to strangle the very life from each other.

Bark hung from some trees in long strips, like peeling skin. Others had soft, fine bark-like paper, which could be peeled off. Once or twice, Hannah made out the three peaks of yellow rock through the thick trees, but they didn't seem to be closer at all.

As well as rough, yellow stone, they also came across strange outcrops of smooth grey rock, shaped like the curves and peaks of the ocean. As the sun climbed into the sky, they came across such an outcrop. There were two basin-shaped hollows at either end, and between them, the rock rose up sharply, and then levelled off to make a flat top.

'It looks like a table and chairs,' said Hannah, laughing.

Molly looked at the rock with her head on one side. Hannah put down the canvas bag.

'We should have a tea-party,' she said.

Molly looked at her, puzzled. Hannah pushed her down into one of the hollows, and seated herself in the other. She handed Molly the water bottle.

'My dear, will you pour?' she asked.

Molly stared at her for a moment, then smiled. 'Of course,' she said, taking a sip and then passing it back.

'So refreshing,' said Hannah, dabbing the corners of her mouth with her sleeve. 'Now, what have we here?'

She took out their last morsel of bread. It was fringed with blue mould, and felt as hard as stone.

'Fresh cinnamon cakes!' cried Hannah. 'Don't they smell delicious?'

Molly inhaled, nodding.

'And some fine French *camembert*,' said Hannah, placing a crumb of cheese on their stone table. 'From the very best dairies in Normandy.'

'What else?' asked Molly, her eye taking on a lustre that Hannah hadn't seen for days.

Hannah reached into the bag again. 'The very finest suckling pig. Roasted on a spit and served with parsnips and potatoes.'

'Does it have an apple in its mouth?' asked Molly.

'But of course,' said Hannah, placing the last of the savages' meat on the table.

'Everything but the squeal,' said Molly happily.

They ate the feast, closing their eyes and savouring the fine flavours.

'Do help yourself,' said Hannah. 'But remember to save room for the second course!'

'What's in the second course?'

'Hand-raised duck pie with plum chutney and stewed vegetables. And collared eels, and a bisque of pigeons with truffles and beetroot. And a calfsfoot pudding.'

Molly put her hands over her stomach. 'Stop!' she said. 'I'm fit to burst.'

Hannah grinned. 'I haven't even started on dessert yet.'

She closed her eyes. 'All the other dishes are removed, and the cloth is changed. Then the dessert course appears. A miniature Vauxhall Gardens made out of spun sugar, twinkling in the candlelight. A little sugar orchestra in the pavilion, a sugar tightrope walker. It is the most beautiful thing you have ever seen. So beautiful and delicate that you don't want to eat any of it, for fear of spoiling the scene.'

Molly looked worried. 'But we do, don't we?'

'Of course,' said Hannah.

Molly sighed contentedly. 'What a lovely feast,' she said. She wriggled a little and rubbed her upper arms. 'But I wish the fire was hotter, it's so cold in here. Do you think you could ask Peter to stoke the fire a little?'

Hannah chuckled. 'Who's Peter?' she asked.

Molly closed her eye sleepily. 'I hope Catherine is warming up my bed, Mama.'

Hannah caught her breath. 'Is Catherine your sister?' she asked.

Molly yawned. 'Goodnight, Mama,' she said.

Molly had never spoken of her life before she had become a convict. Hannah assumed that she had spent her whole life on the streets. She wondered what could have happened to make her family abandon her. Hannah reached out and shook her gently.

'Come on, Molly,' she said. 'We have to keep going.'

Molly raised her head and frowned. 'Where are we going?' she asked.

They kept walking, but Molly was lagging behind. She kept coughing, and her eye seemed unfocussed. Her lips were cracked and bleeding. Hannah took her hand. It was hot and clammy. They walked on.

Clouds began to scud across the sky, and the tree-tops overhead bent and rustled as a breeze picked up. Hannah shivered uneasily. Molly stopped dead.

'Come on, Molly,' said Hannah.

'Rubies,' said Molly distantly. 'I found rubies.'

'Just a bit further,' Hannah said. 'And then I promise we can rest.'

She could feel Thomas nearby, she was sure of it. They must be close. They had run out of food, so if they were not close now, then they never would be. Molly didn't move, just stared at the tree in front of her.

'Look, Hannah,' said Molly, her voice slightly slurred. 'Rubies!'

Hannah sighed and looked.

There was a bright, shining red stone protruding from the rough brown tree-trunk. It was twisted and lumpy, as if it had been melted into place. Hannah reached out to touch it. The tree reminded her of something.

A tree covered in jewels … was it part of Thomas's story? Hannah ran her fingers over the smooth, hard stones.

'It's so beautiful,' said Molly dreamily.

'Yes,' said Hannah, feeling where it fused with the bark of the tree. What did it mean? The memory lurked at the back of her mind, just out of reach. She frowned, and the red stone came off in her hand.

She held it up to the light. It wasn't a stone. It was soft inside, like some kind of sweetmeat.

'Oh, Hannah,' said Molly, swaying on her feet. 'What did you do?'

Hannah looked back at the tree trunk. It was bleeding, a thick, dark, reddish blood. She dropped the red stone to the ground, and stared, horrified, at the bleeding tree.

'We have to go,' she said, grabbing Molly's hand. 'We have to find Thomas.'

Molly began to walk again, Hannah almost dragging her through the undergrowth.

The clouds rushed in, low and full. Thunder rumbled in the distance. Hannah walked faster, Molly stumbling along behind her. As the first few, fat drops fell, Hannah felt despair sweeping over her. She shook it off.

'We'll just get to the top of the next rise,' she muttered. 'And he'll be there, waiting for us.'

But he wasn't. The rain started to fall in earnest, thick curtains of freezing water. The ground beneath them grew treacherous.

They kept walking. He wasn't over the next rise either, or the next. The three yellow rocks seemed to have vanished. Hannah's hands and dress became soaked in mud, as she slipped and stumbled through the forest, towing Molly along behind her. Molly didn't speak.

It grew dark. The rain continued to fall. There was no moon to illuminate the forest around them, and Hannah felt as if she were going blind. As the light faded, the trees stretched into sinister, looming shapes around them. Hannah's hands and feet were numb.

They kept walking.

As the last glimmer of light faded from the forest, they stumbled into a shallow cave and collapsed in the dirt.

Molly's breath was coming in sharp, ragged gasps. Hannah put a hand to her forehead, but snatched it away immediately. Molly was burning.

'Mama?' said Molly. 'Is that you?'

Hannah sat with Molly, horrified at herself. Molly was really sick. Hannah had been pushing her for days.

Molly shivered and burned, muttering nonsense and staring blankly at Hannah with her one good eye. She made Molly sip some water, but it only made her cough and retch, bringing up a stinking greenish-yellow bile.

'King's pictures, miss,' said Molly.

'Shh,' said Hannah. 'Try to sleep, Molly.'

Molly moaned and thrashed about. 'Molly put the kettle on,' she muttered.

'I'm so sorry,' whispered Hannah. 'We should never have come here.'

As the night wore on, Molly slipped into a restless sleep. Hannah sat by her, using Thomas's handkerchief to mop the sweat from Molly's brow.

Hannah spread the damp handkerchief out and looked at it. It was barely holding together, its threads so worn and tattered that it threatened to disintegrate at any moment.

She thought about how Thomas had looked when he had told her that he loved her. Or had he? Hannah went through his proposal in her mind. He had never said it. What if the rumours about another woman were true?

Why would he love her? She had only ever been selfish and cruel to him. Thomas wasn't like James. He wouldn't have loved her because of something she wasn't. He wouldn't have loved her at all.

'What have I done?' she murmured.

Had she made it up? Had he only offered to marry her out of sympathy? Out of obligation?

A churning, writhing despair rose from her stomach. She felt sick. The cave felt suddenly too small, but she couldn't leave it because of the rain. She was trapped.

She never should have let Molly come. She was just a child. Hannah had thought that she had changed, but she was just as selfish as she had always been. She didn't deserve to find Thomas.

A great clap of thunder sounded, and Molly whimpered.

Panic rose in Hannah's throat. They would die here.

'Hannah,' whispered Molly. 'Hannah.'

Hannah tried to swallow her panic. 'I'm here, sweetheart,' she said, taking Molly's hand. 'I'm here.'

'I–' Molly broke off and coughed again, a violent, racking cough. 'I'm the third acorn.'

'What?'

'I'm the third acorn. Like when you gave Mister Bear's spectacles to the brown men. You should keep going.'

Molly's head slumped back onto the ground, and she slipped out of consciousness.

Hannah shook her head.

'No,' she said.

She ducked out of the cave and stood in the rain. The wind in the trees sounded like the whistling and wailing of the *Derby Ram*'s rigging. She looked out for the winking yellow light of Thomas's campfire, but could see nothing but rain.

It had been four nights since they'd seen it.

'No,' she said again.

'Do you hear me, mountain?' she yelled into the storm. 'I'm not giving in. I crossed an ocean to get here. I climbed this mountain. *I will not let her die.*'

The mountain answered her with another rumble of thunder, and a fork of lighting that lit up the sky. Water soaked through Hannah. The rain filled her mouth. She laughed. The mountain couldn't frighten her. She had come this far, and she *would* find him.

She crawled back into the cave and lay down, taking Molly's hand again.

'You *will* be all right,' she said. 'I promise.'

And she slipped into a deep and strange sleep.

Hannah lay at the mouth of the cave, staring out and up at the stars. The Great Bear was there, glittering above her like a shining knight protector. The bear's eye burned yellow on the horizon.

'Where have you been?' she said softly. 'I missed you.'

She reached out a hand to touch the bear – it seemed so close. She brushed the stars with her fingertips. They made a tinkling noise and began to fall. As the stars tumbled gently down from the sky, Hannah realised that they were not stars at all, but snowflakes. They landed softly on her cheeks and lips, icy and tender. She sighed, and drifted back into a dreamless sleep.

When Hannah woke, she was feverish. She opened her eyes, and the world swam before her.

The sky was on fire, glowing pink and orange and gold, burning and boiling. The valley below her was gone. Instead the world was covered in white snow.

A flat, white plain stretched out beneath her, with greenish-blue mountain peaks rising out of it, like great ships at sea. Hannah remembered the Great Bear turning into snow during the night.

'I found it,' she whispered. 'East o' the sun, west o' the moon.'

'Molly,' she called out, and her voice was weak and croaky. She licked her lips. They were dry and cracked. Her mouth felt like it was full of sand.

She sat up, and the world tilted. She was shivering and sweating all at once, and her head was stuffed with wool.

She clambered to her feet, holding onto the rock ledge for support.

'Molly,' she called again. There was no answer. Molly wasn't there. Hannah staggered from the rocky overhang, each step pounding throughout her body.

'Molly, I've remembered. I know the rest of the story.'

She was so thirsty. If only she could get down to the snow, it could quench her thirst.

'Scatterheart *does* find the castle, Molly,' she said. 'She finds it, and it's made entirely from ice, surrounded by fields of snow.'

The snow was before her, only a few feet away, but it looked wrong somehow, insubstantial. The pink and orange light from the burning sky made everything look strange, like she was inside an oil-painting. She leaned against a tree, catching her breath.

'She goes up to the door of the castle, but…'

She pushed off from her tree and plunged down towards the snow. As she reached it, it swirled away for a moment, then reached out to envelop her.

It wasn't snow at all, it was fog.

Hannah remembered crouching in her hallway in London, her head against the front door as Thomas disappeared into the fog. She remembered it swallowing up the Frost Fair.

This fog was different, though. It was pure and white, light and cool. It was not the deadening, dark, sickly fog of London.

She heard a crackle of sticks and leaves, and stumbled forward blindly, not caring if it was James or Dr Ullathorne or the London bailiff himself.

A pair of arms reached out of the fog and grasped her by the shoulders. She sank gratefully into them, feeling dirty linen press against her cheek, and strong hands holding her up.

'But the door to the castle has no key or lock,' she said to the arms. 'Not even a handle.'

Then the mist swirled again, and swallowed them up.

thirty–
three

Finally, Scatterheart came to the castle that lay
east o' the sun and west o' the moon.
The door was closed, and she could find no handle or lock.
She cracked open the last acorn that the north wind had
left her, but was surprised to find nothing but a nut inside.
Scatterheart tossed it onto the ground and wept bitter tears.

Hannah was in a large cave. A fire burned just outside, in a dusty little clearing. Her body felt delicate, as if it were made from glass. Her mouth was dry.

There was a movement beside her, and a hand held out the glass water bottle.

'Here,' said a voice. 'Drink.'

She took the bottle, and held it to her lips. The water

inside was startlingly cold. Hannah blinked, trying to clear
the fuzziness from her head.

'Molly…' she said, her voice hoarse.

'Molly's here,' said the voice. 'She's fine. She's playing
outside.'

Hannah turned her head towards the voice.

She didn't dare speak. Part of her was frightened, he
looked so *different*. But another part felt that there was not
enough of her to be able to shout her joy loud enough.

His body no longer looked soft – it was lean and hardened.
His once-pale skin was brown and creased – from exposure
to dirt and the weather. His hair had grown long, and was
roughly tied back. He was unshaven. He wore dark trousers
like a farmer, and a stained, torn linen shirt, open at the neck,
sleeves rolled up to expose the thick tangle of yellow hair on
his arms. She barely recognised him.

'Thomas,' she said.

He smiled a strange smile, and looked away. Hannah
blushed. What must she look like to him? Dirty and scratched
from her journey through the forest. Her hair short and
ragged. Wearing a muddy and tattered dress. Her face red
and peeling. She put her tongue to the gap in her mouth
where she had lost the tooth in the doldrums.

'I must look terrible,' she said vaguely.

'I can barely see you,' he said. He spoke slowly at first,
as if he were unused to it. 'The light in the cave is poor, and
without my spectacles–'

'Oh,' said Hannah, somewhat relieved.

Thomas took the water bottle back from her, and turned to put it down behind him. Hannah struggled into a sitting position. The silence was uncomfortable. This wasn't how she had imagined their reunion.

'I'm sorry,' said Hannah at last. 'About your spectacles. I had them. I gave them to the savages. Well, I didn't really *give* them. They took your spectacles. I didn't really have a choice.'

She was babbling. Thomas smiled the strange smile again.

'You met them?' he said. 'I've only seen them from a distance. I'd like to meet them properly.'

'I was frightened,' she said. 'The stories you hear.'

Thomas shrugged. 'They're just stories. People are always afraid of things they don't understand.'

Hannah didn't understand what was going on. Thomas didn't seem happy to see her. He didn't seem happy at all. Where was the sparkle in his grey eyes? She snuck a look at him. His eyes were flatter than the ocean had been at the doldrums.

'Is everything all right?' she asked.

'Fine,' he said, with another of the strange smiles.

Hannah tried to work out what was strange about it. It wasn't a happy smile. She thought suddenly of the story she had heard about Thomas falling in love with a convict woman. Was that it? Did Thomas feel he was being rescued by the wrong woman?

'Are you hungry?' he asked.

'No,' said Hannah. She felt sick.

He scrambled to his feet. 'You should eat something,' he said, turning to rummage in a hessian sack behind him.

Hannah looked around the cave. She lay on a rough bed of dry leaves, covered with a hemp blanket. A few glass jars were lined up against the wall, filled with water. There was a large canister of rice, and a black kettle. Towards the back of the cave was a line of little carved wooden figures. Animals. Hannah smiled as she saw a kangaroo and a bear. Behind them was a small pile of rectangular objects.

'You have books!' said Hannah.

A faint blush crept over Thomas's cheeks. 'It's silly, I know,' he said. 'It's difficult to read them without my glasses. I should have brought food and more blankets and a clean shirt. But I couldn't quite bear the idea of being up here alone with nothing to read.'

'I don't think it's silly at all,' said Hannah. 'You can't imagine how often I wish I'd brought some books with me.'

Thomas nodded. Hannah looked away, frowning. This wasn't how it was supposed to go.

There were footsteps outside, and Molly came bounding into the cave. She clutched a little wooden doll in one hand.

'Hannah!' she squealed. 'You're all right.'

'I thought you were the sick one,' Hannah said.

Molly shrugged. 'I got better,' she said. 'But then you got sick, so I came and found Mr Bear, who came and found you.

I followed the yellow star.'

'Oh,' said Hannah, feeling as if she were in a dream. 'Of course.'

Thomas stood up. 'I'll make some food,' he said, and left the cave.

Hannah watched him go.

'Mr Bear has lots of new stories,' said Molly happily. 'And he made me a dolly from a stick.'

Hannah looked at the crude doll. 'It's lovely,' she said, wondering if she would cry.

'Aren't you happy?' said Molly. 'We found Mr Bear. And he told me the rest of the story. We can all live happily ever after, now.'

'Yes,' said Hannah. 'I suppose we can.'

'Hannah?' said Molly. 'You should be happy. We found him.'

Hannah nodded. 'But perhaps he didn't want to be found.'

She stood up, and went outside. Thomas had wrapped some sort of vegetables in thick leaves, and was placing them near the hot coals of the fire to cook. About twenty feet from the fire, the mountain dropped off suddenly in a cliff. Hannah could see the hazy grey-green of the valley far below them. She felt dizzy.

'Thomas…' she said gently, reaching out and touching his hand.

Thomas moved his hand away, stoking the fire.

'You've come a long way,' he said.

Hannah's eyes filled with tears. 'I have,' she said. 'Such a very long way. But I found you, and now we can go home and start again, and this time I won't be so stupid and everything will be all right.'

Thomas glanced away. 'How did you communicate with the savages?' he said, as if he hadn't heard her. 'Was it very difficult? Did you see their camp?'

Hannah wasn't sure if she was going to burst into tears or fly into a rage.

'What's wrong?' she asked.

Thomas turned and looked at her directly, for the first time. Hannah was frightened by what she saw in his eyes. The glittering grey ocean was dark and deep. He shook his head.

'I'm sorry,' he said. 'I know this isn't what you were expecting.'

He turned at the sound of a loud rustling in the trees nearby. Hannah followed his gaze, and her heart sank.

'What a touching scene,' said James, as he swung off his horse and approached the fire.

thirty-four

Scatterheart's tears turned the earth to mud around her, and the discarded acorn grew a tiny green shoot. This shoot grew bigger and bigger, sending roots down into the moist earth and stretching branches up into the sky. Soon, it was a huge oak tree, powerful and strong. The tree wrapped its branches around the walls of the ice-castle, and tore them asunder, reducing the ice-castle to rubble.

James looked dirty and weary, as if he had been riding without sleep for many days. Black pouches sagged under his eyes, and in the harsh white light, his pallor made him look sickly. His eyes flickered back and forth, and his left eyelid twitched.

'How did you find us?' asked Hannah.

James shrugged. 'I followed the road until I found the

workers. They told me about the crazy man hiding up in the mountains, and how he lights a campfire every night.'

Molly crept to the mouth of the cave.

'What a happy family,' James sneered. 'The monster, the runaway and the murderer.'

Thomas was looking at James, frowning.

James smiled coldly. 'Or is that the murderer and the runaway? It's hard to say.'

'What do you want, James?' said Hannah.

James turned to Thomas. 'I don't think we've been introduced. You're Thomas Behr, murderer, deserter and fugitive. I'm Lieutenant James Belforte. Hannah's husband.'

Thomas glanced at Hannah, an eyebrow cocked slightly.

'It's not true,' she said. 'At least, I *did* marry him, but I didn't realise it at the time.'

Thomas turned back to James.

James drew out a pistol. 'I'm taking my wife home,' he said.

'You most certainly are *not*,' said Hannah.

James ignored her, staring at Thomas. 'I brought you a weapon, to make it fair.' He pulled out a second gun, and tossed it at Thomas's feet. 'I believe you'll recognise it.'

Thomas glanced down at the pistol and his jaw tightened. He looked up at James.

'I won't fight you.'

James sneered. 'What are you, a coward?'

Thomas shrugged. 'Perhaps.'

'Pick up the gun.'

'I won't fight you.'

'Why not?' asked James. 'Isn't she worth it?'

Thomas said nothing.

'Well then,' said James. 'Come on, Hannah. I'll take you home.'

'I'm not going anywhere with you,' said Hannah. She looked at Thomas. 'Am I?'

He looked at her. She remembered him looking at her that way on the steps of her house in London. Hannah took an impulsive step towards him. Then he looked away, and she stopped, frozen.

'You should go with him.' His voice caught slightly.

Hannah felt the earth slip away from underneath her. 'You don't mean that,' she said.

'Hannah,' said James. 'Let's go home.' He looked at Molly. 'If you come with me, I promise the … child will be taken care of. We can adopt her.'

'No!' Molly shouted. 'We're staying here with Mr Bear!'

James clenched his fists. 'You *will* come with me!' he said to Hannah, veins standing out in his neck. 'He doesn't want you, did you hear that?'

'What are you going to do, James?' said Hannah. 'Sling me over your horse's back? Tie a rope to my ankle and drag me back to Parramatta?'

James grabbed her by the wrist with his free hand. Hannah tried to pull away, but he yanked her forward and down into the dirt. Hannah tried to struggle to her feet, but James pushed her down again. Why was Thomas just standing there? Why wasn't he helping her?

'Yes,' he hissed. 'If I have to drag you home, then that's what I'll do. If I have to knock you unconscious, then so you shall be knocked.' He planted a muddy boot on her chest, and levelled his pistol at her. 'And if I have to kill you, then so be it.'

Hannah opened her mouth to fling a reply at him, but James was pushed aside by a whirling ball of teeth and hair and nails. He yelped and cursed, dropping his gun. Molly clung to his back, spitting and scratching and biting like a wild thing. He yelled and struck out at her. There was a crack as his arm connected with her head.

Molly fell to the ground, but scrabbled towards James like one possessed. He pushed her down and knelt over her, grabbing her by the throat.

Blood was welling up on Molly's forehead, and her lips were turning purple. Her one eye was rolled back in her head.

Hannah scrambled to her feet and leapt at James, throwing all her weight against him. She glanced towards the cliff, and thought of Dr Ullathorne. If she could just get him over there ...

James struck out at Hannah, sending her sprawling again.

'Stop.' It was Thomas. He was standing by the mouth of the cave, holding James's spare gun.

'Leave her,' he said.

James's eyes flickered down to his own gun, lying several feet away in the dirt. He looked back at Thomas and sneered. 'You won't do it,' he said.

Thomas said nothing, but didn't lower the gun.

'You're a coward. You won't kill me.'

Thomas made a small, cold sound that wasn't quite a laugh. 'What do I have left to lose?'

James looked at Hannah. 'You convict slut, whoring yourself out to this murderer. How can you be so *dense* not to realise what I'm offering you?'

Hannah went over to Molly, and helped her to her feet. Dark marks were appearing on her throat where James had gripped her. Hannah remembered the marks on Long Meg's throat. 'Go home, James,' said Hannah.

He looked at her, and seemed to deflate. He turned to his horse. Thomas lowered the gun, and glanced over at Molly, who was crying.

While Thomas's head was turned, James leapt for his own pistol, making a furious, animal sound.

'Filthy little bitch,' he said, levelling the pistol at Hannah. 'You call yourself a lady of Quality, but you're nothing more than a filthy, disgusting whore–'

There was a sharp crack from the pistol in Thomas's hand, and James gasped. He stared at Hannah, his mouth open.

'How *dare* you,' James whispered, and fell to the ground, dead.

thirty–
five

**Scatterheart looked up from her weeping, and saw
the white bear, lying asleep in the rubble. She ran to him
and kissed him and he woke up, and they were both
filled with joy.**

Thomas disposed of the body. Hannah didn't ask how. When
he returned, they sat together at the mouth of the cave, not
saying much. Molly wandered off down the hill to play with
her wooden doll. James's horse was tethered nearby, cropping
at rough grass.

Hannah thought that she would feel some sadness or
guilt at James's death, but all she felt was relief, and a vague
uneasiness. Thomas had saved her. Did that mean that he
loved her after all?

'She's a sweet girl,' said Thomas, watching Molly scamper amongst the trees.

Hannah nodded. 'I hated her when I first met her,' she said. 'But she grew on me.'

There was an uncomfortable pause. The hope that had kept her going through the mountains was soaking away. He didn't want her.

What would happen to her now? She couldn't go back to the house in Parramatta. Would she be sent back to the Female Factory? She couldn't bear to think about it.

'I think it might rain tomorrow,' said Thomas, looking out of the cave over the valley.

'Oh,' said Hannah. She thought of the long journey back through the mountains. She didn't think she had the strength to make it.

She was going to burst, or fall apart. Something. She couldn't keep feeling like this. The emptiness inside her was too big; it would swallow her whole.

'Thomas,' she said.

'Hmm?'

Hannah thought about Scatterheart and the white bear. It was too easy for her. She just had to find the prince, and then everything would be happy ever after. This wasn't right. The emptiness inside her began to whirl around, and then gathered together into something cold and hard.

'Enough,' she said. Her voice echoed angrily around the cave. 'Enough,' she said again, her voice growing louder as she tried to hold back hot, angry tears. 'What is the matter with you? I gave up everything I had to get here, and you won't even look at me. What happened to you?'

He looked up at her. His eyes were wild and dark, like the ocean that had consumed Dr Ullathorne. He swallowed, and then spoke, slow and soft.

'When I got here, I started working under a man called Captain Mitchell. He was cruel to the convicts, and not much better to us. One day, we were working a team of convict women. They were carrying buckets of earth to build a bridge. One of the women tripped and fell over. Captain Mitchell pulled her up by her hair, and she swore at him. He ordered me to flog her as punishment. I told him I wouldn't do it. I couldn't flog a woman, and she hadn't done anything wrong. He ... he held a pistol to my head, and told me to do it or he would kill me. So I flogged her. But I was so careful. I made the cat crack like it was hitting her, but I was as gentle as a butterfly. I was staring at the woman, praying that she'd realise what I was doing and pretend to be hurting. But she didn't. When I'd finished, Captain Mitchell tore her dress from her back. She didn't have a mark. So he did it himself. He told her to remove all her clothes. Then he flogged her, naked. One hundred strokes, and every one felt like it was hitting me. She passed out after seventy, but he kept going. The ... the light in his eyes, Hannah. He loved it. Loved seeing her scream. Loved watching strips of skin tear from her back. When it was over, he tossed a bucket of salt water over her, to wake her up. Then he sent her to the black cell.'

'The black cell?'

Thomas nodded, biting his lip. 'It's a pit, underground, filled with water. He locked her down there, naked and bleeding, for two days.'

Hannah felt sick, remembering the darkness of the brig on the *Derby Ram*, and the bite of Superintendent Green's cane. 'But it wasn't your fault.'

Thomas took a deep breath. 'Afterwards, I went to a drinking house. I wanted to forget. Every time I closed my eyes I saw her face. I drank too much. Then one of the other officers came in and told me that the woman had fainted again when she was in the cell. She drowned.'

He stopped talking and looked down at his hands. Hannah thought he might have finished, but then he started talking again, faster this time.

'I didn't think. I was drunk. I stopped feeling guilty and started feeling angry. Instead of the woman's face, all I could see was the delight on that bastard's face as he tortured her. So I stood up, walked out of there and over to Captain Mitchell's house. I didn't try to sneak, or be secretive about it. People saw me walk in there. And they saw me walk out again, with his blood on me.'

Hannah closed her eyes.

'I shot him, Hannah. In cold blood. I murdered a man.' He paused, and glanced at the reddish-brown stain close by. 'Two men.'

Hannah let out a breath she didn't realise she'd been holding. 'I don't care,' she said. 'I killed someone too. I pushed him off the ship's deck in the middle of a storm. Do you think his face doesn't haunt me at night?'

Thomas sighed. 'Life isn't a fairy tale, Hannah. I can't give you a happy ending.'

Hannah stood up. 'Did I ever ask for one?' she said, but as she said it she realised she had. She had imagined their happy ending a thousand times. Tears filled her eyes, and she left the cave.

The cave was situated high on the mountain, looking out over the deep series of valleys that Hannah and Molly had crossed. The three crumbling peaks of yellow rock crouched on the ridge, like the sawdust-crone, the glass-woman, and the wax-child from Scatterheart's story. Hannah looked away. Some help they had been.

She thought about her imagined reunions with Thomas, rehearsed and played over and over again in her mind since she had dreamed of the white bear in the doldrums. It now seemed so childish and pointless.

She poked the fire with a stick. Orange sparks danced up into the air and vanished. Hannah watched them absently. She heard footsteps draw close, and then he was sitting beside her.

'I imagined it too,' he said. 'The happy ending. I just never actually believed you'd come.'

The very faintest shadow of a smile – a *real* smile – passed over his face, and for a moment, Hannah recognised him once more as the young man who had made snow-creatures with her in Hyde Park. They were not quite touching. Hannah poked the fire again, sending up another stream of sparks.

'I'm sorry,' said Hannah.

Thomas shifted slightly. 'What for?'

Hannah shrugged. 'Everything. Being horrible to you. Being me.'

There was that shadow-smile again, this time with a flicker of life in his eyes. 'Don't be sorry for being you,' he said. 'You're strong.'

'Stubborn.'

'Same thing.'

He took her hand. It wasn't the same hand as she had held on his first day as her tutor. This hand was calloused and hard. But it still covered her hand completely, swallowing it up out of sight.

'I'm sorry too,' he said. 'I shouldn't have given up on you.'

'You had every reason too.'

'I still shouldn't have given up, though.'

She squeezed his hand.

'I just never imagined it would be like this,' he said. 'I always thought I could protect you, but...'

'You can,' said Hannah. 'You did. We can protect each other.'

He nodded. She reached up a hand and gently touched the side of his face. It was rough and prickly with stubble. He closed his eyes and smiled gently.

Hannah leaned against him. He felt warm and solid. Safe.

Thomas opened his eyes. 'Do you want to go back to London?'

Hannah looked out at the mountains spreading before her, majestic and overwhelming. An enormous brown and golden bird wheeled into view, soaring up into the achingly blue sky. She shook her head.

'No.'

'Good,' said Thomas. 'I'm sure there are plenty of opportunities for an escaped convict and a fugitive murderer in a place like this.'

His eyes twinkled, and Hannah finally relaxed. He was right. This was the land where nothing was as it seemed. There would be a place for them somewhere.

'So,' said Thomas after a pause. 'You married that man.'

'I thought you were dead,' said Hannah. 'I thought that I'd lost you. So I picked up his handkerchief. I didn't realise it meant we were married.'

Thomas looked away and swallowed.

'Are you jealous?' she said.

Thomas shrugged. 'You picked up his handkerchief,' he said. 'You chose him.'

Hannah put her hand up against his cheek and pulled him round, forcing him to look at her.

'I chose you first,' she said.

She dug in the folds of her dress and pulled out the brown scrap of fabric.

'I picked up *your* handkerchief first,' she said, pressing it into his hand.

He looked down at it, then smiled at her.

'Thank you,' he said.

'In London,' she said, remembering him standing before her fireplace, eyes shining. 'In London you said we could have an adventure.'

Thomas raised his eyebrows. 'I didn't think adventures were appropriate for young ladies of Quality.'

Hannah grinned. 'But I'm not a lady of Quality,' she said. 'I'm a doxy convict slattern, didn't you hear?'

He laughed and put an arm around her waist. 'Lucky for us,' he said.

'So where do we start?' Hannah asked.

'Well,' said Thomas, still smiling, 'how about a story?'

Scatterheart and the white bear looked up at the great tree, and saw that it had grown leaves of silver, and acorns made of brightly-coloured jewels. And Scatterheart and her white bear (and the little wax-child) picked these treasures, and lived happily ever after.

Acknowledgments

🖤

It takes more than one person to write a book, and although it's my name on the cover, this book wouldn't exist without the support of the following people.

Sarah Dollard for her storylining genius – every writer should have a professional storyliner they can call up when plotting a novel, and again when the first draft is ready to be torn to pieces.

Justine Larbalestier and Scott Westerfeld, for excellent accommodation, wine and conversation, and for helping me figure out what the field of spikes was. Special thanks to Justine for her first-reader patience and refreshing lack of tact.

Sean Elliot, for fantastically nerdy astronomical knowledge.

Everyone on the aus_convicts mailing list for answering my questions.

Kate Rose for checking that I hadn't confused my masthead with my mizzen.

The staff in Manuscripts, at the State Library of Victoria.

My mother for being both a good reader and a good listener. Also to mum and dad in general for letting me live under their roof while I wrote the first draft.

Thanks also to my colleagues at the Centre for Youth Literature (Mike, Paula and Elizabeth) for their flexibility and understanding, and to my amazing friends for letting me rabbit on endlessly about convicts and pretending they weren't bored.

And abundant, effusive thanks to everyone at black dog books, in particular Alison Arnold and Andrew Kelly, for their endless support, patience and enthusiasm.

One of the best things about writing historical fiction is that you get to do research and find out lots and lots of amazing and interesting things and then steal them for your book. You also get to make stuff up.

Scatterheart is a work of fiction. There was a convict called Hannah Cheshire (she was my great great great great great grandmother), but she sailed in the Second Fleet, in 1790, and apart from her name, had nothing in common with the Hannah in this book.

There was no ship called the *Derby Ram*. It's made up of bits and pieces of other ships, and I apologise if any ship-knowledgey-people read it: I am an absolute novice when it comes to matters nautical. I tried.

Nearly all of the characters are fictional, although many of them were inspired by real people. The only 'real' character in the novel is Dr William Redfern, who was the Assistant Surgeon to the colony, and is the man after who the suburb of Sydney is named.

In case anyone is wondering, the gruesome, violent, cruel things that happen to people in this book (the Black Pit, the man with no skin, the Mermaid Dance) are unfortunately not from my imagination. They all happened, right here in Australia.

I'd like to thank the authors and publishers of the following books, which were not only fabulous resources, but also fired up my newfound passion for Australian history.

The Fatal Shore by Robert Hughes
John Nicol, Mariner, Life and Adventures by John Nicol
The Convict Ships by Charles Bateson
The Floating Brothel by Sian Rees
Orphans of History by Robert Holden
Dancing with Strangers by Inga Clendinnen
Dr Johnson's London by Lisa Picard
The 50-gun Ship by Rif Winfield and John McKay
1811 Dictionary of the Vulgar Tongue by Captain Grose et al.

And the works of Georgette Heyer and Leon Garfield, and the Hornblower mini-series, for getting me in the mood. I used to think Australian history was boring. I've changed my mind.